MEKONG SHADOWS

TALES FROM CAMBODIA

SARASWATI PUBLISHING

https://saraswatipublishingcambodia.com/

saraswati.publishing.cambodia@gmail.com

<u>CONTENTS</u>

Introduction

When I first had the idea of putting together a collection of tales from Cambodia, the intention was to produce a follow-up to 2012's 'Phnom Penh Noir', a fantastic collection edited by the very talented Christopher G. Moore (a big pair of shoes to try and fill). As time went on we decided to drop the 'noir' part of the plan as it allowed us to feature a wider range of story subjects.

A conversation then ensued with Mark Bibby Jackson of Asia LIFE and a plan began to take shape where we would run a joint competition to encourage new and aspiring Cambodian writers. Cambodia has long lacked a solid literary scene or a reading culture, though I have been very encouraged to see that changing a lot in recent times with several young Cambodians not only producing books but also setting up reading and writing groups to encourage others.

Our two competition winners, Voleak Phan and Vorsnar Ses, stood out from a very impressive field of entries, especially when you remember that all the entrants were writing in their second (or even third) language. The majority of our entrants were also under the age of 20 which is another hugely encouraging fact, and our two winners were 18 (Voleak) and 15 (Vorsnar), which bodes very well for the future of Cambodian literature.

I am now looking forward to putting together two anthologies of stories by Cambodian writers – one in English and one in Khmer – at the beginning of 2018. My thanks to all those who entered the competition with AsiaLIFE Cambodia.

I also had the idea that we could donate any profits from the book to a Cambodian charity or NGO. It was Mark who then suggested the excellent – and very apt – Khmer Sight Foundation.

Cataracts are the leading cause of blindness in Cambodia and most of the cases are avoidable. Health Ministry figures showed that in 2007 around 2% of Cambodians suffered blindness in both eyes as a result of cataracts, and more recent figures from 2014 stated that around 5% of the population over five years old had varying degrees of sight impairment (Cambodia Demographic and Health Survey). The good news is that over the last 20 years the prevalence of avoidable blindness has dropped by nearly 70% (The Fred Hollows Foundation). It is still a very real issue though.

In 2015 the Khmer Sight Foundation (KSF) was formed to unify ophthalmology and eye care across the Kingdom, thanks to local philanthropists and to the efforts of ophthalmologists from Australia and New Zealand who regularly donate their time and experience to reducing these figures further and to training young Cambodians. They also arrange scholarships for ophthalmology students to study abroad with the aim of making Cambodia self-reliant.

Each operation costs only $40, an incredibly low amount from a Western perspective, so selling around eight to ten copies (depending on the outlet) could help restore someone's sight.

I am lucky enough to know many very talented people, which made the initial task of gathering material for this anthology very easy indeed. My thanks to all who took the time to write something new or to offer an excerpt from existing work. Take a trip into the dark noir of James Newman in 'La Petite Mort', one of two tales which feature the infamous Heart of Darkness nightclub in Phnom Penh. Share the feelings of a forced returning émigré with Kosal Khiev in 'Returning'. Ek Madra tells a love story with a difference in 'Fight the Enemy, Find Love', while Philip Coggan visits one of his favourite subjects, black magic, in 'The Dark Son'. Thom Locke's 'Two for the Road' has a real twist and some nice cameo appearances, and Mark Bibby Jackson's 'Sleeping Beauty' fills a gap while we wait for the follow-up to 'Peppered Justice'.

Cambodia offers a rich tapestry to both draw on and from. Few other countries have suffered the upheavals and horrors that this nation has in the last 50 years or so. Yet despite all those dark shadows, it is the light and hope of the people that continues to stand out. From city streets to dusty rural lanes, the smiles of ordinary Cambodians are one of the principal reasons so many of us have chosen to make our homes here. With an increasingly young population there are exciting times ahead for this small Kingdom, but it is essential that the past is also remembered; from the glories of the Angkor Empire through to the genocidal madness of the Khmer Rouge. One of the best ways for any nation to acknowledge its past is through the art of storytelling, and in the coming years Saraswati will continue to find and support young writers like our two competition winners.

I think that we have produced a wonderful collection of short stories for you to enjoy. If I recover from the job of putting this one together then there may even be a follow-up in 2018 (or 2019).

I'd like to thank Steve Porte for the wonderful cover photo, Hamid Saatchi at Saraswati for design and formatting, Mark Bibby Jackson and Marissa Carruthers at AsiaLIFE for all their help and ideas, Philip Coggan for his ad hoc editorial assistance, and Bandol Teav at Image Printing for her (as always) amazing service.

Iain Donnelly

Kampot, Cambodia.

July 2017.

Woman

Yulia Khouri

The sun that burned our steps - bled
The wolves that tore us apart - dead
The men that scarred our souls - fled
The destiny snake: its scales - shed.
The curse at its end.
Only emptiness left.
And nothing ahead,
Except. Perhaps Hope.

The Tree of Us; the three of us:
The Root. The Stem. The Fruit.
The Matriarch. The Mother. And I.
Like birds in the cage.
We trembled with fear and rage
But repressing the sorrow
We built our own tomorrow
And invented our own stage
In foreign lands.
We danced for a fool
And we played for a sage.
Latent and ugly coming of age.
...
The Matriarch:
The root of our life.
The orphan by war
Saved by the devil's knife.
Allowed to grow & bloom.
To choose her own groom.
And turn it into a gloom.
To adore her own reflection.

And then to reject her flesh
To hate her blood
And to sever connection
To her own roots.
And to her fruits...
But then to repent and start afresh.
To pray for her sin.
To nurture her youngest kin.
And to sing the songs to her wings.
...
The Mother:
Born to survive.
To endure hell.
And never tell
Of nightmares and pain.
She rang the bell
When she heard the song
When she saw my wings.
She offered her life
With the bittersweet smile,
So I would not cry.
And instead I would fly.
Fly Away.
Away from the bleeding sun.
Away from the hungry wolves
Away from the lost souls.
Away from the evil trolls
....
I expected the fight.
But then I began my flight.
And I conquered the highest heights
And there, I found my knight
And I loved and embraced my Light
With all my feminine might.
And it shines so bright.

And nothing else matters.
Except. Perhaps Hope.

***

Yulia Khouri is a graduate of University of California, Berkeley and London School of Economics. She has spent many years working in the humanitarian field with Human Rights Watch, Amnesty International, and United Nations High Commissioner for Refugees. After moving to Cambodia with her fiancé, she decided to create her own company – INNOV8 - with a strong social responsibility ethos, supporting women & children at risk, and the protection of the environment and wildlife. Yulia is also founder and managing director of Animal Mama Veterinary Hospital and serves as an Ambassador for Wildlife Alliance.

The greatest influences in her life have been mother, Nina, and her late Grandmother Yelena, to whom her poem is dedicated.

Returning

Kosal Khiev

It's 2011, March 15th, and five days after I turned 31. It's been 15 years since I have seen the outside world but the approval of my travelling documents has come and now I am told that today this day is here.

Theday of my return. Return to what I haven't the faintest, only a world beyond bars and chains and grey walls and to people and society.

But Cambodia is foreign; all I can remember are old war-torn stories once told through the traumatic and trembling lips of my beloved grandmother.

She still speaks to me.

I'm in the Tacoma Washington Detention Centre and my journey has begun.
I will fly to Seattle then on to Los Angeles, and then from there to Bangkok and finally from Bangkok to Phnom Penh. We are to take commercial flights and there are two of us.
The other is an older Cambodian gentleman who said he had family in Thailand so that's where he is heading. For me I have no clue. With us are four Immigration and Customs Enforcement (ICE) agents to escort us. Wow. Right? That's a lot of dollars. They say that if we don't try and run then they won't handcuff us. What a laugh. I tell him straight away…
"It's all good man. I'm free. I ain't running nowhere."

The two guys I have are decent enough fellows. Just doing their job and following policies. Can I blame them? No. One was pretty cool.

He collects alcohol bottles from different countries he's been to. We talked quite a bit. About all sorts. It was gonna be a long journey and well…the outside world after a decade and half spent in institutions. I was free. I remember him asking me:
"Are you scared? How are you feeling after being locked up for so long and then being sent back to a country you have never set foot in?"

I sit there for a moment…lost in thought. Prison felt so far away at this point like it was all just a nightmare. I felt like the prodigal son. I looked at him.
"Yeah man, pretty scared...terrified."
And in truth I was. I had no idea what to expect but then I knew this. I said:
"Let me tell you something brother. I just survived through the most hellish of hells. So it doesn't matter where you drop me at. It could be in the middle of a jungle somewhere and I swear to you the next time you see me I'll have a spear in my hand along with a pet panther."
We laughed. But I was dead serious.

Seattle to LAX was smooth and from Los Angeles to Bangkok is not a bad flight either. I mainly watched movies if I wasn't curled up asleep. But the flight from Bangkok to Phnom Penh?

That flight was something else. There was a storm that night. Oh man, a horrible one. At one point there was turbulence for at least 15 minutes. That's a long-ass time. And I'm thinking in my head; please God, don't let this plane go down. Let me taste true freedom before you take me. Real talk. I was petrified. Just my luck, right. Oh man but when that plane landed I was so relieved. But also aware of everything. This is it. Final destination.

I grew wings and flew to the other side of the world,
became a seashell and through hell I became a pearl.
my kingdom,
my throne,
my people,
my home,
my heart,
on a platter,
no bones,
my flesh,
my blood,
my chest
swelled up with love,
and I'm sewn back up
with a piece missing
and I'm drifting along
like a poem unwritten
while sitting
beside a river that
has grown still…
no longer running
I'm only running on will,
determination and skill
crafted through years of walking and talking
he builds from nothing but will…
and I will fly…
Phnom Penh…
My new home.
I'm in a cold zone like Eskimos,
Work hard play harder,
In the land of barters

exchange for martyrs
cold hearted,
Left for dead
till we recharged…
A volt with a bolt to free God.
Lost and found
now we're treasures on this courtyard.
No choice but ball,
it's a free fall.
Heed the call.
We each all,
answer to a higher calling…

Lights are blinding in this city that I'm finding.
Night time Phnom Penh this city's made of diamonds,
And see if u could find them.
Led by little boys are these blind men.
Good girls gone bad,
This city's full of sly men
So on the sidelines u can see the grinding.
Daily in rotation with time steady flying…

Phnom Penh
and you can see the sky rise
it's crazy how they flock by
everywhere I go
you can see the poor wealthy and old
with a bunch of young folks
searching for that pot of gold

So please forgive me I'm a sinner
been sinning ever since I could remember…
It was a cold November…
snowflakes as eyes graze upon an iron gate
18 years old and hell froze over a fiery lake

Baked in the hot sun I perched among snakes
lizards and gizzards pitted against each other in order to break
divide and conquer
can you see the bodies on the crosses…?
long live the King!
We survive only to become stronger

Thoughts keeps coming like pieces of a puzzle keep falling
each piece comes in the forms of the words I'm scrawling.
scratch within a tree bark "I was here."
heed my calling…
I'm balling out tears…
no more fear I'm going ALL IN
my sins are my scars
but my heart is no longer barred in
I'm free...
let me breathe we are all kin
ancestors of my past lead me to the greenest grass
my hands outstretched with fingers open for your grasp

Kingdom of Wonder
Underneath Cambodian thunder.
Tropical monsoons with the passion of lovers
making love underneath thin sheets and warm covers
See these words are meant to caress flesh and undress us
So let's just…
settle back and envision us laid back in several different positions silhouetted in dim black.
Imagine…
flickering flames struck from a thin match
It happened
Like worlds colliding the string snapped
It was magic
We disappeared and never came back

I was born with two tongues
one speaks in cadences and radiates like street sages
a young breed that was led through tragic pages
fill with endless mazes…
I was left for dead…
but what amazes me
how life can go through phases
cause even through the haze of death
there was breath in my dying traces
my eyes reflecting faces
which reflected life
so my eyes reflected love
instead of hatred...
my mother tongue is broken
passed down through the ages
so traces of my ancestors comes through in a broken
dialect, foreign though my tongue is native
I'm ancient
raised upstate
shackled and chained like slaves
I was placed in pavements
see I'm engraved in ink
a visual translation
stories told of me like seasonal changes
so witness my transformation

Features reflect my reflection
his speech speaks of my missing sections
With a toothless grin he sings my lessons
With sad beginnings wishing he had been there from the
very beginning
But life had a different ending
We were both broken without a sight for mending
but as time waned we gained a new beginning

all the while sending unforgotten thoughts as life went on bending
So I was to sidewind
between thorns and vines
while he was tiptoeing behind enemy lines
See Both crept thru and slept thru different kind of mines
Wept thru nights at different points in time
But as the sun darkens so it shines
A new day a new way to say I love you with new prayers to pray
Bless you as I hug you this is newly written thrown into the fray
To change and produce flames from the ashes we raise like Phoenixes
Sleeping now awaken I breath to speak what dream is this
A living one
Surreal it feels how ease the breathing comes
As each season sung
With the turning of leaves as each piece was flung
To the far side
Corners thru borders we was born thru genocide
Survived but a piece did die
So though we cry these tears reflect life
Reflects twice...inspects strife
Only to inject light
So one two check mic in these cold nights
I write sing glory cause these stories should hold might.

Kosal Khiev is a poet, tattoo artist, and survivor of the US prison system. Born in a Thai refugee camp, Kosal's family fled to the U.S in 1981. Instead of the American dream, Kosal's family lived in grim public housing with scarce social services. Kosal admits to making poor choices as a teenager that led him into more violence, poverty, and eventually prison. At the age of 16, Kosal was arrested in a gang fight and charged with attempted murder. Kosal was tried as an adult and sentenced to 16 years in a state penitentiary. While serving 14 years in prison he discovered spoken word poetry from a former Vietnam War veteran. Spoken word became his creative channel to tell his own story and transform his anger, regrets, and experiences into a poetic art form. Upon release in 2011, the U.S. government deported him to Cambodia, a country he had never been. Having won multiple awards for his award winning documentary "Cambodian Son", Kosal was also invited to the 2012 London Olympics representing Cambodia as a Cultural Olympiad in the first and largest gathering of poets, "Parnassus Poetry".

La Petite Mort

James Newman

The funeral party had been rattling bells and chanting since I'd checked into the White River Guesthouse that morning. The staff moved around slowly like reptiles, eyelids a quarter closed, conserving energy for the evening shift. I sat playing with the glass of stout for a while before that third drink accelerated day into night and we entered, as we do, that familiar hazy, chaotic, Cambodian dream.

I'd have had a better chance of finding Peter as the shadows darkened, the drinkers got cynical, and the guilty took chances. On the street outside a stage had been set up. Bronze bodied Khmer temptresses swayed melodically as we worked on the glasses and the dreams. My mind turned inexplicably to the funeral strippers of China, but absent minds often did.

Like any city *The Penh* looked great on a postcard with its glittering temples and dusk-lit river, but the real Asian cities were the cavernous wet markets, the cow-slaughtering districts, dilapidated buildings, ruins, relics of another dream.

Some men were oil paintings, others were flicker-books or movies, but Peter's stork-like body was more like a sketch; a thrown-away scribble by a bad artist on a poor afternoon. I'd spent the morning pulling apart his guesthouse room but hadn't turned up much apart from fragments of his past, the shattered belongings of a troubled mind, notebook with random scribbles, a battered rucksack and a letter from his mum. The boy had weakened as swiftly as his trust fund matured. Unnerved by his new surroundings Peter embraced the ice drug craze slowly tearing apart the threads of society strand by bloody strand. He skipped meals and became paranoid. Peter had once played polo, achieved solid grades at Canterbury, won a scholarship to study law at the London School of Economics. So why did Peter murder Hippie John outside the Long Lin Guesthouse between one and two that previous morning?

Whispering ghosts lead us to strange places. The British upper class were a curious inbreed, they'd get drunk and take their clothes off and throw house parties, they'd simulate congress with a pig carcass, ride horseback, chase foxes; some had been known to burn bank notes in front of the homeless, but there was more to Peter and Hippie John than a rebellious altercation. They'd had history, but just what kind of history? At first I suspected drugs, and then a woman, but the story didn't add up whichever way you twisted it or pulled it apart.

Peter had been last seen before the incident drinking a beer on a tobacco-stained balcony looking over the city. His friends saw nothing unusual in his behaviour. They described his mood as remote and distant, the city was no doubt tearing him apart.

"He'd taken something from Bangkok that wasn't his," red-haired Betty had told me earlier that day. "He never spoke about it, well, not much, but sometimes he would seem distracted, he'd look at the door, as if somebody or something were about to burst through it."

"He was scared?"

"Jumpy," she said as her freckles danced beneath the glow of the strip light beam. She shook her face to illustrate her friend's nervousness. "He was teaching, on and off, but his heart wasn't really in it. And of course he had the money. Who knows what he wanted to do? He used to visit the Heart of Darkness, for goodness sake."

I showed her the notebook and asked what she made of the scribbles. She shook her head, and smiled. Betty shared the guesthouse with Peter but I figured she knew little of his private life. Addicts and snakes dwelled inside nests of secrets, hatching routines, and skits required to serpentine through the day. Maybe he had given the locals some story about a heist or robbery to explain the fruits of his trust fund?

But I didn't take him for a fugitive.

I figured it best to see the boy myself in the holding cell, but before that The Heart of Darkness and Peter's past.

***

Sartre called the orgasm the *little death*, and there wasn't as much death in Cambodia, as say, Bangkok, but the city was catching up fast. Neon bars spat in and out an endless rainbow of lost souls as midnight approached and gold was sought.

Entering the Heart of Darkness was like moving into an exploding cavern, copper-bodied youths stood around flexing their muscles, hustling, hitting the Johns for drinks. A bargirl smiled and made a circle with her left thumb and forefinger. She extended her right index finger and stabbed it into the hole. The sound system coughed loudly and screamed about a *White Wedding* as I found a dark-skinned youth by the bar and flipped him the picture of Peter.

His eyes lit up like a snake catching a mouse's shadow. "He used to come in here," the hustler told me. "Cock tease." He made a face like he'd sucked on a sour lime and said, "Play pool?"

"Sure."

"Follow me," his top lip curled predatorily.

Out of the bar we strolled a few blocks east to a nameless shop-house with a moth-bitten table, a rumbling refrigerator, and a cemented pile of bricks for a bar. "We can talk in here - the music," he said making a circular motion with a finger beside his ear and pointing back in the direction of The Heart of Darkness. "Are you looking for boy?"

A sad shake of the head told him I wasn't.

He ordered a drink knowing that I'd pick up the bill and he'd be due a commission.

"So we play?" I said and motioned towards the table, "I'll rack them. Five dollars?"

He nodded staring at the table.

I took the triangle and loaded the balls inside. Placed the white in the D and nodded for the hustler to break them up. He did so, and took five solids from the break. He played well, a strong cuing arm and thinking two shots ahead of the last. He had enough passion to leave one difficult stripe and the rest blocked behind his remaining two. I potted the difficult ball but gave myself nothing else. He played his game down and missed a few tucked up close to the cushion. I picked off two more and missed my chance. He cleared up and I handed him the Abraham five.

"Next game is for words," I said. "Tell me what you know about Peter. Give me something to play with."

"Can I trust *you*?" He said *you* as if it was a dirty word but we both knew *trust* was the one to be cautious with.

"I'm employed by the kid's family. No risk for you. Just lay it out there."

"Ten dollar," he said.

"Break them up."

This time his game was tight. He took five from the break and left himself in a safe position. I played the ball advantage and left him with a lot of work to do before slowly picking mine out one by one, rolling smoothly off the top right cushion to stop perfectly for the black in an easy middle. Potted that and hung up the cue and leaned against the bar. Ordered the hustler a beer and stout for myself, said, "So, let's hear it."

"Peter killed him," he said a bit too soon.

"You saw this?"

"He attacked him. Hit his head, he fell down, they took him to his room. That's where they found him. He hit him, he died."

"Who found the body?"

"Police."

"That's all you have?"

"It was like that."

I gave him the ten and watched the boy wander off into the dollar-studded night street. I walked up to the bar. The bartender was a young woman with a quick wide smile and a pronounced forehead – Khmer bone structure. She told me her name and we spoke for a while about the passing traffic, the hustle, the slog, the drink. I can't remember how many drinks I had but can remember she matched me. Before too long I popped the question.

"The man you play pool with? His name Tick. Not good guy," she said with a concerned frown.

I paid her with a ten.

For the first time in this town I had found someone I agreed with.

***

The next morning's sun rose like most suns did.

Shards of light stabbing through the thin guesthouse curtain and into the brain causing that brief minute or two before a life-time of regret came stumbling through the mirrored built-in closet in like a thundering cyclone and shook you out of bed.

But, we have no time for memories.

Showered.

Dressed.

Had a cup of rich syrupy coffee.

Tuk-tuk to the police station.

The desk sergeant made life as difficult as possible. He was a large brute in a tight uniform with the face of an angry sloth which would have been comical if it weren't for the tumorous growth sprouting from his neck like a star-faced mole. I had my own hangover to deal with and had little time for the old Khmer battle of wits. I gave it to him simple. "Name's Joe Dylan, hired by the family of Peter Walsh," I slid over a power of attorney. He picked it up and looked at it as if I'd just passed him a comatose sewer rat. He raised a phone to his ear and made a few oriental sounds into it and pointed me towards a chair. I waited. Wriggled in the chair and waited some more. Near the door, on another chair, a plump black cat stretched its claws and yawned. The clock hand turned. The cat yawned again and surveyed me with its disc-like evil eyes. I waited long enough to realise he was trying to break me. The sergeant, that was, not the cat. I'd played the old oriental waiting game before, but I also knew that the waiting game wasn't the only game in town.

Slid out the old crocodile skin wallet and pulled out a fifty-dollar bill, folded it, and placed it under a business card and handed it to the sergeant who considered it for a while, before leading me down to the holding cells.

The sloth waited at the doorway, I guess the fifty meant I had some alone time with the kid.

Peter was the only prisoner in that can; the stalk-like frame was unmistakably experiencing what they call *The Fear*, coming down off a prolonged drug binge, the arms and legs spasming uncontrollably. He was pacing the cell and muttering something to himself, but I had anticipated all of this. Cambodian pharmacies require no prescription, and I'd acquired a strip of the blue tablets.

"Peter your parents sent me, I'm here to get you out, but first you need to calm down. My name's Joe Dylan. Here, take two of these, don't swallow, let them dissolve on the tongue." I handed him two of the blue pills through the bars and he stood there looking at me like I'd just landed there from Pluto or Mars. He hopped from one foot to the other, like an agitated parrot. I held up my right hand, palm towards him, and told him to wait.

It didn't take long before the eyes drew back slightly, the muscles relaxed, and his jaw began to slacken.

"Valium ten milligrams, got me out of some tight spots myself," I said. "Just wait a little while."

"They let you in?"

"Fifty bucks gets you a pass, but I doubt it gets me a season ticket. We may not have much time. What happened, Pete? Did you kill the Hippie?"

"No… I…"

I lit a cigarette.

Blew a purple cloud up to the ceiling and offered him one.

He took it. "Even if you did, we can probably get you out, so it's best to be up front about all that now. You two have a little history together, huh?"

"No, I'd never seen him before," his eyes told another story as he put the cigarette in his mouth with shaky fingers and jerked his lips towards the zippo flame I had blazing in front of him.

"So why did you start shouting and slapping at him in a crowded place, Peter? You went to a good school, good family, probably shot a few pheasants in your time, grouse even, why are you shouting and pushing around strangers in guesthouses, lad?"

Peter became suddenly interested in the ceiling and the smoke he'd just blown up there.

"You signed anything?" I asked him.

"No, well, I 'ad to do somethink." His accent had been mangled by a desire to be part of the lower classes.

Well, it happens. While most of us were crawling out of the gutter we pass curious traffic traveling the other way.

"Given a statement yet?" I asked.

"Yeah, I, er, I wrote it down in English."

"You remember how it went?"

"Word for word, pretty much. I'm good at remembering things."

I made a mental note of that and said: "Okay give it to me."

I took out the notebook and wrote it down. "So the way you sing it is, you were out, you saw the Hippie, you swung at him, and then you left him. Where did you go?"

"To my room."

"Anyone see you? Receptionist, housemaid, other residents?"

"I have a key, let myself in, it was past 2am, I was kinda out of it."

"Okay that'll have to do, for now."

I thanked the sloth on the way out and took a motorbike taxi to the Long Lin Guesthouse. The coffee was as dark and gritty as the youth who brought it to the table.

Tuk-tuk drivers stood their ground eyes hungry like vultures testing for the least sign of disorientation among the loose herd of travelers who wandered by. I paid the bill and walked to the reception desk that doubled as a travel agency

"Bus to Kampot," I told the youth who rummaged around a pile of flyers and ticket coupons, searching for the correct ticket book. As he did so I opened the guestbook, and turned to the 5th of January, the date that the Hippie had registered.

John Anderson.

Nationality: USA:

Passport Number: 90834983.

Occupation: Online Marketing.

The youth found his pad and we agreed tomorrow's bus, 9.30, would do it.

I booked it thinking, what the hell, I might be needing it.

***

The job of a detective is not to bemoan the past but embrace the present. To let the feet lead you to the next place, in this case to the immigration office.

The officer was of a peculiar type to have gravitated towards her chosen profession. In a world of psychopathic xenophobic pen-pushers one thing set her apart - she genuinely wanted to help.

As she scrolled through the records for both Peter and the Hippie I'd regretted slightly my Scotland Yard bluff.

"Peter came here first in 2007," she said, eyes shimmering with admin pride.

"But, how is that possible?"

"The computer never lies," she grinned.

"But he would have been only a child of ten or eleven?"

"He came first, I think, let me check, if I cross reference..." She tip tap tapped but before she had finished her tap dance I had it.

"He came with his parents. I see, yes."

"Yes mum and dad come too."

"And Hippie John, er, John Anderson, was here at that time?"

"Mr. Anderson has been here since 2002."

"He has any criminal..."

"Cannot say. Not my department."

"No...Of course. Thank you for your time. You've been fantastic."

I offered her a five which she declined. Instead I burnt the five to transport myself to street 172 in a tuk-tuk.

I had Peter's past but I didn't have John's.

I did what anybody else would do in that situation.

I logged onto the internet.

Wireless is everywhere in every city, *The Penh* included. Gone were the days when we would look to locals for inside knowledge. The tuk-tuk drivers knew this as did the travel agents and even the street walkers. The internet has brought us closer together only to drive us apart.

A nameless bar restaurant, a plate of fried rice, and a beer for half a dollar and the search began.

I had his real name, his date of birth, and google was my friend.

John had blogged.

He wrote about something called the *Fathership of Love.*

He had lived in a commune. I dug around a little on the *Fathership.* A few magazine articles, some high-brow, others lower.

Later on he had written some pieces for a magazine named *Farangs*.

Then, tip tap tip, I found it.

***

Fifty dollars found me downstairs in the cell.

This time the sloth didn't even put up a fight.

Nor should he. He earned half a month's wages in two days.

Peter was in better shape, I guessed the sleepers had knocked him out for a few hours.

"They treating you well, Peter?"

"Fecking great. What do you think?"

I smiled and lit a local cigarette. "I think you need to be more truthful. If, for example, I were to ask you when was the first time you laid eyes on John the Hippie. What would be your response?"

"Well. I told you, it was two nights ago the night I saw him."

"You were both here at the same time, years ago, Peter, you recognised him?"

"Wha…"

"This wasn't a recent memory, this was a ghost from the past, the little death you'd be carrying around inside for all these years, Peter. You knew what he had done to you. You wanted to repay him, didn't you Peter, you wanted to break him like he had broken you all those years ago. He stole your youth Peter, he stole everything. But it wasn't just you Peter, he stole from other boys too, and you have to let this thing that has been hurting you inside for all these years, you have to let it go."

"I didn't kill him. I SWEAR!"

"But you *knew* him. *Phnom Penh Post,* 2007. Page fourteen. Your parents reported the incident. Of course they never found him…"

"… I did remember him from before we were on holiday, that much is true, I hit him then and I hit him again… But I didn't kill the bastard."

"You were taking revenge Peter. I could have still gotten you out but if we start out on a mistruth, I could find myself in here with you. The Hippie had an underground business here. He was in it up to his neck. You knew about it, were involved in it even."

"I wish I had killed the bastard, but it wasn't me. I was here in Cambodia, that's true, as a kid. Siem Reap. Angkor Watt. I was exploring around alone and…"

"And…"

"And he just appeared from nowhere and there he was, his hands, his face, he was trying all sorts of shit, I screamed, that was it, he tried to do stuff, I didn't let him, I was a fighter. I punched him, I ran. But I'll always remember that face."

"So if you didn't do it what the hell is this?"

I took out the notebook. "Last time I was here, I made notes using *your* notebook, Peter. I took the notebook out in front of you and you didn't comment on that? Especially a notebook, a moleskin notebook, a notebook not too easy to find in this neck of the woods. What's in the notebook, Peter?"

"Nothing, just doodles. Pictures. Ideas," his face was now white with jaw-clenched terror.

"I thought the same, but when you pretended not to recognise it I knew there had to be something to it."

Peter hit the ground as I decided to return his parents' retainer.

"Sleep tight, Peter."

I got the hell out of there.

Maybe another Dick with lower morals would take the case.

I still had the street but that was about all I had.

The scribbles were of course codes, linking clients to punters in the underage sex racket. Numbers, ages, I couldn't dig any deeper than that without finding out the higher-ups and putting myself in the river.

The IP address linked both Hippie John and Peter to the site.

And yes, he was abused.

But the abused becomes the abuser.

Had Peter actually killed Hippie John?

I wasn't sure but I doubted it.

I later heard a more credible story. Hippie John had stumbled into The Heart of Darkness, popped some Viagra and taken Tick the pool player and another hustler back to his apartment.

Took another Viagra and nature did the rest.

I returned to The White River, and paid up for another two weeks, five dollars a night and fifty cents a beer. I phoned the kid's family and suggest another local detective and sat drinking until reaching that familiar hazy, chaotic, Cambodian dream.

Or the little death, as they call it here,

La Petite Mort.

***

James Newman moved to Thailand at the tender age of 24 and has written fiction in the region ever since. He is the author of the popular Joe Dylan noir detective novels and has recently branched out into writing and producing feature films in the region. The author of hundreds of short stories, ten novels, and numerous articles and essays under different guises, James is also the curator of the Bangkok Night of Noir literary festival event, and the co-founder, along with John Daysh of Spanking Pulp Press. He is a frequent visitor to Cambodia and was a guest speaker at the Kampot Writers and Readers Festival 2016.

A Low Sun

Alasdair McLeod

The long-tail boat scraped along the stone bulwarks of the new riverbank by the reclaimed land and two foreign investors disembarked unsteadily. Of the two guides, Bong walked ahead while Sorm extended her hand and helped them clamber up the slope. The Russian investment delegate stumbled and his knee thumped against a rocky outcrop.

After clambering up the bank of new land they stood squinting at the glittering casino hotel. The green windows of the monolith reflected the variations in the layered sky.

"A delicious buffet is waiting for us on the casino rooftop, but we first wanted you to see up close the site where your investments will take shape."

Two diggers were spreading soil in the middle distance, followed around by a roller to pack it down. A tumbling village of corrugated sheds clung to the perimeter wall of the casino gardens. The construction workers that lived there were resting on hammocks and benches in the late afternoon heat. The sound of karaoke music drifted from one of their rooms across the hot dusty space to the visitors.

"Appreciate the scale! And the superb views too, of course. The location is absolutely second to none."
"Very nice, it's really a good spot," said the Chinese representative, mopping his brow and then pulling at his collar.
"Welcome to the modern Cambodia!" grinned Bong.

Sorm nodded eagerly in agreement with a big smile that died moments later as if a switch had been thrown. "But not everything is as perfect here as it may first appear, Phnom Penh is not without its annoyances," she declared, pausing until the full attention of the group was on her. "For example, you can never find a tuk-tuk anywhere in the city when you need one!"
The investors laughed and Bong visibly relaxed and breathed a sigh of relief.

"Ha, tuk-tuk?" said the Russian, laughing longer than the others. "I thought we'd never find one!"
Sorm's mirthful grin faded again in a fraction of a second as she pulled out her smartphone to scroll though messages and updates. The Chinese investor asked Bong about the scale of engineering projects upriver.

Bong gesticulated towards the Central Business District buildings further down the shoreline as he spoke and the Russian investor strolled away along to the corner of the casino perimeter wall to take in a wider view across the Mekong River. He squinted to make out the patterns of settlement on the far shore beyond the scattered tourist boats and freight ships. He looked down to his left and started with surprise when he saw a woman sitting with her back against the wall just a few steps away from him. A serious recent injury had reddened the area around her right eye that was swollen shut. Her left arm was in a sling and a silent baby lay cradled in her right. The vicious beating seemed so fresh and recent that he glanced quickly around to see if an assailant was still in view. Blood appeared to have just stopped flowing from the head wound and caked her skin in winding lines of faded crimson that plunged into her neckline. He looked back for a moment towards where the rest of the group was still chatting. Hesitating as questions and options played through his mind, he finally reached into his pocket and handed her a ten-dollar note. She took the offering from him without looking up at his face. He hurried away to rejoin the group. In these parts it seemed that around any corner one might come across the raw consequences of violence.

He returned to the group, flustered, as the Chinese investor was just finishing another question.

"The electrical needs of any industries and factories will be more than taken care of by the dams being constructed in our country," said Bong beaming with pride.

"What about the impacts of all this development on the environment?" asked the Chinese investor, broaching the sensitive topic bluntly. "There are many agencies working to suspend construction to protect the swamps and river systems. Can you guarantee that the progress won't be stopped by these misguided and confused meddlers?"

"Ah, my friend, you haven't understood the people of this country. That's okay, few have genuinely tried to do so."

Bong turned to the side with a soft sigh to look across the flowing tan waters of the Mekong and continued.

"For as long as people have lived in this region their lives have been closely bound up with the water cycles and seasons. You may have heard about the celebrated irrigation systems that once supported the Angkor Empire? But when the darkness of the genocide spilled across our land, it was as though the nurturing and nourishing relationship with water was over and the element had turned against us. We felt this very deeply. The waters had betrayed us and it was necessary to retake control. You see what I mean?"

"Ah, no, not really," said the Chinese investor, looking hesitantly between the others in the group. "Not yet. But please go on and clarify it for us."

"Consider what has happened with most of the major infrastructure projects. The great Boeung Kak lake of Phnom Penh has been filled in to be reclaimed for numerous condo developments – the details you know, being participants in the funding. The dams along the Mekong, like a chain of giant concrete dominos, will harness and mitigate the power of the river. As a result, the Tonle Sap Lake will cease its annual reverse flow and eventually fill with silt to make an agricultural rice bowl. It will replace the lost fishing grounds and stimulate the economy. It is all about taking control back from the waters. This war on water comes from the very top and we aim to subjugate it so our country will never turn on itself in such a way again."

"It sounds like taking revenge," said the Russian investor.

"We need water, to pretend otherwise would be nonsense. But it will flow through our country on terms chosen by us. We realize this is not something that may be easily understood by outsiders. But when close relationships change, often a degree of viciousness and bitterness may be involved. That is something that can be understood by people of every country, am I right? That is probably the best way to think about the ambivalent view of water in our culture."

"Were your families directly touched by those events?" asked the Russian investor.

"Every family was touched by our country's shame," said Sorm. "But in the long years of reflecting on the aftermath and the deals that were made, it has been hard to know whether it was the disease or the cure that was more debilitating in the end."

The casino shadows slid slowly out across the River of Wonder as the late afternoon Sun dropped lower.

Two karaoke girls were doing their make-up near the entrance to the shed where the scratchy music was playing. They looked out towards the well-dressed group in between applying foundation, lip gloss and mascara.
"Shall we go upstairs to celebrate with our international buffet?" suggested Bong as the group suddenly seemed at risk of pulling in different directions.
"I want to ask you if these embankments and water defences are really safe?" demanded the Chinese representative seriously. "I mean even during the downpours of the monsoon season, can the defences against the river truly hold?"
"It's completely safe, my friends. Built to international construction standards, every block," Bong smiled broadly.
"And, politically? Things seem stable. But in your opinion is there any chance of a relapse back to something like the days before the reconciliation?"

A pained expression passed across Bong's face as he considered the question.
"Look, in the books and movies it often seems as though being the bad guy is a thrill. But we as a people have seen evil, and we know that it is dull and awful. Storytellers are in bondage to the public need to legitimize wickedness, perhaps in service of the possibility that any one of us might need to turn bad at some point in life.... What I'm saying is that we're not going back to that place again."

Bong fretted with the gold watch on his left wrist while Sorm pouted for a series of selfies that she was firing off. The karaoke girls had started dancing with each other in the doorway. They moved with the abandon of women who no longer cared about how their actions reflected on them.

"Thank you for your honest answer," said the Chinese investor as his attention drifted in the direction of the music.

"And thank you for your kind interest in our projects. It is a pleasure to show the fruits of our hard work to good people such as yourselves," said Bong with a sweeping arm gesture to start the group moving towards the hotel.

"So kind of you to say. But this 'nice guy' image is just something I cultivate to make it easier to steal peoples' organs."

"Oh really?!" asked Bong slowly with wide eyes. "How's that working for you?"

"I'm just joking around with you. Well, perhaps. I certainly hope to be able to submit a favourable report to my superiors about the opportunities and operations you have running here. There's a good basis for further talks, that's my impression. Let's continue this discussion, as you mentioned, around the casino rooftop buffet. I have worked up an appetite. Let's see if we can't make a deal."

"It seems we are all rather hungry," said Sorm with a warm smile that died on her face the instant she finished speaking.

Alasdair has had fiction short stories published in Chiang Mai City News and Maelstrom Magazine. In addition to writing the book of poems "The Ashes of the Sun" he has contributed poetry to the book Bangkok Beat and to Works magazine. His photographs have been used by Condé Nast Traveler online (US) and print (India) editions and used extensively in the Thailand Footprint blog. Alasdair conducted and filmed some of the interviews in the Krom documentary 'Songs from the Noir & the Mekong Heart' and his YouTube channel has had over half a million views.

The Genocide Boys and Girls

Jim Algie

This excerpt is from the opening section of the second interlinked novella in his new book, On the Night Joey Ramone Died: Tales of rock and punk from Bangkok, New York, Cambodia and Norway (Magic Bullet Press, 2017), available as an eBook from Amazon Kindle.

The change happened as slowly and mysteriously as a wrinkle appearing on his face. Lek couldn't remember how old he was – Thirty-nine? Forty-one? – when the Thai-Chinese girls in his local shop began calling him "uncle" instead of "older brother." Only around then did he first notice that younger women were looking at him, if they looked at him at all, in a different way.

It was difficult to read the expression on their faces and in their eyes. Was it something maternal? Was it mockery or contempt? Some kind of fear that he was an aging lecher? Indifference or pity?

Maybe it was some mixture of these emotions that he'd never seen before. Whatever it was, he was far beyond the young man's fantasy of seeing his fascination or desire reflected in their eyes.

For his age, Lek didn't think he looked that bad. Not for a musician who'd played as many sold-out concerts, done as many drugs and downed as many drinks as he had. At the very least, he had never displayed the most overt warning signs of aging, heterosexual males: letting their wives or girlfriends pick out their clothes for them, or looking so slovenly and unfashionable that he wished they had a woman to pick out their clothes for them.

Yet nothing he did, not the workouts, the facials, the expensive haircuts, or abstaining from drink and drugs, seemed to help: the ruts corrugating his forehead continued to deepen; the iron filings kept salting and peppering his black hair; and younger women continued regarding him in this strange way.

It wasn't until three years after his divorce, when he volunteered to let his son practice his new interest in psychology and relationship counselling on him, that Lek realized he'd reached a turning point of no return. Getting his twenty-year-old son to advise him on women?

This could only be the onset of a full-blown, mid-life calamity.

"Do you think your teacher and I formed some kind of connection right from the beginning?" asked Lek.

"In about two minutes I'd say."

"That's all it took? I guess so. After that I couldn't seem to stop it."

"You could have, but you didn't want to."

"That was my fault?"

"Both parties are to compliment or blame in any love affair."

"Is that what it was? I'm not sure it was love or even an affair."

"Could you please stop pacing the room and chain-smoking and have a seat on Dr. Dee Dee's couch? Good. Thank you. Now let's go back to the beginning when she came over for my first conversation class."

"Doctor, didn't she seem kind of obnoxious to you at first? I mean, polite *and* obnoxious."

"Sir, were you or were you not wearing ripped jeans, a studded leather belt and a T-shirt for the death metal band Cannibal Corpse?"

"Are you supposed to be a relationship counsellor or a prosecuting attorney?"

They traded smirks.

"Answer the question, please."

"Oh, I see where you're going with this. You mean, right from the start I gave her a license to say and do pretty much what she wanted."

"Exactly. That was your first, and maybe your most powerful, connection. So let's rewind…"

Lek was going to make another pot of Dragon Well Green Tea when Dee Dee walked into the penthouse with a petite blond. "This is my new conversation teacher, Professor Edana," he said to Lek in Thai. He turned to her. "This is my father, Lek," he said in English.

Immediately she smiled and put both of her palms together and raised them in front of her face. She said hello and asked him how he was in Thai. Not many foreigners pulled off the greeting and sang the correct tones like Edana did. Most of the ones Lek had met didn't even bother trying.

Her performance was all the more impressive when he recalled Dee Dee telling him that she'd only lived in Bangkok for a few months.

Because of their size white women had often intimidated him, but Edana was a few inches shorter than he was and just as slender.

"Nice to meet you, *Khun* Lek," she said.

A smile split open his dark and leathery features. "Cool to meet you too. Lek is fine. I try not to put on any airs or graces."

Dee Dee rolled his eyes and said, "I need to start the class soon. I got shit to do tonight."

"Saying 'shit' around your teacher is not that polite. You could use 'things' or 'stuff,' you know."

"That's okay. I talk shit all the time." Edana's smile forced her dimples out of hiding. Until then Lek hadn't realized how pretty she was, nor how a smile filled those big blue eyes with pinpricks of light. Her voice rose. "So let's get the *fucking* class started, shall we?" Her laughter was surprisingly girlish.

Shaking his head and grinning, Dee Dee said to his father in Thai, "Remember? I told you she's cool."

Edana pressed her knuckles against her hips and glared at him like a schoolmarm. "No speaking Thai in my classes." She softened the rebuke by smiling at them, first Lek, then his son; she understood the Thai hierarchy too.

For such a pixie, Edana had a commanding presence that she turned on and off at will.

Lek was mesmerized by this tiny woman with the big mouth and long platinum hair, fine as a child's and parted to one side, so he couldn't think of anything to say, until he finally managed, "Excuse me, but where are you from? I can't put… I can't place your accent at all, and I've never heard the name Edana before."

"I've lived all over the world, but I grew up in a tiny village in the mountains of Norway where it can rain or snow for almost thirty days straight."

"Really? That's one of the few countries in Europe I've never visited."

"Good. Save your money and go somewhere cool like Florence or Amsterdam, because Norway is freezing cold and mind-bogglingly boring." While she spoke her eyes never left his. This was an improvement. He didn't see any mockery or pity in her eyes. Though he couldn't have said exactly what he did see.

"I like that. I didn't know mind-boggling could be used as an adverb, but hey, you're the professor."

Dee Dee held up his arm and stared at his watch.

"Okay," she said. "Sorry to keep you waiting. Let's start the class now. It was really nice to meet you, Lek. I guess we'll see each other again."

"Sure. Cool to meet you too."

Lek went into the kitchen to make some green tea, her voice echoing in his head. "That's okay. I talk shit all the time. Let's get the *fucking* class started, shall we?"

Edana's fashion sense was also striking: the ankle-length, red velvet dress with long sleeves and a string of pearls around her neck, like a little girl dressing up as a Hollywood starlet from the fifties.

Smiling to himself, he washed the same cup three times in a row.

Lek brushed his teeth, combed his long, dyed-blond hair, and put on some underarm deodorant. He thought about changing his clothes, but that would be too obvious.

By the time Dee Dee's class ended he was sitting on the black leather sofa in the living room, under the chandelier strung with models of Japanese film monsters and Hello Kitty dangling from a noose, switching between a subscriber's copy of *The New York Times* (Did that make him look stuffy?) and *The Selected Poems of Anne Sexton* (Was that too literary for her?).

As Dee Dee was showing her out, Lek said, "Hey professor, could I speak to you for a minute, please?"

"Sure." She sat down on the other black leather couch to his right.

Lek offered her a cigarette. "I know I shouldn't but I can't help encouraging certain people to smoke. That way I'll have a lot of cool company in the cancer ward."

She laughed and took the Black Devil. Lek leaned over to light it for her. The shadow of the flame leapt into her eyes.

"Thank you."

"You're welcome."

"What did you wanna speak to me about?"

"Oh, nothing much. I'm just curious about my son's level of English. I don't hear him speak all that much around the house."

"He's really good and his vocabulary is excellent. But he still has problems with the past tense and conditional clauses and phrasal verbs. Nothing we can't sort out."

"That's good to hear. So you said you've lived all over the world. If you don't mind me asking, like where?"

"Well, it's a long story, but when I was eighteen I moved to New York because my boyfriend played guitar in this industrial band called the Riot Act. Then I was teaching English in Prague for a year, and I worked as a rock critic and music writer in Amsterdam for a while, made jewellery in Osaka and travelled around Southeast Asia by myself for ten months. Then, when I was twenty-five, I was supposed to be the trophy wife for this corporate lawyer in LA. Like he bought me a ten-thousand-dollar dress and I remember sitting in a five-star hotel, wearing the dress, really bored and waiting for him, when all I wanted to do was go out drinking with my friends in a scummy punk rock club. But you can't wear a dress like that to clubs like those."

Lek knew she was blunt, but he hadn't expected this torrent of personal details.

Edana spilled some ashes on the glass coffee table, pulled a tissue out of her purse and wiped them up. He appreciated the effort.

"What happened to the marriage?"

"Long story short, my fiancé had this Persian cat that he really loved and one day she got out of the house and I couldn't find her. So I looked all over the yard, on the street and – do you know who lived down the block in another mansion? Alice Cooper."

Lek pushed his bangs back and grinned. "The king of shock rock. I used to worship Alice and still listen to his *Greatest Hits* album sometimes."

"I think the cat got into Alice Cooper's estate. But you know, I wasn't going to ring his front gate and say, 'Hi, Alice. *Killer* is a great album. By the way, have you seen our cat?'"

"Wise move. I suppose Alice was probably sacrificing the cat in a Satanic ritual."

Edana's laughter bubbled up into her eyes like champagne. "So I lost the cat and that was the end of our marriage plans. I guess he loved Cleocatra more than me." In her smile he caught a glint of something cold that suggested the relationship didn't mean that much to her in the first place. Was that it or was it just a trick of the light? Or was he misreading her completely?

Lek reached for another cigarette from Malaysia. The cloves perfumed the air and sweetened his lips. He looked at Edana. It was strange how she sat there with her thighs clamped together, her legs facing the coffee table, palms resting on either knee. Her head swivelled in his direction, but her body and hands didn't move. She seemed so open yet her body language said exactly the opposite.

In a skinny hand with twig-thin fingers (no rings on any of them he noticed) Edana picked up her black leather purse and put it on the table. "I hope this doesn't seem rude or unprofessional or anything." She pulled a half-finished bottle of Thai sugarcane rum out of her purse. "But I'm finished working for the day and I don't have any more classes until tomorrow afternoon. I'd never drink and work, you know. Could I have a glass, please? You can have some too if you want. Sorry it's only the cheap stuff."

Lek picked up the bottle. "Sure, I'll get you a glass. Any cola, soda, or ice?"

"No, thanks. I always take my alcohol straight so that nothing dilutes the taste, and I don't do sugar."

Lek went into the kitchen. He poured some rum into a glass for her. Without even thinking about it, he poured a shot into another glass, added some coke and ice cubes, stirred it up with an index finger and put the finger in his mouth. It was his first taste of alcohol in more than five years.

His stomach buckled. He closed his eyes and rubbed his forehead. For a few dizzying seconds he thought he was going to throw up. This was wrong. He had to throw the drink down the drain.

One glass wouldn't be too bad. It was mostly coke, hardly any rum in it. Lek picked up the two glasses and went back to the living room.

He handed the glass to Edana. She smiled at him for the thirtieth time – did she smile at everybody like this? – and said, "Cheers. I like your T-shirt. Cannibal Corpse is one of my favourite bands."

Lek's eyebrows reached for his hairline. "Really? You like death metal?" She had to be joking.

"Yeah-ahh, the Corpse *rocks*!" Now she sounded like a total LA girl. "I started listening to them when I was nine or ten. That's one good thing about Norway. We have really good scenes for death metal and black metal. Is that what you play? Dee Dee said you're a famous musician in Thailand."

"I've sold about ten million albums here, I guess, and many more millions in pirated copies I didn't sell, but I've had songwriter's block, or just ran out of material and ideas quite a few years ago. To answer your question, no, my music was based more on sixties pop, seventies punk and hard rock, and Motown, country and rockabilly, mostly American and British folk influences, that I sort of patched together into my own sound. I only got into death metal when I was going through my first divorce and drinking a lot and doing too many drugs, went to Cambodia for a while and thought I'd write some songs about the genocide and the Killing Fields that would be a lot heavier than –"

"Oh, I visited the Killing Fields at least ten times when I lived in Phnom Penh."

Lek didn't like being interrupted. He gave her a sharp glance intended as a warning sign. Edana didn't seem to notice it and kept jabbering. Her eyes were glowing like blue candles on a birthday cake. Even so, her body didn't move. Her thighs were still clamped together. Her voice got louder, but her hands remained on her knees. "Yeah, but you know where I wanna go now? They found this other secret prison that the Khmer Rouge had where about thirty thousand people were tortured and executed. That's twice as many as Tuol Sleng in Phnom Penh."

"I've been there, the high school-turned-torture centre, and tried and failed to write a decent song about it. If you don't mind me asking, what's your interest in all of this?"

For once, Edana looked coy and evasive. She took another drink. Without asking she reached for one of his cigarettes. Were they already on such familiar terms?

Pretending not to look at her, Lek smoked and waited. This was one of his specialties: the insightful question that unlocked puzzle boxes in the people around him; he'd tape record their answers in his head and play them back when he was writing songs.

Lek was disappointed by her non-answer. "My interest? I don't know it's just interesting, that's all."

That wasn't it. She was holding something back. One way or another he'd get it out of her. First he'd confess to his own morbid fascination with all the wars in Indochina. Then she'd have to respond.

"If you want to know the truth," he said, looking straight at her, "I grew up on an American air base in north-eastern Thailand. My father was a paratrooper from Bangkok in the Royal Thai Airborne and my mother was a local woman and former sugarcane farmer. So when I was young there were these bombers taking off all the time, but we didn't really know where they were going or who they were bombing. Those missions were secret. I'm not even sure a lot of the pilots knew what was really going on."

He flicked some ashes in the ashtray and continued. "When you're young, everything is black and white. It's us against them, it's good guys and bad boys, the freaks against the straights, the theme of a million rock and punk songs. Later in life, things start to look a lot greyer. So I guess I was in my late teens when I found out about this whole secret war started by Nixon and Kissinger, and how hundreds of thousands of innocent people got bombed in Cambodia and Laos, so that many of them felt like they had no choice but to join the communists. Still later, when the Vietnamese kicked out the Khmer Rouge, and I found out that the Americans and the Chinese and the Thais were all backing the Khmer Rouge, and some of the top brass were even living on Thai soil, and their leader Pol Pot had a holiday home in Pattaya, and had a personal minder who was a top general and future prime minister of Thailand, I was convinced we were on the wrong side, and that our country was harbouring some of the most *evil, despotic, war criminals*" – Lek punched the air with his cigarette like a drummer doing cymbal crashes– "of the entire twentieth century. It was a complete fucking disgrace. So I wanted to go there, partly out of guilt, partly to set the record straight in some new songs, and see it for myself. That's my interest."

Lek stubbed out his cigarette. Surely that would get a reaction out of her. Once again, she surprised him by saying, "Can I use your bathroom, please?" For a few seconds he wondered if she'd been listening to him at all.

He pointed down the hallway. "Second door on your left, one past Dee Dee's room."

Thinking about his son reminded him that he'd left the bottle out in the kitchen. Lek ran and grabbed it. If Dee Dee discovered he was drinking again – and drinking with his teacher no less – all the bridges they'd rebuilt in the last few years would be swept away. Lek poured most of the rum into her glass, saving only a shot for himself. Shooting glances towards his son's door he walked to the kitchen to add some coke and ice.

This was so *wrong*. Here he was drinking again and flirting with Dee Dee's teacher who was only around thirty or so. Yet, he had to admit, it was also the most exciting thing that had happened to him in years.

What was taking her so long? She'd been in the bathroom for at least ten minutes. Was she making a phone call or what? Lek replayed their conservation in his head. He could go along with most of her stories, but one thing didn't sit right: No ten-year-old girl could get into Cannibal Corpse. If not an exaggeration, it had to be a lie. When he'd stayed in New York for eight months, recording English-language demos for a record deal that never materialized, Lek had been to a few death metal gigs. The only women in the audience – outnumbered at least twenty to one – looked like biker chicks, or fetish models, or like they'd been dragged there against their will by their boyfriends.

Lek decided to test her. He went over to the teak cabinet that held a thousand of his CDs, all in alphabetical order, pulled out a Cannibal Corpse album (*Tomb of the Mutilated*), and cued it up. He looked at the cover: an illustration of a male monster performing cunnilingus on a blood-spattered, female ghoul. *Subtle and tasteful*, he thought, laughing to himself. *I should've hired this guy to do my album covers. Oh, they'd love this in Ubon Ratchathani.*

Lek hadn't spun the disc in years. Except during that especially dark period of his life, he only liked death metal in small doses. The speed, the ferocity, the growling vocals and cutthroat melodies grated on him after five or six songs. Glancing at some of the song titles like "I Cum Blood" and "Entrails Ripped from a Virgin's Cunt," he thought, '*this band is beyond over the top. They're like the soundtrack for a snuff movie.*'

After a good fifteen minutes in the bathroom, Edana finally came back.

"I've got a surprise for you," he said. With the remote, he detonated the first track, "Hammer Smashed Face."

She sat down on the couch in exactly the same position as before: thighs clamped together, knees pointing towards the coffee table, not him, her palms resting on both knees. Only ten seconds into the song she smiled and said, "How did you know that *Tomb of the Mutilated* is my favourite Cannibal Corpse album? Are you psychic? You give off some pretty heavy vibes, you know." Again: the LA girl.

Lek shrugged and grinned. "Just a lucky guess." But it was true. Out of the six albums he had by them, why had he chosen that one?

"I think 'Hammer Smashed Face' is one of their best songs."

She'd passed that test. Lek didn't think it was a good omen, though. In disbelief, he watched her while sipping his drink. If she loved the song so much, then why wasn't she reacting? She didn't tap her feet, bob her head, or sway to the beat. She wasn't moving at all. Her eyes were closed, her face a blank. She almost looked like she was dead.

After Lek ordered another bottle of whiskey from the corner store, and they started drinking again, he didn't remember that much the next day, except for the incredible amount of things they had in common: movies like *Apocalypse Now*, novels like *Under the Volcano*, bands like the Jesus and Mary Chain.

As dark as her obsessions were, Edana was a jolly and effusive drunk, telling him anecdote after anecdote about her adventures all over the world. "I thought it was going to be interesting to be a journalist in Europe and write about the EU. Sorry, but I'm not gonna write any fucking stories about passports for pets."

No matter how nasty some of her wisecracks were – "Whenever someone I know has a baby, I immediately delete them as a friend on Facebook because I don't wanna look at their new baby pictures every two hours." – she said them with no traces of malice in her voice, frequently laughing and using smiles for semicolons.

The worst part of the night, he remembered that clearly enough because the encounter had sobered him up immediately, came when Lek bumped into Dee Dee in the kitchen. His son glanced suspiciously at the whiskey and coke in Lek's hand, but only said, "It's almost two in the morning. You and my teacher have been talking and listening to music for about seven hours."

It was like being a teenager again, except Dee Dee had become his father and Lek had to pretend that he wasn't drunk. "Is it that late?" He was genuinely surprised. "I'd better send her home."

Before Dee Dee smelled the alcohol wafting off him, Lek (conscious of every step) returned to the living room. He tried to make it up to his son by calling a taxi for Edana a few minutes later, but Dee Dee was stubborn and lacked the ability to forgive people. Lek couldn't believe that he still wouldn't talk to Ying, whom he'd first brought home on the night Joey Ramone died. After all that she'd been through, the spells of depression, her friend's abortion and giving up music to study library science, the least Dee Dee could do was talk to her. But whenever Lek mentioned her name, he said, "Who's that? I don't know anybody by that name." He was stubborn in a selfish, childish way, possibly, Lek thought, because he was an only child.

Even though it was late Lek didn't feel sleepy. Edana's skill as a raconteur, combined with the energy she transmitted through the power points of her eyes, had charged him up. Lek needed to get grounded. So he grabbed the whiskey and coke and lurched into his soundproofed music room to crank up his '62 Fender Jaguar, the perfect guitar for someone with such small hands. Sitting on a small amplifier, he ran through a set of cherished covers, "Looking for a Kiss" by the New York Dolls, "Gimme Shelter" by the Stones, "Answering Machine" by the Replacements, "Jane Says" by Jane's Addiction, "Picture My Face" by Teenage Head, Patti Smith's "Dancing Barefoot" and Del Shannon's "Runaway," followed by an English version of his most upbeat single, "The Heir to the Throne of Her Heart," with a passion he hadn't felt in years.

His playing was sloppy, his voice rusty, but that was only a matter of practice.

Lek felt like he was coming out of a coma, reawakening to his youth, for the most youthful of reasons: to impress a girl.

After a decade as an underground rock musician, Jim Algie moved to Thailand in the early 1990s to begin penning feature stories, travel guides, history tomes, wildlife documentaries, crime reportage, books like the non-fiction collection, Bizarre Thailand, *an acclaimed short-fiction collection entitled* The Phantom Lover and Other Thrilling Tales of Thailand *and, in 2017, the medley of literature, punk history and his own experiences in music called* On the Night Joey Ramone Died: Tales of rock 'n' punk from Bangkok, New York, Cambodia and Norway, *from which the excerpt in this anthology was taken.*

His website is at: www.jimalgie.club

Sleeping Beauty

Mark Bibby Jackson

The left eyelid lifted but the right refused to follow suit. Reluctantly, Jack rolled over and stretched his left arm across the mattress to the small wicker table where he usually left his phone to charge overnight. In its path lay a body.

Careful not to disturb it, he reached further across and eventually managed to find his phone. Then, squinting his right eye as hard as he could, he managed to make the numbers on the screen come into focus. It was eleven. The rays of light pouring in from the inadequately drawn curtains revealed that it was still the morning… just. As to what day it was only time would tell.

Leaving last night's beauty to sleep, he moved towards his small bathroom and washed away as much of the sins of the night before as he could. The gentle jet of water refreshed him sufficiently to realise that he was lacking two of life's essential ingredients – caffeine and nicotine. As he brushed his stained yellow teeth, he looked at himself in the mirror. The cause of his right eye's earlier reluctance soon became apparent as he detected a large bruise forming beneath it. He knew better than to touch it, but still did. The sharp jolt of pain that coursed through his head was the first proof of life that morning. When it departed he was left with a familiar dull throb. Clearly, there was much about the previous night for him to discover. The identity of the woman in his bed for one.

A towel wrapped precariously around his waist, he moved back towards his bedroom leaving a trail of water in his wake. Then picking up his packet of cigarettes, he walked out onto the narrow balcony. It certainly was a beautiful day, but then again it nearly always was in the Cambodian capital of Phnom Penh. Confronted with the blinding light he squinted as he felt his way into the pack, only to discover a lighter and nothing else.

"Nothing will come of nothing," he mumbled to himself, as he realised he had to venture out into the world, or at least down the solitary flight of stairs to the store below where the cause of his future death lay in wait – all twenty of them neatly stacked with Philip Morris's ringing endorsement. The girl still lay motionless – he had long admired the Khmer appetite for sleep.

"Let sleeping bitches lie," he said more to himself than to his unknown companion, as he left a $50 note by the side of the bed in case she awoke before his return. He was feeling generous. He passed through his doorway into the darkened stairwell, a t-shirt, pair of shorts and flip-flops replacing his threadbare towel. No point in locking up, there was nothing in his pad worth stealing.

"As I said it was amazing, absolutely amazing, you should have seen the size of it. Truly I've never seen anything like it before."

The man's voice kept penetrating his protective wall of silence, with little meaning. Upon reaching terra firma, Jack had resolved that something more substantial than the Marlboro Reds now resting in the ashtray in front of him was needed to kick-start his day. So he had navigated the 50 metres or so to the Rising Sun, an English pub run by a retired Australian soldier who had come to Phnom Penh in the UNTAC days, when the UN in its infinite wisdom had decided to take over the running of the country. Two decades of nepotism, corruption and land grabbing followed, as Cambodia was governed by a cabal of politicians that would make the Sopranos appear like a well-balanced and democratically elected movement. Jack was a much later arrival, drawn by the all-pervasive lawlessness that suited his inner personality.

"Honestly I've never seen one that size before, was the size of a rat."

But upon arriving at the Rising, he changed his stratagem once more, ordering a Beer Laos instead of his fully-intended half breakfast. One look at the congealed mess that lay on his companion's neglected plate had been enough. Anyway, it was too early in the day for solids – never before the sun had passed over the yard arm. He took a gulp of his beer before realising that beneath the cacophony of motorbike horns, cars reversing and the screech of construction noise, the soliloquous conversation had fallen silent.

"You don't say." Jack sensed his mouth open and heard the words emanating from it without registering that it was he who had spoken.

"I do. As large as a rat."

The other man was a permanent fixture at the Rising Sun. Or at least he always seemed to be sat there each time Jack wandered past. The man's girlfriend next to him played obediently on her mobile phone, although her role was that of a strictly neutral observer to her beau's conversation. Clearly, their relationship had progressed to a higher spiritual plane where traditional human norms of interaction were no longer required.

"Me go shopping now," she interrupted the resumed pause in their conversation. The man nodded at her and handed across some notes before she disappeared off into the distance side-saddle on the back of one of the motorbikes parked on the street outside.

"A rat. As big as a rat," the man repeated presumably not for the last time that day referring to the large Tokay gecko he had seen climbing the Rising's walls the previous evening.

Jack nodded once more before taking a long drag on his cigarette, thankful he had not fallen into the same trap that so many of his acquaintances had – just like a rat. He smiled at his own wit, which was all the encouragement that the man required.

"Yes. A rat," he laughed from the depths of his vastly over-exaggerated belly, even though even he must have realised it wasn't in the slightest bit funny.

Jack had lived in Phnom Penh two years now, arriving in the summer of 2008, even though the city had no real seasons. Just hot and wet or hot and dry, rather than summer, winter, spring and autumn. A long-since-forgotten intention to visit the temples of Angkor before returning to the UK from Saigon where he had been attempting to teach English to the willing but misguided Vietnamese youths. He had made it as far as the Cambodian capital, but no further, the ancient Khmer ruins still no more than the stuff of National Geographic documentaries.

His fate had been determined one Saturday night at the nightclub Heart of Darkness, like so many not-so-young men before him. Her name was Mom, although she looked nothing like any mother he had encountered before. They had met on the dance floor and moved with a deftness his feet normally never possessed to the hotel room he had booked just around the corner. Two weeks, one phone, a motorbike, and a close shave with building an outside toilet for her family home later, Jack realised that the path of true love was in reality a wide highway and one on which he had most definitely been taken on a ride.

But all that was in the past now. He felt no bitterness towards his former femme fatale, even regretting the time he had slapped her face when he eventually succumbed to the reality of his folly. Now, when their paths occasionally crossed, they would smile at each other with appropriate vagueness, leaving Jack uncertain whether she would even be able to pick him out from a police identity parade. All that was very much in the past. Jack never allowed any girl to take advantage of him anymore.

Last night was an exception which he very much doubted proved the rule. After the Rising, he had headed to the Green Vespa for a few more beers, then as the clock ticked its way catatonically towards nine he slid around the corner to Street 104, where his sirens awaited. He hadn't intended to take a girl back with him – he never did – but as this morning had proven, he clearly had. His recollection of the evening's events flitted in and out of focus like the cine films of his youth. He could vaguely recall having an argument with some girl on the street, whom he apparently owed some money or something equally mundane.

More bars, drinks, watching the girls dancing on the tops of the bars, hip hop strangling his ear drums in the background. A few uncertain steps along the street. A motorbike drive across the town, the wind blowing through his unfettered hair. A blast of horns. A sudden stop. Careless efforts to extract some notes from his pocket. An argument. Shouting at the moto dup driver. Eventually his notes finding their way to the surface of the road as he staggers off once more towards the sanctuary of the Heart. A queue he bypasses. The smiling security guard's feeble efforts at feeling for his non-existent weapon. And once more at the bar, a gin and tonic resting on the counter in front of him. And then oblivion.

"Looks like you had quite a time of it last night," the man – a large bottle of Angkor now replacing his three-quarters-finished half-breakfast – once more intruded on Jack's reverie. "Does it hurt?"

"Not really." Jack lied from behind his deceptively friendly smile.

"Still, should see the other guy, right?" The man continued oblivious to everything. A false laugh to accompany his failed attempt at humour.

"Yeah, right." The man was really beginning to irk him. Jack could sense the barely-contained rage surge inside him. He rose from his chair and approached the other man. "One more Beer Laos." He said to the waitress just in time, before he made his way to the toilet.

A man attired in women's clothes, his large penis appearing from beneath his dress greeted him. It was a familiar sight. At least here. A caricature sketched many years ago and now hanging on the unisex toilet wall. Jack inspected his face once more. The swelling was settling down, the red slowly turning a darker colour as the throbbing pain resided.

"The other guy." Right. If only he could remember who he, or for that matter she, was. He returned to the table relieved to see that he was now alone, the other man having departed leaving him with his restless thoughts.

The sun was beginning to set by the time Jack left the Rising. Normally he would walk along the riverside. The best time of the day, as the heat was beginning to relent and Phnom Penh's community descended upon the coiffured communal space to do some aerobic dancing or stroll arm-in-arm with their lovers.

Jack was about to accompany them when he remembered he had forgotten to turn off the air conditioning when he left home that morning. He made his way back up the narrow stairwell that now smelt of stale piss. He fumbled with his key for the door, before recalling he hadn't locked it. Pushing it open he made his way through the kitchen to the bathroom. He looked once more at his face in the mirror. The beer had dulled all relic of pain, but the evidence of his unknown assailant was still all-too-obvious. If only he had some make-up with which he could disguise it. He walked towards the bedroom, the only room with air-conditioning. He could feel the reassuring coldness oozing through the open door.

Inside she lay there naked on the bare mattress. Exactly as he had left her. Once more the sudden surge of anger before he realised that she couldn't still be asleep. He tried to recall their meeting the night before, of bringing her back to the room, of their having sex, arguing, anything, but all was blank.

Beside her body lay a piece of foil. Nothing more.

He turned her naked body over and examined it. No sign of a struggle, no marks on her, no cuts nor bruises. Above her heart a tattoo of an animal; a tiger, or leopard or something. A slight scar beneath her knee, no doubt from some motorbike accident. Apart from that she looked perfect.

However, whoever the girl lying in his bed was, one thing was beyond doubt, she was most definitely dead.

***

Mark Bibby Jackson is a freelance travel writer and publisher of AsiaLIFE Cambodia, the leading lifestyle and travel publication in the country that never ceases to amaze. His Cambodian Trilogy has won much international acclaim with To Cook A Spider being the national winner for Best Asian Cuisine Book at the Gourmand World Cookbook Awards 2016. His short story A Slow Death won an award at the Essex Book Festival Crime Writing Short Story Competition. His third novel The Circle Line will be published in 2017, as will the third in his Cambodia Trilogy series, which will see the return of Cambodia's most popular detective Inspector Satya.

Stamp of Approval

John Fengler

The now defunct President airlines was a short lived Cambodian carrier born in the mid-nineties, that flew for about a decade between Phnom Penh and Bangkok. The post-glasnost Russian crew were abrupt but efficient.

I was waiting in the main lounge area of Bangkok's Don Muang airport and struck up a conversation with an affable pint sized t-shirt and flip flop wearing Khmer man who was in town with his family to attend to some medical needs.

The plane was a 737 that had about a hundred and forty seats. On this particular flight there were nine passengers, five of whom were my diminutive new friend and his family. The ticket agents in their infinite wisdom seated all of us together in the three middle rows of the plane. I suppose it made the in-flight service for the fifty minutes that much easier.

My new friend was surprised to learn of my deep interest in his country, which seemed to ingratiate me to him. As we were landing he asked if he could give me a lift to town?

Wanting to be gracious I accepted, although secretly I was dreading the thought of being squeezed into the back of an overcrowded beater car.

As we were deplaning I suddenly remembered that I would have to go through customs and immigration and fill out a time consuming amount of forms. I said that although I greatly appreciated his offer I didn't want to hold them up, but that it was really great to have met him.

He gave me a cryptic smile and told me to give him my passport and to wait across the hall.

Pochentong airport now is a gem of modernity and efficiency. That was not the case two decades ago. Then it was a chaotic third world affair officiated by stern and wary uniform wearing military officers.

I watched my friend approach the line of officials and saw them all nervously jump to attention and salute him.

"Who the fuck is this guy?" I thought.

He had a few words with a couple of the men, glanced over his shoulder at me, waved my passport around, and then walked back over to me. He gave me a warm Khmer smile and said; "Ok, let's go."

As we exited the airport a convoy of three tricked out Land Rover's pulled up. My friend motioned to the lead car and said; "Ok, this one is for you. I will be in the next one with my family."

"Who the fuck is this guy?"

I had a favourite squalid little guest house that I'd stayed in for years. It was on a dark pot-holed road on the edge of downtown. It offered big rooms, a hammock on the balcony, and was only six bucks a night. And best of all it was owned by the most congenial Mr. Vuthy and his wife. I had never really considered just how down market the place was until pulling up in a Land Rover. I also sensed how uncomfortable my drivers were to be taking me there.

The fleet pulled up in front with one man jumping out of each vehicle and taking a forty-five-degree stance. My host came over to me and asked if this was really where I wanted to stay? He gave me his card which seemed to confirm what I already knew about him, which was that he worked in the Agriculture and Forestry department. He invited me to join him on an official Mekong tiger tracking project any night where our schedules matched.

The family wished me well and the caravan drove off. I lost his card soon thereafter.

Mr. Vuthy then stepped out of the shadows to greet me. He regarded me in a way I had not seen before and said; " Nice to see you again, Mr. John. Excuse me but why you know big government official?"

I told him that he was just some nice guy who worked with tigers that I'd met in Bangkok. He looked at me like I was a fool and said; " No, he is minister here. You need to be careful with government people."

Fully aware of Cambodia's recent history and the understandable wariness of the people, as well as their tenuous relationship with the government I acceded to his concerns.

I spent the next couple of weeks touring the capital and environs before deciding to see if I could get into Vietnam by way of the river. It seemed a novel approach. Nowadays it is an over touristic commercial route serviced by many tour companies. Not so back then.

I got wind of a small cargo boat that was heading to Chau Doc, which was a predominantly Muslim inland port town in southern Vietnam. I negotiated a transport rate with the captain of the little boat and arranged to meet him in the morning. It was there that I met Leila. She had apparently gotten the same idea as me, and we would comprise a passenger list of two people. She was an attractive gal, half Swedish, half Iraqi.

It was not common practice then, nor is it a great idea now, to inquire on people's business in the area past basic pleasantries. Most folks were up to some nefarious business in S. E. Asia, and it was mostly better to stay in the dark.

After sniffing each other out and sensing no threat we both relaxed and set off on our six-hour river cruise. We were surrounded by lush jungle several hours in when the captain said that we would have to go to immigration as we were now in Vietnam.

He pulled the boat to the shore and threw a tow line around a bamboo pole. He said that we should leave our bags on-board and walk about a hundred yards down a jungle path to the immigration office, and then to rejoin the boat downstream after we were finished.

Leila and I alighted uncertain as to whether or not we'd ever see our backpacks again.

The immigration office was no more than a shack which was staffed by a perplexed looking young Vietnamese officer who was very surprised to see us. I suspect he would have been surprised to see anyone as this was a fairly obscure outpost.

He tentatively took my passport and flipped through it. He looked at me and then looked back at the document. He gestured excitedly at my passport and then pointed at me. I told him I didn't understand what he was trying to say.

He flipped through the pages again, this time more slowly and thoroughly and then shot me a definitive look. He said; "No stamp!"

"What?"

"No enter Cambodia stamp. How can you be here?"

And then the blinding epiphany of unintended consequences hit me. My affable Khmer minister pal who had expedited my entry into the kingdom, had done so without any thought to how it might affect my departure. Probably wouldn't have been an issue had I left the way I came in, but here I was at a jungle outpost arriving by cargo boat, traveling with a half Iraqi woman and no entry stamp to the country I was now trying to exit.

I decided to go into indignant New Yorker mode, which is the fall-back position for times when you have no argument and your window is closing. It's times like these when military bureaucrats in an authoritarian regime work for you.

They don't assign generals to these sorts of shacks, and the last thing in the world this guy wanted was an incident that would shine any spotlight on him.

And I was well within my rights to be leaving without an entry stamp! Or so I had him believe.

With great hesitation he hefted his stamp laden fist onto an ink pad and slapped my page. He then slunk back into his creaky wooden chair and looked away.

Leila's paperwork was seemingly all in good order.

And sure enough our boat was tied up downstream waiting for us to continue to Chau Doc, our port of entry to the Vietnamese mainland.

***

John Fengler is a traveller and writer, originally from New York City, now residing in Chiang Mai, Thailand. His career has traversed the worlds of film, medicine, and politics. He has travelled extensively throughout SE Asia over the last thirty-five years, starting out with work in a Cambodian Refugee camp. He once swam naked across the Mekong into the waiting arms of a Burmese military patrol, went spelunking in a temple cave with Thai monks, and has been killed off several times in film scripts. John is also the inspiration for a forthcoming book about a semi-retired CIA agent living in Thailand.

Swing the Cat

Bob Couttie

Except for the buzzing of his mobile phone, there was nothing different about Andre Velon's morning. Years ago he would have snatched it up to take orders from his superiors in the organised crime and terrorism division of the Directorate Generale, or receive updates from those under his command, or receive tip-offs from informants who trusted only Velon to keep their identities secret.

Now he was in Cambodia, his own man. All that remained of that past was the frequent pain in his leg, the scar on his thigh and the Marseille waterfront shoot-out that put it there. Now he was at peace with himself, far from the stresses that once triggered his darkest demons, the Black Dog of manic depression that seems to lurk just out of his eye line, waiting.

Forced into retirement, he was no longer at the beck and call of a ringing telephone. It almost invariably meant a pre-recorded message in Khmer encouragingly offering something he neither wanted nor needed. While the device pleaded for his attention, Velon patiently prepared the Mondulkiri coffee in its metal cylinder atop his single coffee-cup as water boiled in the kettle

The phone stopped ringing as he filled the coffee cylinder with hot water and capped it. Later, as usual, he would check the call log and if it was anything other than the usual unwanted calls and consider calling back if it was someone whose ID was in his small, select list of contacts.

A man of simplicity and habit, he donned his usual grey pants, pale blue short-sleeved shirt, canvas shoes and bush-hat while the coffee percolated through the filter and headed out of the door of his one-room apartment leaving the phone beside the computer on his desk. As he closed the door behind him, the phone rang again.

Night rains had encouraged the jasmine flowers in the little garden to open and the air was scented with honey.

He navigated his way through a flash-mob of small children waving and greeting him with happy 'helloes', to a side-street market all but obscured behind a barricade of gleaming black motorcycles and drivers offering their services. There he bought, as always, a still-warm, fresh-baked baguette from a middle aged woman with smiling eyes.

By the time he returned to the apartment the coffee was ready. As he passed the mobile phone on the desk he noticed that there had been two more calls.

He sliced the crispy baguette lengthwise, took a block of unsalted Normandy butter from his polystyrene icebox and a jar of *confiture de fraise* from a nearby shelf, assembled his breakfast and returned to his desk.

The missed calls had a 084 country code. Velon frowned, he knew no-one in Vietnam, certainly no-one who would have cause to repeatedly try and reach him. He took a perverse pleasure in not having answered the calls.

Then, as he held the mobile phone, the incoming call icon appeared on the screen. He hesitated a moment, the swiped the green phone icon.
"Allo?"

"Hey, Andy, how are you?"

The voice was English, modulated, with a trace of Liverpudlian. It was familiar but he could not place it. He had a photographic memory for images and faces but he could not put a face to the voice.

"You're wondering who the hell I am… Kelvin Reith, we met in Manila."

It was the clue Velon needed: Kelvin Reith, a ship's Master, a little under two metres tall, blond hair and short, neat beard, grey-green eyes. He was fit, a man who could swing a fist with the best of them if need be and a boyish sense of humour.

Somebody had been paying the crew aboard Captain Reith's vessel, a containership, to help smuggle cocaine from Manila, a major drug entrepôt in south east Asia, to Marseille inside hidden compartments in 20 feet shipping containers. An accident with one of the containers exposed the drugs. Interpol got involved and French authorities had sent Velon to the Philippines to co-ordinate with the country's National Bureau of Investigation, its equivalent of the FBI, knowing that his Interpol contact in the NBI was one of the most notorious drug smugglers in south east Asia.

Reith turned out to be a solid, courageous man in a situation of immense danger. In Manila there was much danger in those days.

"Hello, Kelvin, it has been a long time," said Velon, "How did you get my number?"

"I heard you were in Cambodia a while back. A friend put me in contact with a chap he thought would know you, Brigadier-General Chamreun in Phnom Penh, he gave it to me."

Velon smiled, he knew Chamreun as a fine judge of character and someone who would not give a number out without good reason.

"Are you calling for a reason, Kelvin, or just saying 'hello'?"

"You're the only Frenchman I know that can pronounce my name. Background: I swallowed the anchor five years back, these days I navigate a desk, investigator for Club d'Indochine in their office in Vietnam. It's a P&I club – Protection and Indemnity, think if me as an insurance investigator" explained Reith, "One of the member companies is Marunishi Bulker Lines."

"And there is a problem?"

"A dead people problem."

"So, more than one deceased, possible murder, and the ship will come into Sihanoukville carrying coal."

"My god, you're fast."

"C'est simple: You would not be calling anyone in Cambodia if the problem was in Vietnam or Thailand. The only other port is Phnom Penh, if it was there then you'd be talking to Chamreun not me. Sihanoukville is the only deep-sea port and it's just an hour and a half from here. There is also a coal-fired power station near there supplied from Newcastle in Australia. Marunishi operates bulk carriers. And you wouldn't be talking to me if you did not suspect murder."

He heard Reith chuckle down the line. Then Reith offered a price for Velon's services that got his attention. He whistled.

"Don't worry, it's not coming out of my pocket," said Reith.

The ship, the Marunishi Mystique would dock in Sihanoukville the next day. They would have just 48 hours before the vessel departed again for Singapore where it would have its normal turnaround of crew.

"Once they're off that ship we may never know what happened," said Reith.

"That is not a lot of time."

"That's why you're getting the big bucks. I'll pick you up from your apartment tomorrow around eleven and we'll get some lunch."

"How will you find my apartment?" asked Velon.

"I can find anything. Besides, you have GPS on your phone."

They disconnected and Velon sat back in his chair sipping the last of his coffee. He wasn't sure that he should have agreed so quickly, he did not need the money. He was a horse long put out to grass after all. And there was the sense of the Black Dog, twitching in its sleep, just out of sight.

He glanced at the bookshelf where the unframed, fading black and white photograph of his father in his Gendarme's uniform topped by a white kepi was propped against a book on Cambodian colonial history. The photograph showed the man standing outside the gendarmerie at the hill station atop Bokor Mountain just outside the town, a place that Velon, despite his years in Cambodia, had never found cause to visit. It was taken in the interregnum between France lifting its protectorate status over Cambodia and the country's independence in 1954, before Velon Senior returned to his family home in the Midi in the south of France.

He took a deep breath and let his simple, regular routine resume. He put his drawing pad and charcoal sticks into a shoulder bag together with some carefully protected completed drawings. He gave no more attention to the conversation with Reith as, moments later he cycled across the old French Bridge and along the quaint river front lined with casuarina.

He dropped by the souvenir shop and discovered that a couple of his drawings had sold. He replaced them with new drawings, collected the money and deci-ded to eat at Pourquoi, a modest bar near the market run by a couple from the Midi who made him feel at home. He satisfied himself with a dish of cassoulet and a bottle of Belgian wheat beer.

Later, he watched the sun set over the mountains, drinking a pastis *perroquet,* young men and women passing on their motorcycles, the elegant tuk tuks and, as night fell, the lights on the old French Bridge and the riverside walk flicker into life. He set off back to his apartment as the last orange ray of sun vanished and the clouds went dark.

At 11am the next morning Velon got another phone call from Kelvin Reith

"I'm at your gate."

Velon checked his go-bag: Spare clothes, notepad, a small handheld recorder and his mobile phone. Then he walked out of the apartment and locked the door.

Reith was parked at the gate in a dark green Toyota SUV and swung the front passenger door open as Velon emerged from the gate. Putting his go-bag on the rear seat Velon climbed in.

A man of few words, Reith simply said "Are you in?"

Before Velon could speak, Reith had the vehicle in gear and the tyres biting dust.

Reith drove as if he was competing in a rally, aggressively and as close to the edge of the vehicle's performance envelope as the law allowed. Velon refused to be intimidated and sat back as the Elephant Mountains passed on one side and small farmsteads and the occasional river tributary that flowed toward the Gulf of Thailand on the other.

Finally, Reith started the briefing: "She's a bulker, carrying coal. Filipino officers and crew. One Able Seaman went missing before she docked in Newcastle, presumed man overboard. Usual accident investigation started but she departed before the investigation got underway. A second man, the second engineer, died of a fall in the engine room on her way to Fremantle. Police nosed around but didn't have time to interview the crew. Then the first officer was found dead in the Air Scavenge Unit."

"What is an air scavenge unit?" asked Velon.

"Part of the engine, like a big tube on top of the engine big enough for a man to get inside, it makes the engine more efficient. Poor bastard cooked to death."

"Wouldn't he have shouted? Banged on the side, got help?"

"Engine rooms are noisy buggers, everyone wears ear protectors, they would not have heard him."

"You think it's murder?"

"The first officer thought so. He emailed the company before he died but his English was not good, it was mixed with Tagalog and their English and Tagalog was not great so they translated it into Japanese as 'accident'. I got them to send me his original email. My Tagalog is still pretty good. He meant murder. But it was pretty garbled."

Velon asked whether the ship could be detained for a police investigation, Reith explained the intricacies and expense of a detention plus no Cambodian was involved and the deaths happened outside Cambodian waters. And there was an additional irritation, the vessel would have a complete crew change at Singapore, the next port of call and whatever witnesses there were would be scattered among other ships across the globe.

"Let's us say it was murder, and we identify the guilty party or parties, what happens then?"

"The company will have to decide what it wants to do. And there is every chance the murderer will get away with it."

"We shall have to make sure he does not," said Velon.

They passed by the silver tanks of the Cambodia Beer Brewery that mark the outskirts of Sihanoukville and 20 minutes later they drove through the gates of the port.

Multi-coloured containers were stacked in the yards, straddle cranes shuttled other containers to and from a ship at the wharf. To Velon it all felt too familiar. For a moment he closed his eyes and the air carried the sounds and smells of the Marseilles port container yard long ago. There was a loud bang and his eyes jerked open.

"Merde!"

"OK, mate?" asked Reith.

Velon winced as the scar on his leg throbbed with intense pain, he massaged it for a couple of minutes until it died down to a dull, nagging sensation.

Past the container yards was the bulker wharf, smaller, older, surrounded by piles of small light-coloured stones that Velon recognised as bedding for the railway tracks being built between Sihanoukville and Phnom Penh. The single-track line already carried a couple of trains of freight a day and a passenger service was promised.

A short distance away from the wharf was the Marunishin Mystique being nuzzled into position by a pair of bustling tugs towards a group of stevedores waiting to tie her up. She was an old ship with none of the greyhound sleekness of the faster containerships berthed farther along the dock. It struck Velon that she had the feel of an ageing whore, well past her prime but well able to do good work.

"A bit more than 10,000 tonnes deadweight," said Reith.

"Deadweight?" asked Velon.

"Basically, what the ship can carry – cargo, bunker, stores, everything except the weight of the ship. - without sinking. That's the short form."

From the deck of the ship seafarers in orange coveralls and hardhats sent slender lead lines tipped with monkey's fist knots snaking towards the stevedores ashore who pulled on them to bring over the thicker mooring lines which were secured to bollards on the wharf. There was the thunk and whine of the mooring winches as the vessel was drawn snug to the dock.

Reith told Velon to stay put while he got out and opened the rear of the SUV, emerging with a pair of yellow hardhats and fluorescent Hi-Viz vests together with a pair of sturdy black steel-capped safety shoes, which he handed to Velon.

"We're the same size, as I remember," said Reith.

Velon opened the door his side, shucked off his canvas shoes and donned the safety shoes, put on the Hi-Viz vest and picked up his shoulder bag.

"They fit like gloves" he said, stepped out of the vehicle and put on the vest and hardhat.

"Watch where you're going," said Reith. "Ships are dodgy places if you don't stay alert."

By now the gangway had been lowered from the ship's side and secured. Three seafarers came ashore, two in orange coveralls, and the leader with a white short-sleeved shirt with shoulder flashes showing two gold stripes carrying a walkie-talkie.

"Second officer," explained Reith, "Filling in for the dead first officer. His name is Mendez. The crew is Filipino."

Velon nodded as Reith introduced himself to the group and showed his ID to Mendez, who spoke briefly on the radio then instructed one of the seafarers in Tagalog to accompany Reith and Velon and pointed towards the ship's bridge.

The seafarer's name was Luis Carlos, an Ordinary Seaman of around 24. Luis seemed shy and somewhat fey, far from the stereotype of the sailor. Velon logged his name and committed his face to his photographic memory as the young Filipino led them up the metallic, echoing gangway, along the deck past the folding McGregor hatches covering the holds and through a watertight hatch dogged open. Up a step flight of steps and through a metal door they found the bridge and Captain Jaime Rodrigo alone working on a thick wad of paper forms.

Reith introduced himself, then Velon: "He's helping with the accident investigation". Rodrigo extended his hand with a smile that Velon felt was a touch too obsequious.

"It is very sad. Can I offer you coffee? Soft drink?" he said.

Before either could answer, Rodrigo turned to Luis: "Get them some coffee."

Luis lowered his head and walked away.

Velon sensed that Reith was taking his time, building a rapport, telling Rodrigo about his own experiences as a ship's master on whose vessels men had died in accidents. "But it's hard to get some crew to do what they are told," said Reith. It was out of character for Reith, thought Velon, to blame it on crew, he was a man who had accepted the responsibilities of his command.

There was a clatter from the other side of the bridge. Rodrigo glared across at Luis who was putting a plastic swing-top rubbish bin back into position.

"Idiot. Get the coffee," snapped Rodrigo and returned to the conversation with Reith. Luis glanced towards Velon, then back at the rubbish bin and left the bridge.

Those who have been into battle together, have faced death together, have an instinctive, almost telepathic bond. Nothing needs be said, each knows the other's needs without obvious communications, the message transfers through some form of osmosis. So it was that Reith asked Rodrigo to show him the vessel's passage plan, where each event happened on the charts.

"I can show you on the ECDIS," said Rodrigo. ECDIS, the Electronic Chart Display and Information System, was a computer screen on the other side of the bridge which showed the ship's position while it was underway rather like a car's GPS display. Right now it showed a static image of the chart around Sihanoukville Port.

"Can't stand computer screens." lied Reith, "Show me on the paper charts."

Rodrigo led Reith to the chartroom, a separate area to the rear of bridge which housed a chart desk, paper charts, and readouts of the vessel's navigational instruments. At night a curtain is drawn across the entrance to the chartroom to prevent interference with the dark-adaption of those on the bridge, where the lighting would be at it dimmest to enable those on the bridge to see as far as possible under night-time conditions. Some experienced officers get into the habit of drawing the curtain even in day-time when it was not necessary.

Reith was one of those officers, apparently. He drew the curtain as he and Rodrigo entered the chart room, the ship's master made no comment.

Alone on the bridge, Velon went to the rubbish bin and pushed open the swing-top. Inside, among biscuit wrappers and discarded forms, was a brightly coloured brochure which did not seem to belong. Removing the top of the bin he took out the brochure and without looking at it, slipped it into his shoulder bag.

A thudding, clanging noise vibrated through the ship. There was an extension to the bridge, the bridge wing, and Velon went out on it and looked back towards the deck. The hatch covers were being pulled back by a winch like a concertina to expose the coal in the holds. A pair of cranes with bucket grabs waited to unload the ship of its cargo and transfer it to tip trucks on the wharf.

The clock was now ticking. Once the ship was unloaded the investigation would end.

He turned as footfalls sounded behind him. Reith handed him a coffee with one hand while supping at his own cup held in the other. "This is not a happy ship. Deaths aboard ship always rattle a crew, it's like a family, but I'm sensing something else here."

"What are you sensing?" asked Velon quietly.

"Fear and anger, I think. We'll interview the crew in the mess. They don't have to talk to us."

"Filipinos don't like being called 'stupid', they are very sensitive about it," said Velon.

"People have been killed for it," replied Reith, "But remember, it may just be an chance series of bad accidents."

"But your instinct says otherwise," said Velon.

"Want to see some bodies?" responded Reith.

"The bodies are still on-board?" asked Velon, "Where?"

"The meat freezer. Ship's carry bodybags, you know."

"Two of them are. In the meat freezer? With the food?"

"Where else do you keep meat?" said Reith.

Moments later they were being lead through the innards of the ship by a young crewman who seemed subdued. Presently they were led through the mess, where Velon saw Luis swabbing the floor, and into the ship's galley.

The galley would have graced a smart restaurant, or an efficient fast-food outlet. Gleaming steel worktops, industrial mixers, ovens, stove tops adapted to keep pot and pans in place in rough seas. There were three crew in the galley, including the chief cook, who opened the walk-in meat freezer.

There were two bagged bodies lying on a table in the cramped confines of the freezer. Velon shuddered at the cold, not at the bodies.

Reith unzipped one grey plastic bodybag. Inside was the remains of an Asian man in his 40s dressed in blue engineer's coveralls. Velon got Reith to help him tip the body on its side, it moved like a marble statue. Velon noted the ugly indentation on the lower part of the back of the skull and the mass of bloodied, matted, hair around it. A note on the bodybag identified him as Carlos Remora. Velon bent closer to the dead man's head, paying attention to the forehead.

In the second bodybag was Raul Velosos, in his early 30s. His body, too, was as stiff as a totem pole. His fingernails were broken, and there were marks of bruises and cuts on his knuckles, as if he's been in a fight. But the most noticeable thing about the late First Officer Velosos was the blistering of his skin, and its colour.'

"Looks like a lobster," said Reith quietly.

The bodybags were zipped up and Velon and Reith left the freezer, the chief cook dogging the door shut.

Outside, Velon felt warmth returning as Reith asked the guide to take them to the engine room.

To Velon the engine room reminded him of a vast ancient temple. There were gantries and instrumentation surrounding the great bulk of the engine itself, laying at the centre of attention like a reclining Buddha. From somewhere came the rumble of the donkey engines keeping the ship's power alive but for now the big engine was quiescent, waiting, like an angry god about to awake.

The chief engineer joined them and showed them where Carlos Remora had fallen to the green painted steel floor. All they heard, explained the chief engineer, was a bang and they found Remora sprawled, dead. No-one had seen him fall. The now-dead first officer, Velosos, was first person not in the engine room to appear after the fall.

"We turned him over and tried CPR, but he was not breathing," said the chief engineer.

Velon scanned the floor, but there was little to see now. He looked up towards the gantry that ran around the engine about ten metres above and imagined the man falling, not once but several times in different ways.

Reith interrupted Velon's thoughts: "Let's take a look up there."

The chief engineer led them up a steep set of stairs to the gantry to the place Velosos was assumed to have fallen from. Against the engine there was a grey instrument cabinet faced with dials and various readouts, push buttons and keys none of which Velon could identify, or needed to. Reith looked over the gantry rails to the spot where Velosos had landed.

Velon looked at the floor: "Kelvin, please move away."

Reith stepped back as Velon crouched on his haunches and examined the floor. There was a series of dark red-brown spots leading towards the rail. They looked like rust spots but Velon recognised them for what they were. He wetted his forefinger with his tongue and ran it over one of the spots leaving a dark red trail.

"Blood," he announced.

Quickly, Reith got the chief engineer's attention: "Show us where you found the first officer."

Again the chief engineer led them to the green-painted cylinder that lay above the engine, the air scavenge unit. It was almost big enough for a man to stand up.

Unscrewing the wing-bolts that secured the dogs of a heavy hatch at one end, the chief engineer hooked up an engine room crane and pulled the hatch open. Then he shone a torch inside.

"He was found at the other end, dead," said the chief engineer.

Earlier in the day of Velosos's presumed death the first officer had inspected the pistons after maintenance at the last port of call with one of the engine room team helping him.

Reith climbed into the cylinder, leaving the chief engineer to stand guard over the hatch. Meanwhile, Velon walked around the gantry to the other end of the cylinder.

Here, the dogs were not secured by the wing bolts; a latch had dropped into its slot, stopping the hatch from being pushed open from the inside and the hatch itself was not tightly shut. A piece of red cloth had been put through the tiny gap of three or four millimetres. In Velon's mind's-eye was First Officer Velosos amid the thunder and heat of the engine, beating and scrabbling vainly at the hatch, knowing no-one could hear him amid the noise and vibration, desperately pushing a tiny piece of cloth through the gap in the false hope someone would notice.

Velon returned to the other end of the air scavenge unit as Reith eased his way out and the chief engineer secured the hatch once more. Reith thanked the chief engineer then asked the guide from the crew to show them the cabin of the AB who disappeared, Paolo Davide.

Again they wove their way through the ship to the accommodation block to the rear of the bridge and to Davide's cabin. It was scrupulously neat and tidy. On a small inbuilt table was a mobile phone and a charger for a Sony laptop. There was a thick book published by the Transport Workers Federation, and another on maritime law stacked below the mirror. Photos of a young woman and a couple of children were taped to a mirror, and clothes were folded away. It had little to say about Davide's story other than that he was a family man.

Idly, Velon pushed the swing-top of the small plastic trash can. There was another of the coloured brochures he'd found on the bridge and now had in his shoulder bag but he left it in place.

Davide was last seen in the mess just after his six-hour duty finished at 8pm. When he did not appear the vessel was searched in vain. The vessel had backtracked in a search pattern but, not surprisingly, had found no sign of the missing seaman in the black, languid waters of a calm night sea.

Soon afterwards, Velon and Reith set up at a table in the mess, with a laptop, notepads, and Velon's pocket recorder.

Reith looked at Velon in a knowing way: "You've got that 'I ain't saying anything but I know what's going down' look on your face"

"I do?" said Velon, with false innocence.

Pointing at the recorder Reith said: "Remember, you have to ask permission to use that thing. That's the code of practice."

Velon pressed the record button. "Assumptions are dangerous. I had a friend in the US Naval Investigative Service – ever heard of the Munns case?" Reith shook his head.

"A Lieutenant Munns disappeared from a US Navy ship in the Philippines in 1968 along with $18,000 dollars from the ship's safe. It was assumed he'd gone AWOL. No-one could find him. Twenty years later a man confessed to killing the Lieutenant. My friend was one of those who got him to confess. He had actually dropped the body into the ship's fuel tank. So it disappeared."

"Great way to dispose of a body," said Reith, "Heavy fuel oil is very corrosive and you'd have to be very convinced that it was necessary to drain the bunker, time consuming and expensive."

Velon switched off the recorder then checked that it had recorded the conversation. Then he put the machine aside.

"What are you up to, Andy?"

"What do they say on ships? There is more than one way of swinging a cat?" Answered Velon.

"Well, there are those who think we should never have abandoned the Cat o' Nine Tails whipping as shipboard punishment. Those were the days when ships were made of wood and men were made of iron."

It was now far into the afternoon. There were 24 officers and crew to get through. Velon and Reith worked on a priority of people to interview. Then they went over the ship's paper records, by which time it was four in the afternoon and the sense of time running-out weighed on them. For Velon this was the slow yet impatient plodding progress of a criminal investigation.

Like all ships of her size, the Marunishin Mystique was equipped with a voyage data recorder, VDR, which recorded instrument settings, navigational information and even the voices on the bridge. But it would take several hours to work through, hours they did not have.

"So what are we dealing with?" said Reith.

"I think you have two killers," replied Velon, "Let's interview Luis first."

Velon reached into his shoulder bag and brought out the brochure he'd taken from the rubbish bin on the bridge. Reith looked it over. It was a gun catalogue offering a range of weapons, mainly 9mm and 45 automatic handguns.

"Guns?"

"I think it is guns and something else," said Velon, "People have been dumping these brochures."

Velon tucked the brochure back into his shoulder bag as Luis came into the mess and sat in a plastic monoblock chair. He was scared, uncertain, and smiled a lot as Reith took down the man's details, ending each sentence with 'Sir' or 'Opo' for a polite 'yes'. Reith asked him what he knew about Paolo Davide's movements on the day he died.

Davide had gone off duty at 8pm and gone to the mess to meet Luis.

“What did you meet him for?” Asked Velon.

Luis suddenly broke into tears: “It's my fault, my fault. I killed him...”

Reith took a neatly-folded handkerchief from his pocket and handed it to the crying seafarer. “It's okay, mate,” said Reith softly, “Take your time.”

The young man pulled himself together after a few moments and handed back the handkerchief, “Salamat po.”

“Was it because you are gay, I think they say 'bakla' in the Philippines?” asked Velon.

Luis nodded. “They always tease me. That's okay. I am used to being teased, made fun of. I laugh with them so they don't know it hurts. But others, they beat me and slap me and shout at me and call me stupid in front of everyone.”

“Who are the others?” asked Reith.

There was a moment's hesitation. “Captain Rodrigo, and the First Officer. Paolo was trying to help me.”

Paolo Davide, explained Luis, had been preparing a letter of complaint about the officers’ harassment of Luis addressed to the ITF. The letter included details of Captain Velosos's gun-running sideline.

Velon's ears pricked up: “Gun running?”

“Everyone had to buy a gun from Captain Velosos. It was $600, and some didn't want to buy, they wanted the money to go to their family. We had to choose on from a catalogue. Then it would be delivered to our homes in the Philippines. After Paolo disappeared, the captain told us to throw the catalogues away before we reached Australia.”

Velon leaned in toward Luis: "You said you had killed Paolo?"

"I got scared. The Captain and the First Officer would hurt me even more if they found out. I told him not to send the letter. But I thought he would anyway. So… so I went to the bridge and told the first officer about it. He said that, he would deal with it. Then I met Paolo in the mess to tell him what I had done, to make sure he did not send the letter. That was the night he disappeared."

"Who else was on the bridge?" asked Reith.
"The first officer and the helmsman," replied Luis.

Reith thanked Luis and assured him that his account would be kept in confidence and Luis left.

"When does the captain take a watch?" asked Velon.

"Reith responded: "He doesn't on this ship. At least not until after the first officer died."

Velon rummaged through the ships records. "The first officer was on duty when Paolo died and the second engineer fell. "

"Yes, so he can't be a suspect."

"Same helmsman as well. Let's talk to the helmsman."

The helmsman was in his late 20s, bright, and very correct. He was a young man who intended to go far. The helmsman was responsible for following the navigation orders of the officer of the watch. The ship's safety management system dictated that the helmsman be on the bridge at all times.

"So you never left the bridge during your duty?" asked Velon.

"No. Sometimes to get coffee for one of the officers from the mess."

After further questioning about nights when Paolo Davide and the second engineer died, Reith let the man go.

"Odd," said Reith. "The First officer tells him to go and get coffee and the first officer takes over the helm. But all the officer of the watch has to do is call down to the mess and have coffee brought up."
"But then the First Officer has to be at the wheel," replied Velon.

"Ships have automatic pilots," smiled Reith, "That would give the First Officer twenty minutes to leave the bridge, do what he had to do and get back before the coffee arrived. I've spent too much time with you, Andy. I know how you think. But he wouldn't have had time to drop Davide in the fuel tank, if that is what you are thinking."

"Ah, no. That is not the way this cat was swung. There was a laptop charger in Davide's cabin but no laptop. The first officer and the Captain had the motives, and opportunity. But, given the time frame, I don't think the First Officer had time to talk to the Captain after Luis told him about Davide's plan. I can only speculate. The first officer left the bridge, went to Davide's cabin, either killed him or knocked him unconscious there, took his body and the laptop, out onto the deck and threw both of them overboard."

"With no-one seeing him?" said Reith sceptically.

"Someone did. The second engineer. It was easy enough for the first officer to enter the engine room, hit the second engineer on the back of the head with something heavy and tip him over the railings. The injuries at the back of the head could not have been made by the fall, and the blood spatters on the gantry confirm that he was hit before he fell. The first officer simply hid himself around the corner of the gantry and when all attention was on the fallen man, he emerged, to become the first person outside the engineroom to arrive."

Reith let out a heavy breath: "We have no proof of any of this."

"Sometimes," said Velon, "the objective is justice, not proof. I think it is time for us to go and eat."

Arrangements had been made for them to stay at a small hotel on a hill overlooking the port. It was not remarkable and had a dull menu and an unimpressive wine list. As they sat to eat, Velon held up his hand: "No business while we eat, it is bad for the digestion. And this food will require much digesting."

Throughout the meal, the wine, and the second rate brandy that followed they spoke about the old days, swapped stories and exchanged banter about their adventure in Manila like old warriors talking about their battles. They did not talk about murder.

Next morning the sky was bright and clear and cool. Velon felt light, as he always did before the kill in cases like this. He ate a chewy baguette and drank some wishy-washy coffee and then went to meet Reith in the lobby.

"We've only got four hours at the most," said Reith, "They unloaded faster than expected."

"There is only one man I want to talk to today," said Velon. "But interview some others, it will not take long."

"So, the First Officer killed Davide and the second engineer. Who killed the first officer?"

"A man who was very angry and very scared and very cruel." Said Velon, "It will not be a surprise."

Back in the mess Velon sat quietly listening as Reith interviewed another three members of the crew separately. There was no new information.

Then, finally, Captain Rodrigo bustled in, all smiles and obsequiousness.

"I have much to do," he said in a slightly pleading voice.

"We will not take long," said Velon, putting the gun brochure on the table in front of him, "I am not sure about the legality of your gun-running business, after all, you did not handle the weapons yourself, they were never aboard the ship. Perhaps forcing the crew members to buy them is a breach of the labour laws. That is not my call."

Rodrigo shrugged and continued his irritating smile but a hardness came into his eyes.

"You are a confident man, an arrogant man, an exploitative man, Captain. You are a brazen-it-out man when you are caught. So you were not afraid of being accused of gun-running. You would make excuses, blame someone else, muddy the waters enough to make it difficult to prosecute. It was not worth your while to murder someone just for that."

The captain shrugged, his smile wavering.

Reith, sitting beside Velon, was poised and alert, a coiled spring under tension.

"And you did not. Your First Officer, Raul Velolos killed Paolo Davide and the second engineer after Luis told him about the second engineer's plans to send a report to the International Transport Workers Federation, about your abuse of the crew, your gun-running, and your relationship with the First Officer."

Velosos's smile vanished.

"He did it out of loyalty to you, to protect you. You were lovers. It is not unusual for men who are secretly gay to express hatred towards those of that persuasion..."

Rodrigo roared and launched himself across the table, reaching for Velon's throat: "Fuck you, fuck you..." before he could connect with Velon, Reith had grabbed the captain's arms and held him.

"It does not matter," said Velon as Reith forced Rodrigo back into the chair. "Now, let us speculate. Velosos decided to blackmail you. Maybe you were threatening to leave the relationship and abandon him, or maybe just refusing to give him enough share in your gun running. It matters not. He was going to frame you for the murders. I have spoken to many men on this ship, their English is perfectly comprehensible, especially officers such as yourself, so when Velosos sent a message to head office suggesting murder, he garbled it deliberately, to give himself an out. You saw that message and understood its import."

"Get off my ship!" yelled Rodrigo, "Get off!"

Velon continued: "When the engine room was quiet, you lured Velosos there, possibly you knocked him out, or persuaded him to enter the air scavenge unit some other way and left the hatch latched in a way that could have accidentally locked him in."

"Get off my ship. You have no legal right to be here!"

Reith, standing behind Rodrigo, looked at Velon and shrugged.

"We shall go," said Velon, gathering his shoulder bag, "You are not a good leader of men, Captain Rodrigo. A frightened, cowed crew is not a good crew."

"Fuck them," said Rodrigo, "They are animals, slaves, scum, they are stupid, stupid, stupid. They are nothing."

"Come, Kelvin, let us go. Our job is done," said Velon.

"You have no evidence," shouted Rodrigo as they left the mess, "You cannot touch me!"

Later, from the dock, Velon and Reith watched the Marunishin Mystique steam out into the Gulf of Thailand bound for Singapore.

"Well, we have nothing, no evidence," said Reith.

"Report it as an unfortunate series of accidents," suggested Velon.

"How did you know Velosos and Rodrigo were an item?"

"I did not. I just wanted to make him angry, to speak with no restraint. But why else would Velosos kill to protect him? There are times when we cannot fill in all the gaps and we must let a guilty man go."

"It is a pity you didn't record Rodrigo, though. We could probably have leaned on the company to do something about him, even if we can't get him for murder."

Velon smiled: "But I did. Everything he said is recorded..."

He patted his pockets theatrically, "Merde! I must have left it in the mess..."

Marunishin Mystique was now a distant spot on the horizon. "A bit too far to swim," said Reith.

It was a week later, while Velon was drinking coffee at Srey Maly's, watching the sunlight play on the big concrete figures of the 2000 monument, that his telephone rang. It was Reith's number.

"Andy, I've been meaning to call for a couple of days. I thought you might like to know that Captain Rodrigo disappeared en route for Singapore. Presumed MOB – Man Overboard," said Reich.

Velon's mind's eye was in the mess of the Marunishi Mystique, Luis's discovery of his recorder on the chair, the gathering of the crew, listening to the recording, the growing anger.

"Did they, by any chance, look in the fuel tank?" asked Velon.

"Why should they do that?" asked Reith, in a tone of voice that suggested a smile on his face.

Velon bid his farewells, disconnected the call and took a satisfied sip of his coffee.

The cat had swung.

Justice had been served.

Kampot-based British writer Bob Couttie draws on 15 years' experience analysing maritime accidents for Swinging the Cat, the second outing for his retired French detective Andre Velon, and a prequel to Velon: Temple of the Leper King. He lives with three cats and several jars of homemade lime pickle.

Fight the Enemy, Find Love

Ek Madra

1.

Nguyen Hung was born to a poor family in 1961. His father worked alongside the American forces during the Vietnam War and he died in a helicopter crash in January 1975 when his helicopter was shot down by the Viet Cong. Hung's mother, Phan Vang Thi, was an English teacher during the war and after the war ended she lost her teaching job and worked as a tailor.

It was spring, and the trees were green and bright with flowers blossoming under the shining sky in Ho Chi Minh City. Hung completed high school in 1978 and was supported by his mother who told him that English would be his vehicle if he wanted to travel the world. So he worked part-time in a factory making uniforms and took English classes in the afternoon.

One day Hung arrived at work and saw a handwritten notice that said "Looking for volunteers to save Cambodia." The news about how the Khmer Rouge had treated its own people had spread across Vietnam. He had heard other workers talk about how the Khmer Rouge had killed and starved so many Cambodians, and of how others had been worked to death on the work farms. Hung had cried when he had heard how Khmer Rouge soldiers had given Cambodian children so little food and how many had been killed with machetes or clubs.

Hung's working day began at 8am and he and his friends would stop talking and focus on their work. One morning the national radio station aired the voices of Khmer Rouge defectors across

Vietnam. The defectors went into great detail about the Khmer Rouge torturing people at the S-21 detention centre in Phnom Penh. The radio broadcast a series of statements by both Cambodian survivors and ex-Khmer Rouge soldiers who had escaped the horrors and fled to Vietnam. The stories they heard on the radio inspired Hung and his friends to want to join with the Cambodian survivors to drive Pol Pot from power.

At 11:30 the factory's morning session finished and it was also time for Hung and his friends to take lunch.

Hung's values were much like his father's. When he was 4, American troops landed in South Vietnam to support the then democratic government in Saigon. Hung's family had lived on a floating house on the Mekong Delta and they narrowly escaped harm during the U.S. bombardment of the Mekong Delta when the U.S. air force were bombing the Vietcong as they tried to invade South Vietnam in 1968. He'd witnessed many deadly incidents so when people talked about torture and killings, he felt his heart pounding. As he was leaving the factory he read the noticeboard again to make sure he remembered the words in his head and heart. He kissed the noticeboard to make a promise, making the white chalk dust go up his nose and almost making him sneeze. When he left he cycled faster than he ever had before; he was sweating and smelt as bad as a horse. By the time he reached his home at the floating village his shirt was wet through. He parked his bicycle against a banana tree and crossed the plank linking the bank to his house. His mom noticed he was sweating and excited and asked:

"Why are you in such a hurry? What is wrong?"

Hung raised his right hand to tell his mom to wait while he regained his breath.

"I am upset because I heard today about the Khmer Rouge killing children." He said.

"Where did you hear this horrible news?" His mom asked.

"The radio in the factory broadcasted stories from Khmer Rouge defectors and survivors and how Pol Pot had treated own people," Hung told his mom.

"So what can you do, tell me."

Hung told his mom what was written on the board - "Looking for volunteers to save Cambodia" – but his mom told him:

"When we save Cambodia it means we have to sacrifice our lives."

Hung was stunned and looked at his mom nervously. All of a sudden she started crying, remembering the husband she had lost in a helicopter crash. With tears rolling down her cheeks she said to him:

"My lovely son, your dad is already gone and I cannot lose you to any fighting or war. Please stop talking about saving others and put me first. I know you are a caring person and that you are upset when you hear people talking about killing children and starving people to death. But you cannot speak Khmer, not one word, so how can you work with Cambodians? The Khmer Rouge killed their own people so there is no way they will spare your life."

Hung listened to his mom attentively. "I am sorry mom, let's have lunch then."

Over lunch Hung tried to smile for his mom but in his mind he was eager to be a volunteer and do something to help. After lunch his mother started her sewing work and feeding the fish in the small fish farm behind their house. Hung carried clean water from the other side of the river so that his mom did not have to do any heavy work. He later left for his English class in the afternoon but with his head still full of what he had heard that morning and the idea of being able to help.

When Hung returned home he did not talk about volunteering as he knew that his mom was unhappy with the idea. They ate dinner with little talking. The moon shone brightly above the Mekong Delta and the birds flew from the other side of the paddy fields to rest in the marshland of bushes and tall grasses. Normally they would sleep well thanks to the gentle motion of the floating house. But tonight was different. Hung closed his eyes but did not sleep as he thought about how to convince his mom to let him join the volunteer group. While his mom lay and thought of ways to convince her son to not go to Cambodia.

Hung's family was a good example of how Khmer Rouge atrocities touched the Vietnamese heart. Cambodia and Vietnam shared the Mekong which brought so much food to their peoples and helped irrigate their farms. Many Vietnamese were like Hung and felt the pain of what was happening in Cambodia. Hung decided it would be a good idea to make friends who are Khmer Krom, ethnic Khmers living in the Southwest of Vietnam whose lands had gradually been assimilated by Vietnam over several centuries.

After his next English class, Hung chatted with some Khmer Krom as he wants to learn Khmer. Hung was a clever guy and within four months of making friends with some Khmer Krom he could speak Khmer quite well. His mother knew nothing of this until he brought his Khmer friends home. He wanted to prove to his mom that he is capable of handling himself if he goes to Cambodia.

It was now January 1979. After dinner Hung approached his mom and asked her to let him go. His mom was unhappy as she still didn't want him to go. Any time he brought the matter up she had sat with a picture of her late husband and said how scared she was of also losing Hung. But after three weeks she had to give up and instead started praying for her son's safety. She made a necklace of platinum with the photo of her late husband as a tag and gave it to her son, saying:

"May the spirit of your father follow you and take care of you wherever you will be."

Hung hugged his mom.

"I love you mom, but I cannot stand to hear what is happening in Cambodia. Thank you for letting me go."

"You have the same values as your dad. He fought the Khmer Rouge and now you will too. It is too much for me to take but what can I do if your good heart makes you want to help Cambodia?"

Hung was thrilled though he was unsure of what to expect as he had never experienced any fighting in his life. He woke up early, had breakfast with his mom, and then cycled to the factory as he always did. After parking his bicycle, he walked into the factory and stood in front of the noticeboard with his legs and arms apart, sending a signal to his friends that he has a green light from his mom to fight the Khmer Rouge.

On his way home, Hung stopped by the recruitment centre in the outskirts of Ho Chi Minh City. Once he got there they weighed him and measured his height. The lady who did this then told him everything was fine and said:

"Please come back next Monday at 9am to collect your uniform, rucksack, rifle, and grenades. Do you know how to use them?"

"I had some training when I was at high school a year ago, though I may have forgotten some of it as I have spent the last year studying English and Khmer."

"Oh, you speak Khmer?" asked the lady.

"Yes, I learned the language from my Khmer Krom friend."

"I am sure that will impress your commander and he may promote you, so you could work as a translator or a spy. They are wary of using Cambodian soldiers in case they are spies for the Khmer Rouge." said the lady.

"Is there anything I should bring with me next week?" Hung asked.

"Any small personal items, such as your parents' photos, that will help you stop from feeling homesick." She answered.

"OK. My mom gave me a platinum necklace with my late dad's photo on it." said Hung.

"What happened to your dad?" asked the lady.

"He died in a helicopter crash during the Vietnam War," he replied.

"Oh, I'm so sorry. So be careful when you go to Cambodia; I have been told that there are a lot of landmines there." said the woman.

The following Monday Hung woke up early to go to the recruitment centre as planned. He kissed and hugged his mom goodbye, and she told him to be careful and to come home to her soon.

"Please always remember to be nice and do good deeds wherever you go. Your military colleagues are one group of friends but another important group of friends are the locals. They are the ones who know how things are there and could be the ones to save your life. If you face hard times or are in danger, kiss your dad's picture and ask his spirit to help you. I will light incense and ask all our ancestors, but especially your dad, to watch over and protect you. Write to me as often as you can."

Hung gave his mother a final long hug then got on his bicycle. He arrived along with hundreds of other young Vietnamese who had also signed up.

Hung changed into his uniform and, with his handgun in its holster and a couple of grenades attached to his belt, now looked every part the soldier. He packed his personal items into his rucksack and got on the truck that was waiting to take the new recruits away to fight the Khmer Rouge.

There were some 600 soldiers from Vietnam that day, and they moved into the border area. Hung and his comrades had thought that Khmer Rouge forces were strong but once they got to the border they did not see any soldiers but only thin Cambodian men and women planting rice seedlings.

Because Hung could speak some Khmer, he spoke through a loudhailer and told the Cambodians to not be afraid as they had come to free them from the Khmer Rouge. His comrades raised a Vietnamese flag while the trucks kept moving and crossed into Cambodia from the Vinh Te canal. But about an hour later as they reached 5km into Cambodia a gun battle with the Khmer Rouge broke out. A group of young Khmer Rouge in black started shooting at his convoy hitting some of the trucks and puncturing tyres. He jumped off the truck while a support team of tanks moved quickly from the other side, spraying bullets at the Khmer Rouge, killing six and making the rest flee the scene.

Hung and his team were proud of chasing the Khmer Rouge away. One of his comrades made a call for air support and about half an hour later a military helicopter arrived and began shooting at the rice paddy from a distance where they had spotted what they thought were Khmer Rouge soldiers. Luckily Hung's team made a quick radio call telling the air force to cease firing as the people in the rice fields are ordinary people.

Because the Khmer Rouge were poorly trained and equipped the Vietnamese forces moved relatively fast into Cambodia, though the guerrilla tactics employed by the Khmer Rouge sometimes made them move more slowly. At one point the Vietnamese troops had almost reached Takeo province when the Khmer Rouge attacked from the rear, but the combination of air support and tanks soon smashed this tactic.

It was now February of 1979. Hung had now seen many corpses and piles of bones in pits and scattered across fields. His team was resting at one end of a village when Hung spotted a skinny child crawling across the rice field. Hung was shocked and ran quickly to pick up the sick child who had lost his voice. As he picked up the child his comrades also found dead children dumped at the corner of the paddy field. As Hung walked back he saw a landmine next to a pond. He shouted through his loudhailer to warn his comrades and saved them from certain death.

Within three months Hung's troops had chased the Khmer Rouge all the way from Phnom Penh to the northwest provinces of Battambang, Oddar Meanchey, and Preah Vihear.

2.

It was early in 1986 and dry season. Hung was now 25 and in the Vietnamese infantry supporting Cambodian troops from Phnom Penh fight the Khmer Rouge who were now operating near the Thai border and trying to recapture the power they had lost after the Vietnamese invasion in early 1979. There had been a lot of fierce fighting between the two forces with both sides gaining and losing ground. Hung's Vietnamese commander, General Van Linh, came up with a new strategy to try and defeat the Khmer Rouge forces.

Linh held a secret meeting with only three Vietnamese spies, including Hung, at a location in Oddar Meanchey. They sat and talked in the shade of the trees and discussed their plans. Hung was assigned to spy on the Khmer Rouge. As well as his usual military equipment, he had binoculars, a map, and a pen to mark enemy positions on his map, as well as medicine for malaria.

The three men had missions to three separate battle fields. One was assigned to spy on the area where forces were led by Son San, leader of Khmer People's National Liberation Front (KPNLF), and another was sent to collect information about the areas operated by the royalist forces, FUNCINPEC, led by Prince Norodom Ranariddh.

Hung was assigned to spy on the Khmer Rouge forces. He travelled at night and slept in the day so as to avoid being spotted by the enemy. His mission was to collect information about the strategic locations of the Khmer Rouge and how best their forces could attack them. It was a tough mission as he knew little about the area though he had a map provided by Hanoi. Some could have described the trip as a one-way ticket, but not Hung.

For the first five days things went fine. He made his way deeper into the jungle and marked his position on the map. At one point he saw Khmer Rouge soldiers patrolling and he hid in the bushes till they had passed. In the second week he found the going more difficult as he was deeper into enemy territory in Along Veng district, the last major stronghold of the Khmer Rouge. Hung started to worry as in this area the Khmer Rouge patrolled day and night. To avoid detection, he would often climb into a tree and sleep in his hammock. Some nights he could hear Khmer Rouge soldiers talking as they passed below him. For the first time since he left his mom, he kissed his dad's photo and asked his dad's spirit to help him from being spotted by his enemies.

Sometimes he thought about killing the patrols by dropping grenades from above or shooting them, but he realised that such action would attract other soldiers who would likely discover and kill him. So he remained quiet and let the patrols pass.

Two weeks passed, including three days hiding in a tree. No soldiers patrolled that weekend as they were all drunk on Thai rice wine, so he climbed down and ran through the forest for half an hour before stopping to rest. For the first time in almost three weeks he had a chance to bathe under a waterfall. But he kept his rifle in one hand while he bathed in case some of the enemy soldiers should discover him there. As a spy in enemy territory he knew he could only bathe for a few minutes. The priority was to collect as much information as possible before returning to base.

But Hung was in trouble; his compass was broken and he was unsure in which direction his base lay. The thick forest canopy meant he was unsure of the sun's position so he used his knife to chop bark from the tree and find which side was hotter as that would tell him which way was west. Though it worked, he could still not find his way out.

By Hung's third week in the forest he had no food left. He started to eat whatever he could find; red ants, grasshoppers, sometimes he would kill lizards and eat them. He would also eat wild fruit, some sweet, others bitter, and on one lucky day he found bird eggs. Hung was now completely lost and could not find his way out of the jungle. He walked and walked and fell asleep on the ground when he was tired. He did not see any Khmer Rouge soldiers patrolling like before. He never used his guns during his mission even when he hunted for wild food as he knew that any gunshot could attract the Khmer Rouge. Now he was lost in an area covered with dense forest that meant he hardly saw the sun. He had no idea where he was and could not find his location on the map.

He walked for days and days looking like a wild man; his hair was long and his beard and moustache were untrimmed. He had lost weight and found it difficult to carry his equipment. Luckily he found an area by a waterfall where there was fresh water and lots of wild fruit. He ate as much as he could then fell asleep. The next day he decided to stay at that location in order to gain some of the strength he had lost before once again trying to find his way back to his base.

After three days at that location he headed off again, walking down the other side of the mountain. Suddenly he spotted a girl bathing alone in a pool about 150 metres away. He was unsure if she was local or if she was part of the enemy forces. He took out his binoculars and focussed on her. She had long black hair that she was washing in the clear water. Then she turned around and he saw her face. Soft brown skin, round eyes, full lips, and dimpled cheeks; she was as beautiful as an Apsara image from one of the Angkor temples.

Though attacked by insects and mosquitos he could not stop watching her. He saw all her things beside her on the rocks; her red and white Krama, her white blouse, her red slippers, her black bra, a buffalo horn comb, and a bar of soap. He focussed on these items as he wanted to make sure she did not have a weapon with her. To her right he also spotted a walkie-talkie and some jewellery; a gold watch, and a bracelet, necklace, and earrings that looked like they had diamonds in them. These looked expensive and made Hung think she was not from an ordinary family. Her necklace made him think of his own and he touched it for a minute, thinking about his mom and dad. He had decided she did not pose a threat to him and he remembered his mom's words about being nice to any locals he met.

It was the first time in his life that Hung had seen such a girl. She was the most beautiful Khmer girl he had ever seen. But he was still cautious as he could still be in Khmer Rouge territory. He kept his rifle in one hand while he watched her. Now she turned to face Hung but did not see him. With her standing naked in the water, the sun shining through the trees, and the choruses of birds, bees, and cicadas, the atmosphere was heavenly. As she began to dress Hung looked away. But he was still totally lost and wanted to approach her. But he was still afraid that she may be connected to the Khmer Rouge and he was a Vietnamese spy who they would definitely torture and kill.

Hung had to make a quick decision before she left for home. Hung could see a path to the left leading away from the waterfall and he guessed this could lead to her house. He removed his grenades and hid them with all the ammunition from his guns by a tree where he could easily retrieve them. Then he walked and stood in the middle of the path he hoped she would take, placing his unloaded pistol and rifle a few metres away from him.

Sure enough the girl, who he could see was in her early 20s and looked like one of the models he had seen in Ho Chi Minh City, took the left hand path and started walking in his direction. The girl saw the weapons lying on the path and, as she was about to pick them up, Hung stepped forward with his hands in the air and said:

"Please help me. I am lost."

The girl was shocked to see him and quickly grabbed the pistol before pointing it at him and saying:

"Don't move! If you move, I will shoot you."

Hung replied in a low voice, "No. I will not move."

"Who are you?" The girl asked.

"I am a Vietnamese spy." Hung answered.

"Why are you here?"

"I am hunting for food." said Hung to the girl who walked toward him while pointing the pistol at Hung's face until she was about one metre away.

"I do not believe you. You must have been spying on us. That's why we can never win against the communist Vietnam forces. I cannot stand this war any more, and we have lost too many lives to the fight against your side. It must be because of you. I need to call my dad's forces to come and arrest you." Said the young girl in an angry voice.

As she was about press the button of the walkie-talkie, Hung snatched the radio from her hand while pleading:

"Please let me explain. I have no intention of killing you. If I did I would have taken your life while you were bathing in the waterfall. The two guns you hold have no bullets in them but I need you to spare my life. My life is in your hands and I will tell you the complete truth."

The girl struggled a little to understand what Hung said, given his Vietnamese accent and that he had only learned Khmer for four months.

"How can you convince me you are good man?"

"You can put me on a probation period for as long as you want," Hung replied as he knelt down to show respect to her as he would his mother.

The girl, whose culture restricted her from close conversation with men, looked around before she asked Hung, "what is your name?"

"I am Nguyen Van Hung," he replied, and then added, "and what do I call you?"

"It is too early to tell you my name. But my first test for you is that you have to handle your own situation for a time. I will come to see you right here where you dropped your guns tomorrow morning, ok?" Said the young girl as she pointed to ground while Hung listened attentively before answering.

"Yes. It is no problem at all. I have survived on my own for weeks so I can wait another day."

The girl also wanted to test Hung's honesty so said, "Here, take back your guns."

Hung replied, "No. I don't need them now I have met you."

"Are you sure you don't want them? If not, I will throw them away on my way home." The girl told Hung sarcastically as she grasped the weapons and left him behind, saying lastly, "See you tomorrow. Do not lie to me or you will die. Remember you are in my land."

Hung, who survived for weeks in the jungle, found himself difficult to hold on for that one more day as his mind was full of mixed feelings as to whether the girl's dad would spare his life or whether they would turn him over to the Khmer Rouge force. But at the same time he felt happy that, out here in the middle of nowhere, a beautiful girl had spared his life although he had admitted that he was a Vietnamese spy.

That night Hung stayed close to the waterfall. He made a mat by cutting a banana leaf with his knife and used his military bag as pillow. He was so tired as he had no food left. He walked slowly to the waterfall and drank as much as he could to fill up his empty stomach before dropping like a dead man on the banana leaf.

He woke about midnight and lay listening to the noises of the jungle and looking at the moon through the trees as he thought back to his mom pleading with him not to go to Cambodia. 'Maybe this is my karma.' He thought. Eventually he fell back to sleep but it was a troubled sleep plagued by nightmares. He woke in the morning light to the red sun rising and the birds singing their dawn chorus. He rose from his mat feeling weak and ill then went and bathed, ready to see the girl again.

After seeing him yesterday, the girl had returned home and told no-one about the strange Vietnamese man she had met in the jungle. After a bad sleep similar to Hung's she had risen and made herself breakfast before packing some noodles and canned food to take to Hung. As she started making her way back to see him she thought to herself; 'Why did we find each other in the jungle yesterday? And why am I thinking about him? Is this good or bad karma?'

She had also noticed that the man looked quite ill with pale skin and yellow eyes. So she brought some medicines her dad had brought from Thailand, such as malaria treatment and some vitamins. When she got to the spot she had left him, Hung looked in a terrible condition. He was sitting shivering and looked so frail. She was shocked and urged him to take the medicine and eat the food she brought but he felt too ill to eat.

"I am grateful to you for everything, but I don't think I could eat anything."

Finally, the girl told him her name. Reach Bopheak. Even though he was tired and ill Hung repeated her name many times till he could say it correctly.

"Can I ask? What does your name mean?" Hung asked.

"It means 'Royal Single Flower'," she replied.

"What about your name? Does it mean anything," she asked.

"I wish I could tell you but my Khmer is not good enough to give the meaning."

"Don't worry for now. You stay here and I will go home to get more medicine for you. If anyone finds you here, tell them that you are a friend of Reach Bopheak. All the Khmer Rouge soldiers in this area are under the control of my dad so they will spare you. I will be back soon."

Bopheak ran all the way back to her house about 300 meters and collected medicine her parents had bought from a drug store just across the border in Thailand. She also brought back a pillow, blanket, mosquito net, and some soap. When she returned, Hung tried to get up and greet her and used all his remaining strength to give her a big smile.

Bopheak spent hours talking with Hung, grilling him on all the details of his adventures.

"I hope you won't kill me after I tell my story." Hung said.

"Why do you think I would kill you?" Bopheak responded.

"Because I have been told by Cambodian survivors that the Khmer Rouge kill prisoners after their confessions."

"Yours is a different story my friend. Please look into my eyes. Am I a brutal person?" she asked.

"No. I do not think you are. But I am afraid of your parents and the Khmer Rouge soldiers," he replied.

"You are right. But a daughter like me here…I am like the queen of all who live in this area. You name it; from birds to bad boys and even my dad, they listen to me. You will learn about this one day," said the girl.

"I am lucky to know you and I thank you for all your kindness," said Hung.

"You may have noticed that this waterfall is only for me," Bopheak told Hung. "Wealthy people in Bangkok may have a swimming pool but they do not have nature like this."

"I have never been to Bangkok, but my mom and I spent years living on the Mekong Delta so all I knew was the fresh water of the Mekong. I sometimes swam with the fish behind my floating house and one time I narrowly escaped from a hungry crocodile which swam after me. Thinking and talking about my home, it makes me miss my mom so much."

Bopheak interrupted. "You have mentioned your mom twice, but not your dad. Do you not miss him too?"

"Yes, but he died in a helicopter crash in 1975. I was 14 when he died."

"Please tell me a bit more about yourself and your work. I promise you that you will be safe and can live here as long as you want," said Bopheak and handed him a Coke and couple of slices of apples that had been in the refrigerator. Hung sipped the Coke and ate a slice of apple.

"My Vietnamese commander trusted me because I can speak Khmer and sent me to observe the battlefields here and collect information on strategic locations." Hung said as he pointed to his map.

"So, what information have you collected and what are you going to do next?" Bopheak asked.

Hung looked embarrassed since he was now in the company of an enemy commander's daughter and had no way out. However, he kept telling himself to be strong and have hope.

Smart Bopheak looked into the eyes of Hung, saying, "My friend, it's as if I have been dreaming about you but this is not a dream but real. But there is one thing I want you, and all your Vietnamese and Cambodian comrades, to realise. Not all of the Khmer Rouge, or their families, are bad. My dad is 53 and has spent many years fighting for the Khmer Rouge, but after the fall of Pol Pot in 1979 he sent me to study in Bangkok so I could help build a better world for all Cambodians. I'm sorry I seemed so mad when I first met you, but I didn't know how true your heart was. Now I do."

Hung was touched by her words and said: "One of the key reasons that I joined the army was to save children and innocent people from the bloody hands of the Khmer Rouge."

"Hung, I shared those same values, but there was nothing I could do at the time. We should learn from the bad experiences and learn how to do good deeds together. Like how you and I are now friends."

Hung was curious to know what factors made her have different values from other Khmer Rouge supporters and asked, "So, do the young Khmer Rouge now share your values?"

"I would say almost all of them did not share their parents' values in the past, but still the outside world saw us as no different. Maybe we need time to change our image from Khmer Rouge to Khmer Rose. What do you think?" She asked.

"It is not a bad idea as the rose has a good smell. But they must get away from their bad reputation and there can be no more atrocities, such as killing people or overworking people in the rice fields," Hung replied.

As they talked, Bopheak got a call on her walkie-talkie from the deputy Khmer Rouge commander asking when her dad will return from Bangkok. She pressed the button and replied, "Next Monday. Wait; please do not send any soldiers to patrol the area within 5km of my house, and especially the waterfall area as I like to bathe there."

The deputy commander replied, "Yes, I will make sure no troops will disturb you. No problem. I will follow your instructions."

As Bopheak talked, Hung heard the man's voice as loud and clear as the voice of the state radio in Vietnam.

Bopheak looked at and smiled at Hung because her words were helping to protect him from being found by Khmer Rouge soldiers. Hung smiled back in thanks.

The sun showed that it was around noon and Bopheak needed to go back home and prepare lunch for her mom as she was alone at home.

"I will come to see you in two days. Here is everything you need. Stay safe and do not do anything crazy or I cannot protect you. I can visit you in the jungle, but not in jail."

"Ok, thanks for your kindness. Please come to visit me when you can as I am alone," Hung said as he gave her a respectful Cambodian sampeah.

"Would you like me to bring anything when I come to see you next?" she asked Hung.

"I need a bigger knife, an axe, nails, and some rope please as I need to make a bed. There are lots of bamboo trees here I can use for materials," he said.

"Oh, you know how to build a hut or house?" asked Bopheak.

"Yes, and could you also buy me a krama please?

Because of his accent, Bopheak misheard him and said, "What? I cannot buy you karma."

He tried to say it again and explained, "It is the Cambodian scarf I see many people wear around their neck."

"Oh, I see you mean krama, not karma. Your accent is a problem because if you leave this area and people hear you speak they will know you are Vietnamese because of how you speak Khmer. I will get you two of them, one blue and one red." She said as she started walking down the path. Hung watched her leave and she again reminded him of a young Vietnamese model in Ho Chi Minh City.

While Hung was lost in the jungle and befriending Bopheak, the other two Vietnamese spies had returned to their camp and reported to their commander. But there was no sign of Hung and his commander sent a report to Hanoi that he suspected Hung had either been killed or taken prisoner. This news then reached Hung's mother as she sat sewing at home. She cried for hours when she heard as Hung was her only child and now she believed she had lost both her son and her husband to war. She could not sleep and lay calling out Hung's name. And she would not eat; the Mekong fish, previously so delicious, now tasted foul to her, and the fresh pork from the local market tasted as if it had gone off. From the moment she received the news that Hung had been classified as 'missing in action' she was distraught. She placed Hung's photo next to that of her late husband in the family shrine and lit incense and offered food to their spirits. She could not sew or make dresses which meant she earned no money. But the Vietnamese government paid her a pension in recognition of her son's sacrifice. Each month she now received more money than she spent, as she ate very little and lived a miserable life as a widow with no children, just waiting to draw her final breath.

3.

Days, weeks, months, and years had passed, and Hung was still hidden deep in the jungle. He had recovered from his illness and built a hut and latrine, ensuring the latrine would not pollute the waterfall Bopheak loved so much. It was now 1989. Dry season followed rainy season followed dry season. Flowers and plants grew and bloomed and then faded again. Animals mated and produced young who in turn then went off to begin their own lives. And the friendship between Hung and Bopheak had grown and strengthened and become a bond of love in their quiet jungle hideaway so close to the Thai border.

One day in April on Khmer New Year's Eve, Bopheak brought more food than usual and some new clothes for Hung who was waiting in the hut and doing his Khmer and Thai homework as Bopheak had been teaching him. She arrived earlier than usual.

Hung was surprised and said "I am so happy to see you so early". Hung reached out and took the food from Bopheak.

"Here are your new clothes, some underwear, t-shirts, and other items," said Bopheak as she handed them to Hung who looked into her eyes with love and thanks.

"Where did you get these from?" Hung asked. One hand held the items, and with the other he touched Bopheak from her head all the way down other waist, to show his love for her. He kissed her on the forehead and asked her to sit down with him and enjoy lunch together.

"What a special day for me, Bopheak. I cannot thank you enough for bringing me these."

"It is ok, Hung; I have no man to give them to. I have no one I like as much as you. I have no place to go to but your hut. And much more than that, my love for you is deeper than the ocean and larger than the galaxy."

"Me too. Since the day I saw you bathing in the waterfall I forgot everything. My life was transformed from being foe to friend, like a caterpillar turning into a butterfly. I hid the grenades, removed the bullets and threw away the guns onto your path. I told myself that there was no point in shooting people, that there was no point in killing you, but there was a point in making you my friend. More than a friend. I love you, I love you, I love you, Bopheak."

Hung kept repeating these words over and over again till she used her left hand to close his mouth and her right hand to pull Hung against her. They embraced and fell to the bed, their passion rising as they made love, the heat between them as hot as the jungle outside.

"Hold me close to your heart, Hung. My life and love belong to you now. You are not a prisoner of war, but of love."

"That is true, Bopheak. The power of love has so much power to make people see each other as friends not foes." Said Hung. "I don't know if your parents told you that the Khmer Rouge and Vietcong were brothers who fought common enemies; American and its ally South Vietnam. They loved each other then they hated each other."

"But we are not like that; our love will last forever even if the earth is destroyed." Said Bopheak.

They lay together for nearly two hours, savouring the feeling of their first intimacy. Finally, they rose and dressed before enjoying their lunch by the waterfall.

"Why is today special?" Asked Hung.

"It is the 17th April and Khmer New Year's eve." said Bopheak.

"What? 17th April?" Exclaimed Hung. He remembered that 17th April was the day the Khmer Rouge had captured Phnom Penh but did not mention this to his lover.

"I don't know what is going on in your head, but Cambodia celebrates New Year for three days from 15th to 17th April." She replied.

"Ok, I understand," said Hung. "So can I visit your parents?"

"They left for Thailand to celebrate Sankranta, since the Thais and Khmers share the same culture in many ways."

"What is Thailand like?" Hung asked.

"The country's development is far ahead of yours or mine. That's why my parents like to spend time there. They asked me to go with them, but I said I had spent 12 years studying in Thailand, so it's nothing new to me. This means I can spend the whole night with you for the week before they return home. I will be home when they get back so that they will not find out about our relationship."

"Tell me more about your time in Bangkok."

"My lover, if you just want to know about my time in Bangkok, then you miss out learning about Cambodia's civil war."

Bopheak tried to summarise the complex story of Cambodia's civil war into 20 minutes, constantly checking that Hung was awake and not sleeping from their earlier exertions in bed.

Bopheak started: "Eight years after I was born, my dad joined the Khmer Rouge movement after the call by Prince Norodom Sihanouk who was in exile in China after the America-backed coup by Lon Nol in 1970 who set up the Khmer Republic."

Hung interrupted. "I'm confused already. You said two Khmer groups?"

"If you get confused this easily no wonder you got lost in this jungle." Bopheak joked. "The Khmer Rouge were pro-China and Soviet Union and of course pro-Viet Cong and the Khmer Republic were pro-America."

"I see now, thanks." said Hung.

Bopheak continued, "So the Viet Cong supported the Khmer Rouge but after the Khmer Rouge took over Cambodia in 1975 they soon became enemies. Because once they had power, Pol Pot and his minions killed more than two million Cambodians including children through starvation, execution, disease, and forced labour."

"Hearing about the children dying is why I joined the army to fight the Khmer Rouge!" Said Hung. "But I had no idea that I would end up here with you."

"So maybe we should thank the Khmer Rouge for bringing us together." Said Bopheak.

Bopheak continued, "I was lucky because my dad was a Khmer Rouge commander controlling the northwest of Cambodia. After the fall of Khmer Rouge in early 1979 my parents fled to hide near the border of Thailand and later joined Cambodian refugees living in a camp there. My parents sent me to study in Thailand and I was later moved to study in the outskirts of Bangkok. My dad tried to avoid Cambodian survivors who might take revenge on him for being a Khmer Rouge commander so he moved from one camp to another, but he always visited me and supported me. My parents then decided to move back into Cambodia when he was asked by Pol Pot to join the Khmer Rouge fight against the Vietnamese invasion of Cambodia."

"Wait a minute. How did the Khmer Rouge survive for so long after the fall of their regime?" asked Hung.

Bopheak was a bit nervous and looked at Hung, "You are my real lover, aren't you?" She wondered if Hung, as a former Vietnamese military spy, would find a way to report any information she gave him back to the Vietnamese.

"Why do you ask that?" Hung replied, "I just want to know. I cannot find a way out from the area and even if I could I would not leave. I chose the girl over the gun. I chose you."

"I believe you, Hung. Now let me continue. The Khmer Rouge and other Cambodian resistance groups have survived for so long thanks to support from China, the U.S., and other western governments who provide their supplies and weapons through Thailand. But you will see things keep changing over time."

"Yes you are right. My life has changed from student to factory worker then to a soldier and now as your lover."

Bopheak said, "That's good though, don't you think?"

"Yes, but I miss my mom so much," said Hung and he began to quietly cry.

"Don't worry, darling, you will see your mom again one day, we will both go and see your mom."

Bopheak, who had finished high school in Thailand in late 1986, had never returned to Bangkok to pursue higher education as she did not want to leave her Vietnamese soldier behind. She regarded Hung as her husband in all but name.

Bopheak had told her parents that she loved the waterfall and the area behind the house and she wanted no strangers there. Her parents had no idea about her relationship with the Vietnamese soldier she'd found nearly four years ago.

Hung taught Bopheak Vietnamese and in return she taught him more Khmer and sometimes some Thai. Both of them shared food, values, and also the bed which Hung had built. One day Hung asked Bopheak, "Will your parents kill me when they find out about our love?"

Bopheak answered with a giggle. "It is too late to kill you now because I am pregnant and they cannot see me and their grandchild live without you. I must say that you are no longer a foe but a friend, and much more than that, you are my husband."

There soon came a time when Bopheak could no longer hide her pregnancy so one night she approached her parents and prostrated herself before them as a sign of respect. She apologised to them for her violation of Khmer culture by having a relationship with the former Vietnamese spy and without their permission.

"I asked you to please forgive me for what I have done. I did not speak out because I was so afraid that our troops would kill him because he was sent to spy on us."

Her dad said nothing. Her mom asked Bopheak to bring him to meet them after dark so that no Khmer Rouge solider would see him.

Hung's Khmer was now quite impressive and he quickly prostrated himself before Bopheak's parents and asked for forgiveness.

"I would have been killed if my wife Bopheak did not protect me."

Her dad spoke. "I am happy as long as your love for my daughter will not cause us trouble. If the supreme commanders who are close to Pol Pot learn about this, then my wife and I could be jailed or even killed. So it is for the best for you both to stay away from this house and live in the jungle to avoid discovery."

The young couple agreed and hugged the parents before returning back to their hut in the jungle.

After nine months it was time for Bopheak to deliver her baby. Her parents were worried about Bopheak so they sent her alone to Bangkok to give birth. After more than three years away, Bopheak was surprised at how many changes she saw.

Hung could not go to Thailand as he had no passport, so he stayed and looked after their hut and waited for Bopheak's return. The couple and her parents believed that they would have a baby girl and had decided on the name 'Thomacheat' (meaning 'nature'). But they were all wrong; a day and a half later, Bopheak gave a birth to baby boy.

Bopheak was asked to give the boy a name but she told the hospital staff that she had to wait till she got an answer from her Vietnamese soldier husband who lived in Khmer Rouge territory. This news surprised the Thai nurses as they knew Vietnam was the enemy of the Khmer Rouge. About two days later, an answer came from Hung saying that he wanted to name the baby 'Nguyen Hung Prey' ('Prey' is Khmer for jungle). The news of the unusual birth attracted the media, both local and foreign, and journalists rushed to the hospital to interview the mother and photograph the baby.

Bopheak, who spoke fluent Thai, was totally exhausted because of the amount of visits and phone calls from journalists. But very quickly the story spread via wire agencies and other outlets with many using the headline "Vietnamese MIA is now father of jungle baby."

The story was eventually picked up by Vietnamese newspapers in Hanoi and Ho Chi Minh. The same day a neighbour of Hung's mother saw the story and ran to her house, banging on the door to wake her as she was ill in bed.

Hung's mother opened the door, asking "What's wrong? Why do you knock on my door like that?"

"Look at the newspaper. Your son is still alive," the neighbour said as she gave Hung's mother the newspaper.

"Oh, I am so happy to hear that. Where is he?"

"He is in the jungle and married to a Khmer Rouge commander's daughter and they have a baby boy called Prey." said the neighbour.

Hung's mother, who had been ill from the thought of losing her son, grabbed her glasses and read the article over and over again. She sometimes kissed the newspaper where her son's name appeared, and that of her daughter-in-law and her grandson, Prey.

Hung's mother was sure that the story was real, since the article also said that Hung's mother is a widow called Phan Vang Thi and that his father served as military and died in an American helicopter crashed in January 1975.

On the same day, she went to the cemetery where she had placed a stone with her son's name on and removed it. When she returned home there was an official letter from Hanoi who had received a diplomatic note from Vietnam's embassy in Bangkok which had interviewed Bopheak about her husband Hung in great detail.

Though there were ongoing talks between Cambodia's Hun Sen and the leader of the Khmer resistance forces, Prince Norodom Sihanouk, from 1987, it took until the fall of the Soviet Bloc over 1990 and 1991 for them to officially end the conflict. The news of the fall of the Berlin Wall had reached Hung in the jungle, as did the domino effect which followed as the communist states of Eastern Europe gradually fell. And after more than ten years, the Vietnamese troops finally left Cambodia. But not Hung. He was too busy taking care of his wife and baby.

Back in South Vietnam, Hung's mother was healthier now that she knew her son was alive but she was still unhappy as she saw the Vietnamese troops return home but not her son. But about a month later several concerned parties, including the American Red Cross, took up Hung and Bopheak's case though it took nearly two years to solve the complexities. But finally the couple were registered as Cambodian refugees and moved first to Battambang and then to Siem Reap.

In 1992, for the first time in 13 years, Hung spoke to his mother via a military radio in Siem Reap.

Hung spoke in Vietnamese: "Hello mom, this is Hung in Cambodia. I love you and I miss you so much. We are going to come and see you tomorrow."

Hung's mother listened to her son's voice for the first time in 13 years and was so thrilled that she lost her voice and began sobbing.

After talking for five minutes, Hung could hear nothing from his mom, and he worried that the shock of talking to him had made her ill or caused a heart attack. But then he could hear her crying, even above the high winds outside.

To try and alter the sad mood, Hung got his wife and son to come and stand by the radio then he passed the microphone to Bopheak. She spoke in broken Vietnamese which she had learned from Hung and said:

"Hello mom, can you hear me? This is Bopheak, I am Hung's wife and we have a son, your grandson, and he looks just like Hung."

As she was speaking, Prey called for his dad, and Hung's mother heard her grandson and said;

"I love you all and I miss you so much. Please come home now. I am getting old and cannot wait to see you. But please, do not fly from Cambodia to Ho Chi Minh City. I'm scared you will die in a plane crash like how I lost your dad in a helicopter crash. You have survived all these years so I do not want you to die on your way to see me. Put on life jackets and get on a boat and sail all the way from Tonle Sap down to Phnom Penh and then to Vietnam. I will be waiting for you all here, no matter if it is raining or thunder and lightning or even an earthquake. And the spirit of your dad will be there with me as well."

"Yes, mom, we will be there soon."

Once they had said their goodbyes, Hung and his family, along with Bopheak's parents, headed to the Tonle Sap River and caught a boat. Bopheak's parents knew the lake and river well, so told the driver of the boat which route to take. It took them six hours to reach Phnom Penh and they arrived at midnight. They could not see many people, just a truck belonging to United Nations Advance Mission in Cambodia (UNAMIC) driving back and forth close to Wat Phnom.

After the devastation of the long years of conflict, there was still very poor infrastructure, and they had no way of contacting Hung's mother. They sailed to a dock on the east side of the river and spent the night at a Buddhist temple before resuming their journey the next morning.

They left before dawn and watched the red sun rising over the Mekong as they sailed towards Vietnam. Hung was impatient to reach home and asked the boat driver to speed up, but he said that it could not go any faster though he hoped to buy a new engine if Hung paid him a good fare. Hung laughed and said:

"I hope my father in law will give you an expensive gemstone he got from Pailin."

Bopheak's dad whispered to Hung, "It's not a good idea telling people I have such precious stones because I do not want anyone to kill me for them. I need to give some to your mom and your son. My wife and your wife have enough."

"I'm sorry, I won't mention them again." Said Hung.

Even though the darkness of night now covered the Mekong Delta, Hung recognised the area after growing up there. It was about midnight when they reached his home and he asked the driver to move the boat in such a way that it would create a wave to hit the house. The driver did as he was asked and the noise of the engine combined with the wave ricking the house woke Hung's mother and she came outside to see what was happening. When she did, she saw Hung standing at the front of the boat and smiling at her.

Hung, carrying his son, jumped from boat and hugged his mom.

"I am home now. When I left I was alone, but now I return with my new family." He said, pointing at his wife and parents in law who were struggling to walk on the floating house.

Hung introduced his family to his mom, and for the first time, Hung's mom saw and held her grandson. It was the middle of the night but it was like a party as all the neighbours came and hugged Hung and welcomed him home.

Hung's mom and all her neighbours listened as Hung told the story of meeting Bopheak and falling in love.

Hung's mom thanked her daughter in-law and her parents for saving her son.

Bopheak's dad said with Hung translating, "I could prevent the enemy from reaching my area, but I could not prevent these two from falling in love."

And Bopheak's mother said, "Since I found out my daughter had fallen in love with your son I can understand your feelings. They have shown that we can overcome differences. It is time for bygones to be bygones."

After a couple of days touring Vietnam, including the areas where Cambodians lived, Bopeheak's parents left for home, telling Hung and Bopheak and Hung's mother to all look after each other.

"You can live in Vietnam or you move to Cambodia as you wish since Cambodia still has plenty of land." Bopheak's mom told the couple and widow as they kissed their grandson Prey goodbye."

Hung's mom replied, "I thank you all for saving Hung's life. We are more than just good neighbours who share a border. We share the same feelings of sadness and happiness and we now share blood as our children are married and have a son who is both Vietnamese and Khmer. I do not know what will happen in the future but let us do good things together a better world for our grandson and for generations to come."

***

Ek Madra worked as an interpreter for United Nations Transitional Authority (UNTAC) in Cambodia in 1993. He then spent three years (1994- 97) working as a reporter for the Cambodia Daily newspaper in English before studying journalism at the University of Southern California (USC). He spent more than a decade as a correspondent for Reuters News Agency (now Thomson Reuters), beginning in early 1998. Madra has worked with the Royal Government of Cambodia (RGC) as deputy director of the press department at the Office of the Council of Ministers since 2009. He is the author of 'The Factors Contributing to Cambodia's Civil War 1950s - 1980s; Lessons Then & Now.'

Two for the Road

T Hunt Locke

"Bye, bye, Daddy! Bye, bye, Daddee!!"

I turned around one last time and blew a kiss to my effervescent four-year-old daughter. My wife also smiled. It was a smile which could light up any room including the cavernous departure hall of Don Muang Airport. Together their beauty emitted a glow which seemed to get bigger the further I walked away.

I don't like these short departures truth be told. Why should I? Rarely is it told that a person actually does stumble upon the end of the rainbow but I am among the lucky few. A nice house in northern Thailand, a bustling test preparation business, and the two sets of magical eyes that were now guiding me to my departure gate. Oh, not to mention, a handful of self-published novels which have made their way on to an Amazon bestselling list or two.

So onward I walked. Past the suspicious glares of the burka clad Muslim women huddled closely by their children who clung fearfully to the loosely wrapped cloth. Past the hungover farang whose empty stare hovered over his Starbucks cup while waiting for the next stop on his debauched itinerary. Past the Chinese tour group which shouted angrily in unison that their flight had been delayed while casually tossing aside plastic waste which began to look like a small mountain of refuse.

Finally, I came to my gate. The full service Dairy Queen, cheesy hot dogs and all, beckoned. But my wife had packed a lunch consisting of a banana, a sack of papaya, along with a box of rice and veggies. If Dairy Queen fast food junk was my past, a healthier present sat in my lap. Yes, life was good. But the glance over at DQ did provide a gift.

His name is Bill Barnwell. In some corners of the globe that may account for little, but here in Southeast Asia his name was instantly recognizable. Bill was an old hand. He had been living in various Thai locales, intermittent stops in Laos, and recently Cambodia for the better part of thirty years. For the longest time his was the name everybody knew even if his face was known to relatively few. His legend grew from the occasional magazine or newspaper article regaling adventures in far off exotic outposts. But his true fame came from his harrowing suspense novels. Bill Barnwell was a literary giant. For me, Bill was somewhat of a role model.

We are friends too. Well, at least on Facebook. I have never met the man. In the flesh that is, and the urge to go up to him and introduce myself was strong. There was much to talk about. Still, perhaps in Cambodia, at the Kampot Literary Festival, would be a more appropriate time. Now my time was better spent summing him up from afar.

His strong muscular frame did not suggest seventy-two years of age. Neither did his busty curvaceous twenty-something girlfriend. Mimi Wow Wow was her Facebook handle and, as Bill has posted, the reason he had ventured onto social media in the first place. Mimi was hot. Kampuchea hot. Bill had met her in the jungles of Cambodia. In fact, he had met her while doing research in the Dângrêk Mountains. Her dazzling features, an ability to make a delicious buffalo kebab, a fascination that Bill could live in her world and, well, a love story, walked down from the mountain top hand in hand. It only added to Bill Barnwell's legend.

And so I observed.

The hour long Air Asia flight to Phnom Phen was uneventful. As was getting my tourist visa and off into a taxi to make the long herky jerky ride to the city center. My itinerary was simple. One night in Phnom Penh and then a bus ride down to Kampot where I would participate in a couple of events planned for the writers' festival.

I had booked a room at the Frangipani Royal Palace Hotel. Located just off the riverside overlooking the Tonle Sap and Mekong Rivers, it suited my needs and with a dash of style to boot. I had a free day. But it was one with which to prepare as well. With that in mind, I quickly checked into the hotel, tossed my lone piece of luggage on the bed, and was off to the riverside.

It was only my second time in Cambodia so I barely knew my way around. But that well could work to my advantage. On trips such as these it was often best to affect the bumbling tourist persona. I was even wearing my straw fedora hat. A casual stroll along the river, snapping several photos, I finally found my first destination: Bohr's Bookstore.

It was a dingy affair. An old beaten up red bike sat outside serving as a sentinel for the dusty bookshelves which appeared they might collapse at any provocation. My type of place. A quick glance showed a bevy of worthy titles but I walked straight to the back. A frumpy woman looked up at me blankly. She slowly arose and with great effort extricated herself from an old wicker chair.

A head peered from behind the back office door. A pair of dull green eyes looked me over before disappearing. The man quickly came to the front desk carrying two books. *The Final Dock* and *A Fatal Dose*. Both authored by Bill Barnwell. I lifted *A Fatal Dose* into the air with the palm of my hand. Satisfied, I quickly stashed both books into my knapsack and left.

I settled down for lunch at a ramshackle restaurant a street or two from riverside and was at a loss as to how the corrugated tin roof was held aloft. But the myriad of aromas emanating from the rundown building guided me to my seat. I ordered fish amok and pong tia koon (the Cambodian version of balut).

Amok is a common enough dish throughout Southeast Asia. But in the Cambodian style, with the use of the local herb slok ngor, the taste simply jumps off the plate. Pong tia koon is the fertilised embryo of a duck. If you can get past that, and the rather unpleasant smell, a culinary delight awaits.

And that is when I began to feel the pangs of homesickness. I missed my girls. One of our favorite hobbies is to dive into a weekend of Bangkok street food. I would have taken them along as well, but with my wife six months pregnant she wasn't up for it. I took a snapshot of the food and sent it back home via Facebook.

After lunch I returned to the hotel, opened up *The Final Dock* and prepared for an afternoon by the rooftop pool.

Keen observation is an art. Perhaps a dying one in this selfie infused age. Most people stumble through their own lives and fail to observe the world that surrounds them. For that I pity them, such a waste. Observation is a professional skill. And those who refine it, an author, a jury consultant, a detective, or any number of professions, can develop a successful career.

She knifed through the water effortlessly. I studied her. Though, if someone were to observe *me* they would likely think I was enjoying an afternoon beside the pool reading a book. Mimi Wow Wow was athletic, her body firm. A childhood living in the wilds of the mountains will do that I suppose. Her fluid movements, like her beauty, were natural.

Her formal education would have been minimal. A small village school at best. Her innate intelligence, however, was considerable. One could surmise this by a simple glance at her Facebook page. But the fact that Bill Barnwell had taken up with her could also lead one to the same conclusion.

And, truth be told, my fascination with Mimi Wow Wow was to gain a greater understanding of the man himself. Her pace increased. The strokes became more focused and her muscles tensed. Underneath her soft curvaceous features there was an animal strength. Underneath her soft caress of a smile lay a tenacious spirit.

Spent, she lifted herself up from the pool, walked over to her man, and pointed into the distance. My eyes followed. Far off towards the horizon the outline of a mountain chain could be seen. Bill put his arm around his love. They both smiled.

I too flashed a brief grin. It was almost as if I had sat down with them both. A friendship had begun. Finally it was time to emerge myself into *The Final Dock*.

Barnwell wrote with a rare compassion. Yet this story of a young Rohingya lady sold into slavery was a story of strength and conviction. Torn from her home, locked into a shrimp peeling shed in Thailand, she slaved in horrific conditions, her labour for the benefit of the five star international hotels and restaurants serving the privileged.

He wrote with a sense of certainty. This young lady, perhaps she was a composite derived from gritty research, never lost sight of regaining her freedom. And she did. Taking a rare opportunity, this lady of steel broke free from the ramshackle factory and raced through the jungle. Finally, coming to a small police station, she begged the authorities for help. It was not to be. She was returned to slavery. Beaten, raped, and left crippled with despair, she was thrust back into her eighteen-hour work day. But hope still shone through.

Barnwell was expert in keeping that dull flicker alive. His writing captivated me. He was writing with a clear purpose, as if he had somehow cast off shackles as well. There was a sense of activism in his voice. I admired it. But activism, at any age, can have consequences.

The lady? Yes, she finally gained her freedom. A bright light was turned to the practices of the shrimp peeling sheds run by large companies such as CP and their clients including the luxury hotel chain Hilton. Reforms were promised. Bill Barnwell's light had never been brighter and his regional fame gained an international audience.

The relaxing afternoon had put me in the mood for a night on the town. And I did get a nice, if brief, feeling for Phnom Penh. However, the night had gone longer than planned. And it was festive.

Krom is a band that recently has gained international acclaim. A mixture of Mississippi Delta Blues and traditional Cambodia Folk, the sound of Krom was entrancing. I had made a Facebook friendship with the band's leader and was eager to hear them perform live.

The Jazz Club was the venue and Krom did not disappoint. The music rocked and the Angkor Beer flowed. I hung in back. It was neither the time to mingle, socialise, or shed a light on my presence. I clung to the shadows.

Bill and Mimi were also there. This was no surprise. He had long been friends with Krom's guitar virtuoso and founder, the King of the Mekong Delta Blues, Chris Minko. In between sets the leading lights of the burgeoning Southeast Asian art scene gathered around Bill and Mimi's table. Writer's, musicians, and artists all vied for Bill and Chris' attention.

But that was not what caught my attention. Sitting to the right of the stage and behind the throng of creative talent sat a striking lady. Alluring would go too far in describing her. Still, she had a magnetic quality. A tablet set on the table, bespectacled in the John Lennon way, she scribbled away with a pencil into a worn notebook.

This was alarming. She was a reporter. More to the point, we seemed to be focusing on the same subject. Bill's booming voice could be heard throughout the room. He was in his element. A man of peculiar jocularity, Bill Barnwell enjoyed weaving a tale.

Perhaps because of this, realizing she would not further her story, or maybe not wanting to jot down the ramblings of a drunken older man, this attractive scribe packed up her things and headed for the exit. I followed.

The scent of Bor Bor, Cambodian rice porridge, jolted me into the present. The strong cup of black coffee sorted my senses. What needed to be done was done. And it was done well. Better to focus on the future. The breakfast finished, I collected my things and checked out of the hotel.

'*Be prepared and be on time,*' my father had always preached. Good advice. The Giant Ibis bus line was recommended to me and I sat awaiting the three-hour journey to Kampot. The bus hostess proudly pointed out that this coach had Wi-Fi. I shrugged, gave a smile, and pulled out my book. To this she looked at both me and the book rather oddly before retreating to her duties.

Out the window I saw a familiar face. Mimi WowWow was helping an obviously hungover Bill Barnwell to their awaiting chariot. Not surprisingly, they had organized a private mini-van for their trip. Having deposited him to his seat, she came back out looking perplexed. She held the shiny mobile to her ear, frantically pacing beside the van, and kept looking at her watch. She was waiting for someone and none too pleased about it. And this was how I left them as my bus lurched out of the station.

'Big City, Sin City,' Krom sang hauntingly last night. And it was with that same dark feeling with which I left Phnom Penh. Then my mobile jingled to life alerting me that my wife and daughter were on Facebook Live. My mood instantly changed. Looking at the somewhat barren landscape, I also took time to note that this land was not so long ago a war zone. One could only imagine the dire plight these itinerant farmers who dotted the distant rice paddies had had to endure during their downtrodden existence. My life, in comparison, was paradise. And if I had to attend to some unpleasant work at times then so be it.

The ride itself was as advertised. Three hours on the dot. I had not booked a hotel. Still, I told the tuk-tuk driver to bring me to the Kampot Riverside Hotel. I was met in the reception area by a bright eyed young lady. She was quite cute in the buxom Khmer way. Neatly attired while proudly filling out her uniform she led me to the reception desk.

"Can I help you, Sir?"

"Yes, I would like to see a room."

"This week we are very busy and only have one room left. It is the standard room, but no view of the river. Is this ok?"

She had great command of English which quite impressed me. It also gave me pause as it spoke of a keen intelligence. "Actually, I was interested in the Deluxe Room with the river view. But I will be coming back with my family in a months' time. Can I have a look?"

My response was a beaming smile. The room itself was none too large but had a balcony overlooking the busy riverside street. And during the Literary Festival it could prove to be noisy. There was a safe in the room which could hold your average sized laptop. The bed was king sized. Satisfied, I motioned I was through with the short tour.

The receptionist led the way out and I followed her to the staircase. Her sway was entrancing. "Do you like?" she asked over her shoulder.

"Yes," I answered. "Indeed I do. In fact, I'd like to book for next month if possible."

Our flirtation continued as I confirmed my reservation for the coming month. Before leaving I held her gaze just a bit longer than appropriate. She did not try to wrestle away. This was intoxicating. I truly wanted her to remember me.

Having completed that, I breezily walked into the comfortable Kampot afternoon air. The cool season was just upon us. I pulled out my map and set on a leisurely stroll to the edge of town. There would be little time for sightseeing and even less for socializing but I did want get my bearings straight. It was a bustling little town. Bokor Mountain loomed on the near horizon as the river dominated the surroundings.

I found my way to the La Java Bleue on Old Market Street. In fact, this is where I was slated to appear on the next day. A panel of expatriate crime writers had been put together to opine on some rather undefined topic. The organizer of the festival was rather elusive on details. Then again, perhaps that added to the charm.

To my relief the bathroom was empty. And it had a mirror. I rummaged in my backpack for what I needed and addressed my appearance. One final look in the mirror confirmed my satisfaction. I gave myself a smile, walked back into the small café, and ordered scones and a stiff coffee.

Then I completed my walk to the outskirts of Kampot. It was as if I had been transported to a different world. The Creek Kampot Guesthouse was set beside the narrow road that paralleled the river. It was located in a small bustling Cham fishing village. The smell was pungent yet alluring.

I walked up the path which led to the reception area where a short plump lady greeted me with a genuine smile. She looked up, heartily giggled, and said: "Welcome!"

Clearly I had selected the right inn for this trip. Sitting on the rooftop lounge the prahok and cucumbers made for great companions to the Angkor Beer. I sat blissfully looking over the Prek Kampong Kandal.

A couple of Americans also came up to enjoy this little nook of paradise. "Are you here for the literary festival?" one of them asked.

I smiled and shook my head, "No." Tomorrow I would engage the world, but for tonight, this rare slice of solitude, the food, the drink, and the intoxicating flow of the river would be my partner.

The festival was in full swing when I reemerged from the fishing village. So here I was. The Kampot Writers and Readers Festival was my first public appearance as a writer. And, I must confess, it made me a bit skittish. I would read a snippet from my latest novel and then participate in a panel. *'Something Fishy: Crime at the Creek!'*

I followed the river road. A beautiful stroll actually, though my mind was otherwise occupied. Today would be an eventful day. After the Bokor Mountain Lodge I turned away from the river. The colonial charm of the sleepy riverside city was hard to resist. The smell of rich coffee and delectable croissants guided me towards my destination.

And that was exactly what I ordered as I took a seat at La Java Bleue. This boutique hotel would be hosting the event so I arrived early to get comfortable with the surroundings.

The panel consisted of five white gentlemen of whom I seemed to be the youngest. We had all written novels set in Southeast Asia. A sparse crowd gathered around as we sat in rattan chairs ready to espouse our expat wisdom on the burgeoning artistic scene which had emerged over the previous decades.

Surveying the surroundings, it struck me that this was perhaps as lily white a crowd imaginable in this part of the world. And I was fairly certain that a conversation in the Khmer language would be hard to come by. But as the crowd filled out, and the people ordered generously from the menu, the owner allowed herself a smile.

For me, the main event was to occur after our round table chat. Bill Barnwell was to hold court in the early evening. I would keep my comments brief and drab. And that proved to be easily attainable as Justin Ashley Ferguson was eager to take charge.

"*Can you talk about what you consider to be good training ground, a certain career perhaps, that can help develop a writer's talent?*"

Ferguson clapped his hands as if he had been waiting to be asked that question all his life. "*Difficult to say really*", he began before going into a long-winded and quite detailed talk on the mundane jobs Charles Bukowski had had to endure. Finally, upon finishing, he remarked, "*Honestly, I never trust a writer who has never endured a soul crushing job.*"

My compatriots then jumped into the ring attempting to outdo each other and, I suppose, Bukowski on who actually had their soul crushed more thoroughly. Holding to my plan I remained silent. Finally, all heads turned towards me to which I could only shrug.

Expecting something more, I decided to row against the current. "My jobs have been mostly satisfying. As a kid during the summer time I was an ice cream maker before graduating to a lifeguard. Great memories there! After University I *did* have a job which I detested."

Now those in attendance as well as my peers perked up in interest. "I worked as a stockbroker on Wall Street. The hours pounding the phone were true hell." I could see my audience was held in rapt attention expecting a diatribe against unbridled American capitalism. "But the money was great, the job perks awesome, I got more ass than when I was on the beach, and after two years I was off to graduate school."

The let down from Ferguson and the rest of the crowd was obvious. I met the assorted sneers and frowns with a smile and was pretty much left alone after that.

Later, clinging to the shadows of the late afternoon, I watched as Barnwell and Mimi Wow Wow made their grand entrance. She was stunning. Her hair had recently been restyled into a cropped geisha look. Her low cut black mini left just enough to the imagination and if you were a leg man you might just be tempted away from the main course. Bill Barnwell had long ago perfected the shabby chic look. But today his black on black attire hinted at the cloak and dagger novel he had recently launched.

A cigar was lit, three fingers full of Scotch in his left hand, Barnwell flashed his waiting fans a smile.

'Let us talk about something truly interesting', Bill began. *'Many of you have read my book. The main thread of the story, ranging from the Golden Triangle to Marseilles onward to South and Central America deep into inner city America, follows an old grizzled pilot. And I'll gladly take any questions in that regard. But for today, I'd like to talk about the true drug kingpins, the real drug lords, the CIA. And it is good that we have this chat in Kampot where not so long ago Corsican mobsters along with their CIA sponsors sipped coffee by this beautiful riverside.'*

A loud round of applause filled the air as Bill Barnwell paused. His topic was a winner. America bashing was always sure to rally the crowd and he certainly knew how to work one.

With all eyes riveted on the stage I quietly exited. I made my way back towards the river road. My eyes spotted a small tavern. Finding my way to the toilet I reemerged a new man. The gray goatee, I had to admit, was soon going to be a reality. For now, it served as a disguise and one that found itself walking back towards the Kampot Riverside Hotel.

I took a seat in the hotel lounge and ordered a beer, lit a smoke, and surveyed my surroundings. If all went according to plan, I would return to this chair for a nightcap. I traded small pleasantries to the friendly staff. Mostly, I wanted to be seen.

The bill being settled, I then walked up to the top floor. A rather inebriated man clumsily avoided bumping into me as he shakily made his way back to a barstool. The hotel door, not surprisingly, allowed me an easy entrance.

The room was awash in darkness which I did not want to disturb. In any case, my brief tour from yesterday provided ample assistance in allowing me to set the scene. Two glasses, a bottle of Jack Daniels, a bottle of Coke, and a bucket of ice were placed on the table. Satisfied that everything was in order, I retreated to the balcony.

The moon had settled in to its nightly arc. It danced in and out of the clouds and provided a sense of serenity to the bustling activity ongoing below. The moon's ascent alerted me that my time was coming. Then I heard the rustling of keys hidden amongst the murmur of drunken conversation.

The door opened letting in a loud laugh.

"You drink too much, Boo Boo," I could hear Mimi Wow-Wow chastise.

I quietly and slowly stepped through the opening of the balcony's sliding door.

"Oh, just for this event. I'll slow down once we get back to the…"

Barnwell stopped abruptly once Mimi turned on the lights. She was about to scream but was silenced by my gun pointed at her head. I produced a knife. I put it close to her neck while shifting the aim of my pistol to Bill Barnwell.

"Mr. Barnwell and, if I may, Mimi, please sit here at the edge of the bed."

Mimi obeyed while he let out a resigned sigh. "You may as well shoot me right here, son."

I shook my head and motioned for him to sit. "And then Mimi would have to die. Is that what you want, sir?"

I turned on the desk lamp, turned off the overhead light, and mixed each of us a drink. Mimi shook her head 'no' when I handed her the glass but I insisted. With her husband's nod she slowly took a sip. He returned the gun's glare.

"So, they finally sent somebody for me. The journalist, last night, that was you?"

"Unfortunately, yes. And I was enjoying Krom so much. A wonderful fusion of traditional Cambodia folk and the Delta Blues, wouldn't you say. But a job is a job."

"Why now?"

I looked at him oddly. "Really? That little show you gave earlier tonight. At least you should have had the decency to admit you were right in the middle of that drug trade."

"A long time ago, kid. Anyway, just a story now. We're either dead or getting there so, I figured, what's the harm."

It then struck me. Perhaps he had, after all his travels and travails, turned the bend. Maybe truth had turned into fiction. This man had been a mountain in the agency. Flown through anti-aircraft batteries, delivered bombs, carved his way through jungles, and been an assassin's assassin, Big Bill was the stuff of legend.

"It is, I must say, an honour to meet you, even under the circumstances. To answer your question, I'm not sure. Perhaps going the Hollywood route, the Ron Howard and Tom Cruise movie, raised some eyebrows." If he was a target, he was also a man due respect. I looked at my watch.

And he knew there was no talking himself out of the situation. Mimi's head began to bob and her shoulders slumped. Finally she fell over onto the bed.

"You should be feeling the effects of Viagra about now, Mr. Barnwell. So, as it were, one last rodeo."

He snorted in response. "Two bullets I take it?"

The imminent thought of death raised other emotions than the amorous kind. Still, he understood that this life was better left with a roar.

I then mixed myself a drink. The grunts and moans grew as Mimi lay lifeless. Two bullets, the CIA's suicide calling card, was indeed the order. It would send a message. The last of the Jack and Coke was downed. I crossed to the bed and discharged two bullets into the side of Bill Barnwell's head.

A slight murmur, a sweet groan, could be heard from Mimi. I didn't hesitate. That was stopped as I strangled the life out of her. Bill's hands were then positioned on her throat and I squeezed. Then I gently laid him over to the side with the pistol placed in his right hand. A lover's murder suicide would be the coroner's finding, when and if these bodies even made it to autopsy. That was that. Not even a sweat was broken. I thought about returning to the lounge, and I would have, but the goatee was providing an awful itch. In any event, it was better to socialise a bit, snap some photos, and enhance my social media profile.

Fellow writers James Newman, Steven W. Palmer, and Kevin Cummings were seen drinking the night away in Oh Neil's Irish Pub. I joined and was thankful for the good company. The ale, the laughs, and the late closing time only added to my good mood.

I rubbed my temple as the Air Asia flight eased into the sky. My thoughts returned to my wife and daughter who would be waiting for me at the gate. Yes, the pot of gold at the end of the rainbow. I truly had it made: A wonderful and growing family, a satisfying and growing business, and the ability to take a trip on the government's dime on occasion.

And there, just there, a thought for a novel entered my mind.

The Assassin's Code!

***

Thomas is the owner and director of the N.U. Test Prep. Center in northern Thailand. In this capacity he helps prepare doctors, lecturers, university students, and business people for their academic careers abroad. It is rewarding work. Living in the beautiful foothills of the Himalayas, Thom and his lovely family enjoy to traveling throughout the amazing Kingdom of Thailand.

Along the way Thom, T. Hunt Locke, has written five novels. They can be found at his Amazon Author Page: https://www.amazon.com/-/e/B0089HIMTW

Little girl and the Hat

By Vornsar Ses

(Editor's note: This was our second-placed prize-winner in the joint competition between Saraswati Publishing and AsiaLIFE Cambodia magazine.)

"Hey, move out the way you stupid girl!" a man in a Lexus RX330 screamed at the girl carrying five jasmine garlands to sell on the street.

"Mister, please help, buy one of my beautiful garlands."

She walks past all the cars that are close to the road. People are getting out of their car to go to the riverside and some are just crossing to the other side to visit the Royal Palace. People with nice clothes, high heels, silver hair, wearing golden earrings, holding a big bag, or wearing a hat to help cover their face. Compare them to us; my sister wears old dark blue pyjamas and on the right side of her shirt is a big hole with some poor sewing, just to cover her waist. I wear big flip flops from my sister that actually are much too big for me while she walks with bare feet. The warm hand that pats my head is rough, full of bandages and blood from making the garlands and the sun is ruthless on her curly black hair. I can see sweat falling down her cheeks onto her shirt.

I can't believe she is just 12 years old. When I look at her, I can feel her beautiful smile and how tight she holds my hand as we walk to the other side of the road. But at that moment, I released my big sister's hand and ran to the garden. The pigeons who are eating corn from the people feeding them are distracted by my little feet with the big red shoes. While I run, I keep thinking about what happened this morning.

Before I came to the Royal Palace I saw one of the girls asking people for money, then they gave her 500 riels. If I can get that much many times, I can help my sister to buy a hat. I imagine her soft face that she used to have, but now it's become red, rugged and dark. Her little lips are peeling, but she still keeps singing a lullaby from the radio or a Khmer song called "*In love with the Moon*" every night before I fall asleep.

"Mister, please give me some money!" I walk straight to one of the guys who's about to buy some corn. I put my hands together and bend down gently. The wind from the Tonle Sap river blows my curly black ponytails to the left then when it stops, it sticks to my sticky cheeks.

"Go away, who let their kid out on the streets to beg for money in front of the Royal palace? You are really disrespectful! Where are your parents?" he screamed at me and pushed me aside.

"I don't have parents, but I..." I try to say something but I immediately stop. My sister comes and grabs my hand from the man.

"I am sorry Mister! I am really sorry." she repeats her words a few time and takes me to the other side of the street.

We walk to the right side of the garden and sit under the tree.

"Stay here okay? I am going to finish selling these garlands and I will come back with food." she pats my head again and walks away.

The more she grows up, the more she looks just like our mother. It reminds me of the time when our mother slept on the bed two years ago. I was just four years old and my sister was only 10 years old. My mother looked pale and weak but she still smiled at both of us. I kept asking when will our father come back from work? It's been one year, and I haven't seen him. Is he okay? Is the construction work alright? My sister looked at me and said he had forsaken us and run away with another woman. I still smiled because they didn't act sad at all. I guessed it might be a good thing, but when I touched my mother's hand it was shaky, it was cold, and her eyes were red and painful. Deep down inside, her heart beats and her tears fell down without a sound. I started to cry when my sister looked away from us. My mother can't even speak. She can't even lift her hands up to pat my head. She promised my sister to buy her a hat, but she couldn't.

Because she just stopped breathing.

"M-M-o-m! Mom, wake up!" I tried to shake my mother's body but she didn't move.

This was my first time seeing my sister cry. She covered her face with both hands and fell down to the floor. She groaned louder and louder. I felt like I was in the middle of a sinkhole. I ran and hugged my sister as tight as I could like my mother did when I fell down.

Our mother had HIV, but we can't afford the medicine. Also Stung Meanchey where we lived was full of trash which made our mother's health get worse. We didn't have a choice about moving. This is why we ended up moving near Phnom Penh, just to avoid the place full of bad memories. Until now, my sister and I walked around Phnom Penh just to sell the garlands from one spot to another, never getting tired. She promised me that she could replace my mother and become both mother and father to me at the same time. She is the best sister and I love her even though others said she's terrible. But in my eyes she is the most precious girl in the world.

"Hey, are you having a daydream or something?" my sister waves her hand in front of my face a few times.

"I am okay." I reply, then we both start to eat the food she got together. The food is nothing more than rice with fried pork that cost 2000 riels. Sometimes we only had fruit or salt with rice. I never thought of eating fancy food because there is nothing more delicious than eating with my sister.

After we both finish the food, my sister starts to do her job again. This time she's not selling the garlands, but she sells the lotus flowers for praying. People usually pray in the afternoon because it isn't that hot.

Suddenly the wind blows my hair and I have to turn to the right against the wind so that it doesn't stick to my face again. Then I saw a black trucker hat, and it still looks new. I start to run and grab the hat before other people take it. I am very lucky but....

Bang!!!!

The car turns to the left side of the road immediately because it was swerving away from me. It bumps me a bit, which is why I fall down. It hurts a little, but I am okay. I just feel a little burn on my knees. I am happy because at least I've got the hat. I look close to where a tall girl stands, her tears dropping down on the hat I carry, her face is pale and her mouth is purple.

"Sister!" I whisper,

She grabs my hand and pulls me to her. She hugs me so tightly. I really want to see her face but the way she hugs me only allows me to pat her back.

"I am sorry sister! I make you worry, But I am okay." I comfort her with my little whispering voice.

"I've got a hat for you though. You use to ask mommy for a hat, but she couldn't get you one and now I have one for you, so smile." I pull her to look at my face. She takes the hat and wears it. Her tears still flow, her face is so red, and I hear her teeth clash together and her mouth is also dry and shaking.

"I love you sister."

"I love you too."

We both hug each other like we never did before. I don't care about other people's money; it can buy anything but it can't buy happiness. I don't care about getting nice clothes because with the same outfit you don't have to wash more clothes. I don't want to be rich without my sister because it will be so lonely and hopeless.

I just want my sister to be happy. People may say that we are homeless, but with my sister, anywhere we go is my home of happiness.

Vornsar Ses is fifteen years old and comes from Takeo province. In 2012, she got a scholarship to the Liger Learning Centre in Phnom Penh. She is particularly interested in writing and reading, especially novels and adventure books, both in Khmer and English. She also loves to draw and explore different places. This is her first time entering a competition.

Oun Srolanh Bong

(Girl loves Boy)

Steven W. Palmer

1.

Boy meets girl, it's one of the oldest stories in the world. From casual meetings outside a cave through to spilling her drink in a club, little has changed in the basic format for thousands of years. A glance across a crowded room leads to a nervous introduction and a whole lot of hormones getting overactive.

Even this meeting had little new to offer. Yet another seedy bar in a seedy Phnom Penh street, its clichéd name marked outside in flickering neon. Bored looking girls sat outside eating kuy teav or bai sach chrouk while they awaited their overweight white knight to arrive in a haze of happy hour beer. Those that weren't eating gazed into the heat of the night with methamphetamine glazed eyes, the soul-destroying embrace of the drug a more attractive option than full awareness of the sad trade they were trapped in. Vacant gazes turned to fake smiles every time a prospective customer walked by, and should any choose to venture in, the girls transformed into a busy scourge of mosquitoes round a pool of stagnant water.

Transient nobodies escaping humdrum existences in humdrum towns were granted temporary royal status as they chose which peasant wench would have the privilege of releasing their alcohol tainted seed for that night. For a few hours and a few dollars these tourists' self-esteem would be temporarily boosted, beauty they can only gaze at on dating sites at home suddenly ripe for the plucking and ripe for the fucking. Beauty that should have stayed untainted on the farm or in the village but which is forced by poverty and desperation to be little more than vessels for the empty dreams of empty men.

There's an almost magnetic tragedy in watching these spectacles unfold; pity and disgust mixing in equal parts, yet you cannot tear your eyes away, cannot close your mind from knowing how the rest of the night will play out.

Her name was Bopha, which means 'flower' in Khmer, and she was 19. But it wasn't her real name, it was the one suggested by the bar's mamasan as she knew that when she explained it to the barang customers it would always elicit a positive response. Her real name was Makara but now no-one called her that except on the rare occasions she went back to her small village of Kampi on the banks of the mighty Mekong in Kratie province. She spoke good English, better than most of the other provincial girls in the bar, thanks mainly to the tourists who flocked to Kampi to see the endangered Irawaddy dolphins. During the tourist season she had worked on one of the many boats which took the tourists out to see the dolphins, and in low season she mainly worked helping her father in his butchery business. But then a year previously her father had died of a heart attack at the age of 45 and suddenly the family went from being comfortable – but not wealthy – to being close to destitution.

It was her friend Chantavy who had suggested she move to Phnom Penh and work in a bar. Chantavy had moved the year before and sent back $400 almost every month to her family in Kampi. She told Makara it was easy work, that someone as pretty as Makara could choose who to sleep with, and that even if she didn't want to have sex with customers she could still make a good salary just from lady drinks. Makara didn't know what to do; she was still a virgin and the idea of sleeping with strangers made her feel sick. But she had two sisters and a brother at home, all of them still at school, and she knew she could never earn enough money in Kampi to pay all their school costs. So she finally summoned up the courage and made the move to the capital. She felt the worst thing about it was having to lie to her mother, telling her that she had been offered a good job at a restaurant popular with tourists. Chantavy had arranged a room in the same building as her, and also an interview in the bar next to the one she worked in.

She had never been to Phnom Penh before, and when she got off the crowded minivan she felt claustrophobic with so many people and buildings around her. Chantavy was waiting for her and her friend's infectious excitement at Makara being there soon cancelled out any nervousness. Once she was settled in her room Chantavy took her shopping, telling her than none of the clothes she had brought with her would be suitable for work. So two hours later Makara had three bags of new clothes, none of which she would ever have dared wear at home, and which if her mother ever saw her in them would probably lead to a major argument.

Chantavy had arranged for her to see the boss of the bar at 5pm so they spent an hour getting ready, her friend doing her hair and makeup so she looked good for the meeting. Makara was now very nervous, unsure if she would get the job, but Chantavy assured her that it was an almost certain thing.

The owner of the bar was a Khmer woman of about 50, who took Makara into the office along with the bar's mamasan, an imposing woman with a hard face but kind eyes. When they found out that Makara was a virgin their faces lit up. They told her that she could make lots of money from losing her virginity and that because she was so pretty she could choose which customers she would sleep with from the bar once she was no longer a virgin. Makara wasn't sure, she'd always thought of her virginity as something to give to her husband, not to be sold like some piece of meat at the market. But when they told her that they may be able to get as much as $2,000, half of which they would keep for arranging things, she suddenly saw in her mind her sisters and brother at school and heading for a better life rather than seeing all her own dreams defiled in a hotel room somewhere in Phnom Penh.

And so she began working in 'Sexy Girls' bar the next night, though she was not available to be bar-fined while the owner looked for someone willing to buy her virginity. She was soon popular, her innocent looks and good English ability proving a winning combination with customers only too happy to buy her lady drinks for a few hours of her company in the bar. For a time, she even wondered if maybe she could just keep working like this, especially as she didn't like alcohol which meant she could make more from the drinks bought for her.

But two weeks later the mamasan sent her up to the office to speak to the owner, who told her she had found someone who wanted to spend the night with Makara. He was a Chinese business owner, the boss told her, very wealthy and willing to pay $2,500 for one night with Makara. $1,250 was a lot of money, and would pay her siblings' school fees for a long time as well as ensuring her family back in Kampi would eat well for months to come. So, for the sake of her family, she agreed to sleep with the Chinese businessman.

When the day came, her boss, Sopheak, took her to a fancy salon to get her hair, nails, and makeup done. Then she took her to buy a new dress, black and sleek but nicer than anything Makara had owned before. The man was going to pick Makara up from Sopheak's house, take her to dinner and then back to his hotel for the night. Sopheak gave Makara a small blue tablet called diazepam and said it would help relax her since Makara didn't want to drink alcohol. She wasn't sure about taking it but trusted

Sopheak so put it in her bag. The time came, the man arriving in a white BMW SUV. He looked old. Old and fat. Makara was even more nervous now but Sopheak hugged her and told her it would all be alright, and that she should make sure the man drank a lot at dinner because that way he would fall asleep quickly after sex. When the man came into the house, Sopheak introduced him as Liu Haifeng. For such a large man he had a soft voice and was charming and polite to both Sopheak and Makara. He handed a large envelope to Sopheak who discretely put it away in a drawer then he announced they would have to leave as their dinner reservation was soon.

He drove them to a small restaurant on Street 294 called Mok Mony, with a leafy courtyard setting or modern looking interior their options.

"It may not look that fancy," said Liu, "but it serves some of the finest food in the city."

To Makara, a girl from a small riverside village, it was fancier than anywhere she had been before. Liu ordered drinks for them both, beer for him and water for Makara. He talked about his business; he owned a factory on the outskirts of Phnom Penh making shoes, and Makara nodded politely and smiled at what she thought were the right times. He also ordered all their food, though he did first ask Makara if there was anything she didn't like. Grilled Betel Leaf with Marinated Beef and Deep Fried Wonton for starters, Blue Mekong Prawns and Mun Char Kern for main course. She remembered Sopheak's advice and constantly refilled his glass, so that by the time the main dishes arrived he was already on his fifth beer. To be fair to him, he was attentive, asking her if she was enjoying the food, then questioning her on her life in Kampi. There almost came a point when she forgot what was to happen after dinner but all too soon the meal was finished and he was ushering her to the car.

She had remembered to take the pill Sopheak had given her while Liu was at the toilet in the restaurant and by the time they arrived at his hotel, a nice four-star place just off Monivong Boulevard, she felt relaxed and almost sleepy.

But then anything that had been almost pleasant about the evening disappeared in the reality of the situation. Once they reached the room he became a different person, pawing and groping at her then commanding her to undress. He poured himself a whisky and sat on the edge of the bed, leering at her as she hesitantly removed her clothes. Once she was naked he ordered her to go and take a shower. As she took her time washing herself she wondered if she would ever feel clean again after tonight.

If the thought of what was to come had been frightening, the reality was far worse. His gentleness from the restaurant had now disappeared completely and she had to stifle a cry as he pushed her onto the bed and began pawing at her body again. Then came the pain as he forced himself inside her and this time she could not hold back a cry of pain, a cry he ignored as he continued to thrust on top of her. The only saving grace was that it seemed to be over before it had even started and he rolled off her, satiated and uncaring and asleep within minutes. Makara lay there for what seemed like hours, her shame a red stain on the bed between her legs, her innocence flowing away with the tears that streamed silently down her face.

Eventually she forced herself off the bed, leaving the now snoring Liu in the bed. She stood under the shower for nearly 40 minutes, trying to wash the memory of what had happened off of her. She dressed and crept back into bed, careful not to wake him in case he wanted more. Sleep took a long time to come, and when it did her dreams were filled with memories of home that took her away from the horrors of the night.

She woke in the first light of morning to Liu's hands and mouth invading her. There was no point in resisting, he would only have forced himself on her, and so she remained passive and let him hurt her once again. When he had finished this time he immediately got out of bed and went to the bathroom and she heard the shower being switched on. She lay there unsure what to do or what he wanted her to do. After about ten minutes he emerged and started dressing. When he was finished he looked at her, threw a five-dollar bill on the bed and said;

"I have to go to work. There's some money for a tuk tuk."

And then he was gone. She gathered her things together and phoned Sopheak who told her to come straight to her house. She was hardly in the door when the tears came, Sopheak enveloping her in her arms and holding her close till every last sob had escaped her body. Once the tears had subsided, Sopheak made her some food then handed her an envelope.

"There's $1,250 in there. I know it seems horrible to put a price on something so precious, but think of the difference it will make to your family. One thing, don't send it all at once or your mother will be suspicious."

Once Makara had finished eating she thanked Sopheak – who told her not to come to work that night – then headed back to her room. As she lay in her lonely bed far from home and family, she swore that no man would hurt her like that again.

From that day almost a year had passed. Sopheak had stayed true to her word and kept Makara as a 'special girl.' She could choose her own customers when she wanted, and always charged $100 or more depending on how generous she thought the customer could be. She never went with Chinese men; the night with Liu had ensured that she could never allow herself to be touched by another one. Her preferred type was under 50 and slim, perhaps both factors also influenced by that night her innocence had been stolen. And although she was a girl very much grounded in reality, she had succumbed to the same hope and dream so common among the working girls of Phnom Penh; that one day someone special would walk through the door, someone who wouldn't care about her past and who would marry her and free her from this life of slavery.

There had been several who had spoken sweet words to her, promising her happiness and escape while in the haze of cheap liquor, but in the cold morning light of sobriety their promises quickly became unmasked as the lies of sweet mouthed barangs. The hope and the dream faded a little each time this happened and cynicism was slowly creeping in to take over.

So here she was, on another Friday night in the big sin city. December in Phnom Penh yet the city seemed quiet. Perhaps the spate of murdered tourists over the last nine months, seven bodies found eviscerated in various cheap guesthouses across the city, made people more hesitant to venture out to the bars and hostess joints. And reflecting just how cheap people thought the lives of working girls were, the fact that half a dozen bargirls had been strangled in just seven weeks had been relegated to inside pages of the newspapers while the dead barangs claimed the headlines and the outrage on social media. Such was the way of the world in South East Asia. The ones with money in their pockets had more value than those forced to sell their bodies in order to survive. Yet take away the dollar signs and which of them were the more noble creatures? Life was cheap here, it seemed like it had always been that way, and the skewed views of those who visited weren't going to change that perception any time soon.

Makara was sitting at the bar, bored and listless, and talking to Saray the cashier about nothing in particular. The bar had seen less than ten customers all night and it didn't look as if that was going to change much. Nights like this had been too common recently and the girls all hoped that January would see a big increase in custom. If it didn't then a few girls would likely have to be let go, returning to their villages or to work in one of the sweatshop factories that surrounded Phnom Penh like a Berlin Wall of exploitation.

The door swung open, greeted with the familiar deafening chorus of 'Hello!' from all the girls as they all flocked round the newcomers in the hope of being chosen. With the month so quiet the two men entering were deluged with girls eager to earn some dollars. Makara sighed, she didn't like hanging out the front so always lost out to that initial rush, and neither of the men looked her type anyway. She picked up her phone, choosing to play on Facebook for a time while Sarey sorted drinks for the customers. As usual there were multiple friend requests from men she didn't know, and as usual she deleted all of them. Some of the other girls accepted all these requests in the hope that one of them would be the man of their dreams, but the reality was usually a succession of sleazy messages and pictures of their dick sent by private message. Little did their suitors know that what they thought were impressive photos ended up being the source of much hilarity for all the girls at work that same night.

The door swung open again. This time it was a lone wolf. When a single man came into a bar, it was pretty much a certainty that he was looking to take a girl home or back to his hotel. When they were in pairs or groups they might choose to stay at that bar or merely use it as one in a succession of venues on a night out, but a single guy was always looking for sex.

Some of the girls still attached to the previous two men detached themselves from the group and went to greet the new customer. Like sexual limpets they clung to him and steered him to an empty booth near the pool table, hoping at the very least he would buy multiple drinks and that at best he would choose to bar fine one…or even two of them for the night. She sighed again. Shame. He was actually more her type than she had seen for a couple of weeks. Aged about 35 he wasn't handsome in a movie star way but neither was he ugly. He had kind eyes and was well groomed and seemed a little shy at the attention he was getting. Makara returned her attention to her phone, occasionally glancing at the mirror behind the bar to observe the flirtatious machinations of her workmates.

On her third glance she noticed he was staring intently at her, the girls beside him oblivious to the fact he was showing no interest in them. She blushed a little, a natural reaction she often had that only added to her innocent charm that so many men liked. She tried to keep her attention on the phone but found her attention drawn back to the reflection in the mirror time and time again. And every time she looked the man was still staring. Should she go over? No, let him ask to speak to her. A certain degree of aloofness was another trait that had served her well over this last year. Forcing herself to stare at the phone screen she resisted every urge to look again. After about ten minutes one of the girls who had been sitting with him came over and sat beside Makara at the bar.

"The barang doesn't like us," she said quietly in Khmer. "He wants you to go and sit with him."

Makara looked over her shoulder. The man was still staring straight at her and when she looked, he smiled, a warm smile that made her feel a little funny inside. She made her way over to him and he indicated she should sit beside him. The other two girls giggled, but Makara could see the annoyed look in their eyes.

"Soursdey." He said in clumsy Khmer. "Sok Sabai?"

She smiled. "It's ok, bong, I speak good English. I'm good thank you, how are you?"

"Good too," he answered hesitantly. "Sorry, my Khmer is not very good."

"At least you try." She said.

He ordered drinks for them both, Jack Daniels and Coke for her – without the Jack Daniels – and a beer for him. They chatted easily. As they always did, he loved her name and its meaning, the trap set and sprung before the drinks had even arrived at the table. His name was Ryan, he was 32 and from Nottingham in England. He told her he was a freelance web designer and was considering relocating to Phnom Penh. As the vast majority of his work was carried out online there was little need to actually live in England and with the way the politics and prices were going, he didn't really want to. Makara nodded and smiled at all the right times. He'd been in Cambodia for eight weeks now and had rented a small apartment. He had spent a week in Siem Reap but had been in the capital since as he needed to finish a major work project so had little time to travel, though he did plan on getting to Sihanoukville and Kampot soon. He asked about where she was from and her family back home and seemed genuinely interested. When she told him about working with the tours to see the Irawaddy Dolphins he asked if she would take him to see them. She looked at him sadly at this point and said that she couldn't as it was her home town and too many people would talk if she was travelling with a barang.

"You're a very special girl," he said.

Makara knew he wasn't drunk – yet – as she had become very experienced at judging how drunk a barang was. Was this just more sweet mouth lies? Nineteen seemed too young an age to be cynical and world weary but that's what working in this trade did to you. He hadn't tried to be sleazy, as many of the customers did, at any point. In fact, the only physical contact had been when he took her hand before telling her she was beautiful.

"You probably think I am just saying nice things, but there really is something special about you." He said.

She liked the words. But she didn't know if she believed them. Ryan didn't seem to have that same desperate aura that so many male visitors to the bar had, but she had travelled this road of hope before only to find that the destination left a bitter taste. He ordered more drinks, but switching his own choice to water as he said he had an important Skype call with a client early in the morning and that he didn't want to be too fuzzy headed. Once the drinks had arrived he went to hold her hand under the table and she let him, yet still wondering if the hand would want to go travelling elsewhere while out of sight. But it remained a tender gesture that let her stay on the road a while longer.

She had expected any new direction in conversation to involve a query around bar fines and availability, but instead he surprised her again.

"Bopha, I do mean it when I say you are special. I know it sounds stupid but I have never been in one of these bars before and I had no idea why I came in this one tonight. But when I saw you I realised that something had made me come in."

Sweet mouth.

"I want to ask you something," he said. "I need to go back and sleep soon. This Skype call is due at 3am. Is there any way we could meet for dinner tomorrow night and talk more? I know you need to pay fines in bars like this and am happy to pay the bar so you can have the night off. And I do mean only dinner and drinks. I'm not asking you to come back to my place; you really are too special to rush things."

Sweet mouth. But sweet too.

"I don't know," she said. "I'll have to go and ask my boss."

Leaving him alone, she made her way up the narrow staircase to the small office where the mamasan held court.

"Do you like this boy?" she asked once Makara had explained the situation.

"Yes," she said. "He seems honest, not like all the other customers."

"Okay," said the mamasan, "let me come down and talk to him."

They came down together and sat down either side of Ryan.

"Quite a handsome boy," said the mamasan in Khmer.

She then grilled the poor Englishman, asking what his plans were for the following evening, where he would take Makara, and how much was he willing to pay for her to lose one of her best staff for the night. Thus began the haggling dance, though to be fair to Ryan he didn't try to hard but realised it was almost a traditional part of the ritual. Finally, they agreed on a price of $40 for Makara to have the next night off. Little more than the average cost of a good dinner in the West or a mid-range hotel here, but also the cost of owning a human life for one night in Asia.

Satisfied, and with the money in her hand, the mamasan retreated to her eyrie and left them alone again.

"Where will I meet you?" he asked.

"Easiest just to meet here. It's close to everything. Is six o'clock okay?"

"Sounds good to me. I am really sorry I have to go." He said. "But it's clients like these that mean I will probably be able to live here."

Makara called for his kit loy (bill) and paid it, leaving a dollar tip for the cashier and handing five dollars as a tip to Makara.

"I guess I'll see you tomorrow then," he said.

"I'm looking forward to it. See you six o'clock."

Ryan leaned forward and kissed her on the cheek.

"You're very special," he said.

Sweet mouth.

"So are you," she said, and meant it.

Once he had gone the gossip started, the girls giggling and asking her lots of questions. She fobbed them off with the minimum details she could till they finally grew bored and drifted back to the captivation of their phone screens, counting the minutes till another quiet night was over.

2.

Makara had made an effort for that evening's date. Though part of her, jaded by a year of lies and broken promises, thought that Ryan was just another tourist with a willing wallet, there was still enough of the innocent country girl left to hope that this could be true romance. He had been so polite and had seemed genuine. So she had her best dress on, not too sexy but not overly demure either. She'd visited the salon in late afternoon and her hair was now a cascade of exuberant curls and her makeup was, unlike so many Khmer girls after a visit to the salon, enhancing her beauty rather than transforming it into a pale mask of horror. She took a tuk tuk to the bar, conscious that her carefully prepared hair would suffer irreparably on the back of a moto. There was the usual early gathering of girls at the bar, cleaning up, doing makeup, and the inevitable Khmer habit of calorie-defying eating. The girls were almost as excited as Makara, teasing her about her new 'boyfriend' and asking when the wedding would be.

Ryan was on time, arriving outside the bar virtually bang on six in one of the weird bubble tuk tuks that dotted the Riverside catering for tourists. He looked good, crisp white linen shirt and freshly pressed chinos and Makara was relieved he hadn't turned up in shorts and sandals. He got out of the tuk tuk in order to help her in, a sign of a true gentleman she thought, and greeted her with a chaste kiss on the cheek, much to the amusement of the watching audience of half made-up bar girls. They set off, heading up the street towards Riverside then taking a left.

"Where are we going?" asked Makara.

"Just wait and see." Ryan had an enigmatic smile as he replied.

They drove up Sisowath Quay, Ryan lightly holding her hand as they looked out at the bustling activity of life by the river at dusk, Khmer matrons performing synchronised aerobics, young couples playing badminton, food vendors serving a variety of succulent wares, and tourists recording the moments for posterity and memories. They slowed just after passing the night market then stopped on the river side of the road by the large, mainly tourist-orientated, Khmer restaurant across from Mao's Club where Makara had been with some friends the month before.

"I thought it seemed appropriate given your name." he said.

Makara looked up at the sign. 'Bopha Phnom Penh Titanic Restaurant.' She wasn't sure where the 'Titanic' part of the name came from, she only remembered it was the name of a ship that had sunk in the film, so she didn't know if that was a bad omen.

They walked through the main entrance and were greeted by a woman in traditional Khmer dress. She gave the couple a Cambodian sampeah greeting, her eyes and smile warm for Ryan but her gaze at Makara saying that she knew this was a relationship based on a foundation of dollar signs. The waitress led them to the table Ryan had reserved, down on the riverside terrace with views onto the Tonle Sap. Ryan asked her what she wanted to drink and she asked for a mango shake while he ordered a Tiger beer. The waitress went to collect their drinks while they looked at the menu.

The restaurant was nice, but was obviously aimed at tourists. It was all a little too…well, Khmer. Like they had tried too hard to be authentic and had then passed their planned destination by a couple of dozen miles. A small stage in the main part of the restaurant hosted a couple of Apsara dancers and some traditional musicians, their show being lapped up by the surrounding diners by the look of the multiple camera flashes going off.

Makara looked over the menu. So expensive. She could make most of the dishes on here for a fraction of what they were charging.

"Do you see anything you like?" asked Ryan.

Makara wasn't particularly hungry. Unlike her workmates she usually ate sparingly, trying to save every spare dollar and riel to send home to her family.

"I think I'll have the Mango Salad," she said. "What about you?"

"What I really like is sitting across the table from me," he replied.

Sweet mouth still. But still so sweet too.

"I know it makes me look like a total tourist – which I suppose I still am – but I'm going to have the Chicken Amok served in the coconut shell. And maybe some Chicken Satay for a starter, but we can share that."

The waitress returned with the drinks and took the food order, leaving them alone again. There was a silence between them, but comfortable rather than awkward, and they gazed out at the Tonle Sap, still bustling in the early evening, content just to be in the other's company. When conversation returned, it was as comfortable as the silence had been. Ryan told her about growing up in Nottingham, about his two brothers who were both in the army, of weekend camping trips with their dad in the Peak District, and of how he had shown aptitude with computers and programming from an early age. She felt she knew him better than the timeframe of 24 hours would suggest, and she dared to hope that maybe this time the road could lead to somewhere permanent.

The food arrived and Ryan ordered more drinks. They shared their plates, though Ryan was not overly fond of the Mango Salad, and Makara declared that her mother's Amok was far better than what they served here. Their conversation continued to flow as easily as the river mere metres from their table and Makara relaxed more and more as the evening went on. Once the meal was finished Ryan paid the bill and they left the restaurant, ignoring the plaintive cries of tuk tuk drivers outside and instead choosing to walk along the riverside pathway.

Even with the occasional waft of sewage assaulting their noses, there was a feeling of romance in the air. Young couples sat entwined on the wall by the river, this their only location for unchaperoned courting. Children still ran and played around their parents, and the only negative was the occasional young solvent sniffer separated from the world and reality by the fumes they were inhaling. Ryan led her over to the wall and they sat, gazing at the reflection of the half-moon on the water and not needing to say anything at all.

"Bopha…" said Ryan. "I really am being honest when I say you are special. Is there any way you would stop working in that bar if I was living here all the time? I can't bear the thought of other men touching you or even looking at you. I want you to be all mine."

Sweet mouth. But the oh so sweet she wanted to hear.

"I will be honest with you too. I hate working there, but since my father died I am the main provider for my mother and siblings. I like you too but I need to think of my family before myself."

"Can I ask? How much money do you send home to your family every month? I know it's rude but it is important."

"No, that's ok," she said. "Some months I manage to send $400 or more, others a little less, but always enough to keep the children in school and food on the table. And I try and save a little for myself too so I can one day open a business back in Kampi."

"Look, my work is good and it pays well. What if I covered all the money your family needs so that you don't have to work there and we can be together?"

She smiled. Had the path finally taken her to the place she wanted to be?

"If your words and heart are true, then yes, I would happily stop working. But I cannot live with you until you have met my mother, and even then we must make plans to marry if you really want to be with me."

"I am true and I am happy to meet your mother. If she likes me and gives permission, I would marry you too though I know nothing of how it is done here. I know it is crazy to talk like this after one day but I know what I want."

"Do not worry about what to do, the women take care of everything." Makara laughed. "You just change outfits when we tell you and smile for the family. I am sure my mother will like you very much."

They embraced, and held each other like that for a long time.

"Do you want to come back to my apartment?" he asked. "You don't have to, but I want nothing more than to wake up beside you."

Sweet mouth, true mouth, happy heart.

"Yes darling, I want to be with you too. But I must tell you one thing if we are being true. My real name is Makara, not Bopha. Bopha is the name the owner of the bar thought suited me."

He frowned.

"I like Bopha though. You will always be my Khmer flower."

They walked over to the road and hailed an enthusiastic tuk tuk driver. Ryan told him to take them to Street 134, not far from Central Market. Makara was surprised as she had expected him to live in a condo block but she supposed he didn't want to get a more expensive place till he had made a final decision about staying. Street 134 was a typical Phnom Penh Street, businesses on both sides varying from phone and computer shops to pharmacies and beauty salons, all with two or three levels of apartments above them. Ryan's apartment was two levels above a phone shop, the entrance a rusted and solitary gate with little lighting.

"This is just temporary till I decide I'm here for good," he said as if sensing her previous uncertainty. "Though I think now I know I will be staying."

He led her up the poorly-lit stairs, holding her hand to reassure her and keep her from stumbling. He had a padlock on his door as well as the normal lock and it took him a few minutes to unlock the door but finally he opened it and ushered her in, switching on the lights as they entered. It was a typical small Khmer apartment but Ryan had made some effort to make it homely to his own tastes. A few tasteful pictures adorned the wall and there was a large flat screen TV across from some of the usual rattan furniture. A stereo unit sat in a small shelving unit and he lifted a remote control, pressing some buttons to play music that sounded much like what she heard in the bar all the time. He pressed the control again and the volume rose, worrying Makara that he could upset the neighbours. Taking her by the hand again, he led her through to the bedroom, and she placed her bag on the side of the bed before sitting down. She looked up at him and noticed dark shadows that were hiding the smiles of before.

"You're just like all the rest," he said. "Another lying whore."

Where had sweet mouth gone?

"Ryan, what's wrong? Why are you being like this? Maybe I should leave."

"You're not fucking going anywhere, bitch."

Makara was in shock. What had caused such a change in so short a time? She made to get up from the bed but he stepped forward and struck her across the face, sending her sprawling backwards on the bed beside her bag. Tears began to rise in her eyes.

"You want to know what's wrong. Then I'll tell you. You left it to the very end to tell me your real name, proving you're just another liar. You think this is the first time I've been in Cambodia? I first came in 2006 and met a girl who I fell in love with. I gave her money, bought her gifts, and she promised she would stop working in her sleazy bar and wait for me to come back from England. Said she was working in a hair salon instead, and while I was gone I would send her money every week to live. But when I came back eight weeks later, I arrived a week early to surprise her, went to the salon where she said she worked but they had never heard of her. So that night I went back to the bar where we had met and there she was with some fat German's hand up her skirt. You can't help yourself; as soon as you become a whore you learn to lie, and a soon as you learn to lie you start hurting people. Well just like the others, no-one is going to care about another dead whore."

Others? Dead? Ryan opened a drawer and took out a short length of rope and moved towards Makara.

"There's no point in screaming, my neighbour downstairs is stone deaf and the stereo will drown anything out for the others."

He struck her again and pushed her back before straddling her and looping the rope around her neck.

"Another dead whore, another dead bitch. No great loss in a country full of whores and liars."

He began to tighten the rope, his eyes ablaze with the insanity only killers really know, and Makara could feel her breath gradually disappear. Ryan was so focussed on what he was doing that he didn't notice her hand reach into the bag beside her. Nor did he see her slip the Citadel Kukri knife that had cost her nearly a month's wages to buy out of her bag. But he did feel the 10.5cm blade as she pushed it into his stomach. And he also felt the cold pain of steel as she slit his stomach open and his intestines began to spill out on the bed. She pushed him off her and he fell back, hands uselessly clasping at his stomach in a vain bid to save his own life.

Now the tables were turned and she straddled him, the skills she had learned from her father in evidence as she expertly disembowelled him. As the last vestiges of light began to fade from his eyes, she stared down at him.

"Did you never stop to think what makes us whores and liars? Do you think we were born this way? Poverty turns us into whores and the empty promises of bastards like you makes us into liars. Every whore is a daughter, a sister, a mother, a woman. We do not choose this life; this life chooses us. You come here with full wallets and arrogant thoughts, you use us and throw us away and then you wonder why we lie?"

But Ryan was gone and could not answer. She looked at the bloody scene and sighed. Another bitter ending but this time it seemed she had gained revenge for her murdered sisters. Who would have guessed that his sweet mouth was masking such a sour heart? It was time to clean up and leave.

As she had done seven times before, she carefully cleaned up after herself, memorising the few spots where she may have left fingerprints and wiping them thoroughly before stripping off and placing all the bloody clothes in a refuse bag. She then showered slowly; making sure every spot of blood was washed from her body then dressing again in the spare outfit she always carried in her bag.

As she made to leave she looked back one last time at Ryan's body lying on the blood-soaked bed. Such a shame. She had really hoped that this was the one. Maybe next time.

Steven W. Palmer is a Scottish expat living in Kampot. In his working life he has worked as a social worker and counsellor in the drugs field, as a social worker and probation officer in criminal justice, a DJ and promoter, a sales and marketing manager, the editor of an arts and entertainments magazine in Cambodia, and as managing editor for three magazine titles in Phnom Penh. He now runs a boutique publishing and marketing/design/digital strategy company.

He is currently working on Angkor Cloth, Angkor Gold, the third and last of the Angkor series, as well as Bangkok Drowning, a dystopian noir novel set in the near future.

In his spare time, Steven enjoys making quirky music tunes, riding his vintage Vespa, and training hamsters.

The Tuk-Tukker of Doom

Chad Evans

Une stèle portant des inscriptions sanskrites et khmères [...] se rapportent à la foundation du temple de Dvijendrapura, ancien nom du site de Prah Einkosei [. . .] fondé à la même date (968 A.D.) [. . .] au sud-ouest, le Travān Khmoc (bassin des morts) [. . .]

Georges Cœdès, INSCRIPTIONS DU CAMBODGE, 1952

I

The dry season sun was rising over Cambodia. In the dawn twilight matrons emerged from houses, shades sweeping oxide-red dust and leaves off the concrete street with no name. Towering pillars, cylindrical trunks of chheuteal trees appeared, spaced along the tumbledown sandstone wall of Wat Leur. A sudden flush of dispersed light captured Buddhist monks departing the vihear hall after pre-dawn meditation. Robed in vivid saffron and gold, a few with shoulder bags gathered in a group for their alms round. An old nun, toothless and hairless, carried an urn towards a stupa. Carey Clayson enjoyed the early street sounds: the guest-house lady preparing rice porridge in her road-front courtyard, the small shophouse roller door rising, women talking in Khmer. Indolent dogs with mange bickered over warm patches on the road. Invisible tailorbirds and bee-eaters rustled and chattered. Geckos clicked goodbye and retired up the wall for the day. A viscous yellow frog squatted free of care on the balcony railing. You knew where you were.

Soon the rear gate of the wat would open, then school students would arrive and enter on bicycles and scooters, each an upright, perfect Khmer promise, wearing collared, starch-white shirts, long navy blue skirts or pants, most with tell-tale plastic thongs on their feet. Wat Preah Enkosei school resided on the same site as a tenth century temple built by a Brahmin lord named Divakarabhata, which Khmers all nicknamed Wat Leur, it being the *leur* or uppermost of a string of Buddhist wats along the Siem Reap River. They had no idea of its Hindu pre-Angkorian heritage, its ancient slave culture, Carey realised … today all temples were Buddhist to Khmers and never once the home of Vishnu or Shiva.

Carey sat alone, second coffee in hand, up on the high, modern deck of his son's new house, Stonewall, overlooking the road and the expansive grounds of the wat, a botanical garden given the lack of old growth greenery elsewhere in overdeveloped Siem Reap. Monks were the first conscious environmental conservationists, he mused. They still blocked capitalist developments designed to wipe out nature. Gnarled frangipanis, strangler banyans, vines, and crocodile ferns framed the Chinese cemetery in the foreground below. The cultural historian brushed fine blonde hair off his brow and filed a note in his sixty-five-year-old eidetic brain: *search similarity between Cape Dutch rounded gable design and Chinese headstones, painted white with inset vertical inscriptions.* He had left his tablet downstairs, dammit. The graveyard was backed by a monastic cell, flat-roofed with a door and square window papered with Cambodian fake news. And now its interior light vanished-- *no power line, candlelight?* --and the newsprint that was backlit all night long was struck by strong sunlight. "What are they doing in there?" Drake had said last night. "I never see shadow play in the window. That door never opens." Both their minds had wandered towards visions of ordained monks having illicit sex with novices.

Through a blind of banana tree leaves Carey could now glimpse the first motorcycle and tuk-tuk taxis occupy their police-sanctioned spot beside the wat's rear entrance. From the gate a dirt thoroughfare ran all the way down to the river, bisecting the wat. In a while their headman, Saroeun, would roll up in his Korean Daelim motorcycle trailing a canopied carriage with two bench seats. *Note for mental clipboard: the early nineties development of the four-wheel Cambodian tuk-tuk is based on the French bicycle-driven remorque. Khmers still call them remork or remork-moto. High transverse pivot connector, no ball coupler. Tuk-tuk is an Anglo misnomer, onomatopoeia for the sound of the original two-strokers.* Drake and he had drunk beer outside until late the previous evening, after his daughter-in-law Seyha had served up a fine dish of spicy duck with rice, and his grandson had reluctantly gone to bed. Carey had asked about his driver, Saroeun.

"The Tuk-Tukker of Doom," said Drake. "I have known Saroeun since temple-town was a quiet village. Two accidents with him, one serious one, a jackknife and rollover which wasn't at all his fault. Some other idiot was driving the wrong way on a one-way street. To his great credit Saroeun never wavered and just plowed straight into the dude once it was clear a head-on was inevitable. If he had tried some kind of defensive manoeuvre, then we just would have jackknifed and rolled over at greater speed while missing the other cunt who would have walked away without his beating. Saroeun pulled me off him. He calls me Kheatakor, killer, in his smiling friendly way. I'd say by now he has figured out you are Aupouk nei Kheatakor, sire of killer."

II

Somreun rolled up knowing things were about to turn crazy in Siem Reap. Dith and Sin had already departed with rides. It was the day before Bon Om Touk, the three-day Water Festival, when thousands of rural Khmers came to the flooded, mud-yellow river to party amongst food and goods stalls, and to watch dragon-boat races and entertainment on the big sound-stage. As if all the construction along east River Road would stop, and he knew all the bridges near town would become choked with pedestrians. Going would be slow but tuk-tuks were all underpowered anyway and he could hardly hit thirty klicks even on Vithei Charles De Gaulle to Angkor. But the many, wobbly remork-motos would protect barangs from the throng of rice farm families and provide chariot views. His old remork was solid and rustic … young drivers, some who knew barang talk, were nowadays more into flashy personal touches … like Samay's with his blaring sound system, which suited that Pub Street tourist mob.

Shaded under his carriage canopy, like lords in palanquins, barangs loved his airy rides in the heat, the pitted roads, the squeaking leaf-springs and constant near misses he provided. Somreun understood courting death got their adrenaline going and they enjoyed what would be illegal fifteen ways in their countries. He knew something about law and disorder, and death, as a former police major. His moto-dups were aware he had served with the famous A-3.86 Unit fighting Pol Pot's jungle ambushers. He had risen in the civilian force during UNTAC and became a provincial major in the National Police. Then, his dismissal . . . the fall guy for a corrupt general ...but as he had accepted this stoically he and his moto gang were given operating territory and a few expensive Icom UHF handheld police radios to report anything and everything. The tuk-tuk telegraph was the link between unpackaged barang tourists coming to see Angkor Wat and the salaried uniforms. Information about resident barangs filtered up to the high command, the big collectors, and the Party. They were watched closely.

Somreun let others take walk-ups or phone calls. He would wait patiently until Kheator's old man, up there on the deck of Stonewall, came to him for his morning ride around town. First stop was always the pharmacy near Phsar Cha market, where the barang would magically unfold his walking stick, then disappear. Eventually he would emerge from the market labyrinth and go walkabout before sitting down for an early beer. Somreun would stretch out across his bench seats, wait and watch citizen cane eat his paw-paw salad and Hanoi rolls at the Soup Dragon. By midday they would head back to Wat Leur, stopping at a supermarket for the barang to shop for snacks, juices and liquor. No sightseeing. Of course his son had the double-cab truck with its extremely evil NGO logo to take him to the temples. Aupouk nei Kheatakor was late this morning and had wandered over to the shophouse to pull some cans of beer out of an ice chest, a kick-starter after the night before. There was never any hurry for a Siem Reap suburban tuk-tukker, particularly if you had one good passenger and could count on ten dollars for the day.

Ponlok, one of the few with an Icom tasked to observe Stonewall and its famous barang owner drove up beside Samrouen. He relayed the story given to him by Narith, who understood English and worked nights. Narith knew the family of three and visiting grandfather in Stonewall by their proper names. Ponlok told Samrouen that father and son had been as Khmers say, riding the panther, until midnight, emptying countless cans of Black Panther stout. Narith had overheard their animated conversation...

"I am here for a good life not a long life," Drake said.

"Well, you have obviously made an enemy after all these years as the cultural cowboy. The Kalashnikov swat team at the airport? The truck's slashed tires. Now you are stonewalled."

"I am over it. The Khmers hate me. The French hate me. But I am too high profile and connected to kill."

"The BBC and Duke of Gloucester love you. International press. I suppose stone walls work both ways for protection," Carey said. "And Seyha handles the locals, all your domestic stuff, properties and douses your behavioural bushfires."

"It is never going to make it. Cambodia will always be a corrupt mess. Stonewall has no address. There is no post. All you see is a mafia run headset video."

"And the barangs love the ancient theatre sets, the raw chaos of the colonial streets...*The Gods Must Be Crazy*."

Translated second hand by Ponlok, only the gist of Narith's report survived for Samrouen to digest. Khmer language was short on inflections, lacked tonality, conjugations, articles and so forth, but Narith's gesticulations were intact. He had told of the late night's events. Drake had morphed into Kheatator and abused Narith when he shuffled past Stonewall to the shop, his Icom crackling with messages. Drake shouted in Khmer and mocked Narith's thonged shuffle, his inability to lift his legs, and in the end threw palm fruit at him while mimicking the sound of his walkie-talkie.

"Ssshoooka, ssshoooka, ssshoooka…" the sound of Narith's lethargic shuffle…"kt-shhhh, kt-shhhh, kt-shhhh…" for the squelch of his Icom. Somreun could not repress a laugh, and secretly hoped Drake had indeed tormented the police rat.

When the palm fruit were thrown, Ponlok continued, father went downstairs to bed. Drake then walked outside, went up the pitch-black cross-road to his rear neighbour's vacant, gated apartment block. He threw stones at the guard dogs and walls of other residences where dogs were barking. Kheatator despised rabies-carrying Cambodian dogs and temple cats, a Buddhist untouchable caste.

Samrouen shifted under his tuk-tuk canopy, now feeling mid-morning heat. The rice porridge breakfast his wife had made sat well in his stomach. Nothing new, he thought…the women would sort out any neighborhood grievances, save face and return all to harmony. Seyha was good for tea-money offerings…her budget would cover the double-trouble expected of reunited father and son. The lazier moto-dups, who only pretended to work to get away from their wives, were setting up a thong-toss game on the wat roadway. One held a squashed rat by its tail and flung it, as others chuckled, into the bushes.

III

Dusk light faded quickly as Carey examined the tenth century inscriptions in the sandstone doorframes of the two surviving sanctuary towers. He had left the villa and walked into the sacred grounds of Wat Enkosei twice today, with a pool swim and lunch break during the midday heat. Now, excitedly, he set the flash feature on his smartphone camera to accentuate the glyphs in the hard stone. French scholars had provided him with detailed epigraphic translations beforehand of the Sanskrit and transliterated Khmer, this medieval hybrid language. He thought of Roman inscriptions in England describing things Celtic, but this was more fused, the Hindu and Buddhist more integrated. Likewise, Carey could see, nothing here other than grandeur was intended to be understood by peasants or slaves…*all written communication was for an elite…the stone polished off-site…a Brahmin scribe wrote the King's text on palm-leaf…a painter rendered the lettering in linear form onto the stone…a mason without a clue then engraved each letter…the builder's slaves placed the stone for the foundation ceremony.*

"There you are," Carey whispered to himself. Much of the inscription was simply a ledger of chattels gifted by the King, dedicated to the local aristocrat, Divakarabhatta and his wife, a princess, who would in turn bestow gifts on the Brahmins of the sanctuary. The priests were well-heeled in the pecking order,

Carey mused. The gold palanquin and 171 slaves listed charged his imagination with grandeur and inequity, as did the silver fly whisks, gold handled parasols, and jewellery all in exchange for the estate supplying the King with rice and honey. Striking slave girls would doubtless have been offered up for the King's harem. The lettering itself would be familiar to modern Khmers but they could not be faulted for their inability to understand the Indic words before him, which read My Holy High Lord at Dvijendrapura.

Carey flashed several photos, hoping for one image without the blur of his excitement. He had come for this, the family, and this moment. It was the original name of the temple site and land granted to Divakarabhatta who already had an estate at Prasat Komphus near the Kulen Mountains, but it represented much more than that…this was also the name for a vast district, including the rice peasant settlement across the river now called Siem Reap. *Aymonier's map depicts Enkosei as the only temple along the entire length of the river in 968…150 years before Angkor Wat was being erected. An inscription at Prasat Komphus clearly mentions Divakarabhatta's foundation school in the town of Dvijendrapura. Bingo. The village Dvijendrapura was renamed Siem Reap after a defeat of the Siamese, perhaps in the sixteenth century.*

It was a darkness now filled with ominous forms outlined with a faint backdrop of house light from the distant, nameless street. The waxing, gibbous moon was blacked out by the vaulted canopy of massive fig trees. Carey felt for his walking cane resting against an inner wall, his thoughts turning to poisonous snakes, and a strange waft of incense…sickly vanilla and balsam, which would ward off living creatures surely. It was coming from the direction of the monastic cells near the cemetery. No light came from these kuti, most of the bikkhus having left the wat after the rainy season Vassa, the Theravada Buddhist Lent. The cell with the papered window was a minor detour on his way back out, so he would take a look, avoid burial stupas and box-shrines, use his phone flashlight if needed. He felt for the warm silver amulet chained around his neck, which Seyha had gifted him . . . perhaps Pra Upakut could indeed provide protection from the miasma of ghosts in the pond of the dead.

Carey tapped uncertain ground with his aluminium cane like a blind man in search of truth. *La nuit au Cambodge.* When he neared the rear of the mystery cell the intoxicating odor of incense overwhelmed him. He felt a touch of vertigo. *Frankincense? Gum bejamin, benzoin resin?* He could make out brick vents across top of the wall below the sheltering overhang of a flat roof. An over scale portico adjoined the side of this kuti, under which the mundanity of a monk's robe drying on a clothesline protected from any rain comforted him. Then a bat flicked past and unnerved him. To hell with it, he thought, he would try and peek through the front window, find a gap in the newsprint…after all he would not be backlit…invisible, but any sound this windless night would undo him. If someone came out the front door, he was a dead duck. As he walked around the side he was surprised to discover a side door under the portico. Two doors for a one-room residence.

A tiny tear in the newsprint sent a thin ray of soft light into Carey's pupil. He positioned his face against the glass for a fish-eye view. The composition of the interior seemed at once shockingly deviant and arresting. Angkorian brass oil-lamps burned on either side of the window. Along the left wall was a cot and a table littered with vials of brownish oil, some bowls, a pestle, and a cook's blowtorch. Some vials were tied with coloured string and hung from the ceiling, slowly rotating. The rear wall was lit by beeswax candles which captured smoke drifting up from nuggets of resin sitting on coals aglow in a large incense bowl. A man, naked except for his loincloth, sat in a lotus position, his back rippling with Isaan tattoos. He faced a grotesque corpse laid out across a low bench. A woman's body withered except for its open, distended belly. A large meat hook was fixed high up on the far right wall. Below that, on a small table, Carey could see a charred joint of meat sitting on a wood slab, and beside that a cleaver, knives and other implements. Another small table served as an altar with small figurines, a bowl of trumpet flowers, an upturned hermit's mask. The mad monk rose slowly and turned, his face contorted in a drugged shaman's death-trance, his eyes black holes, strings of teeth and amulets around his neck. He came steadily towards the window, picked up a Naga knife from the table, then went for the side door.

Carey fled as best he could, blood pounding, past headstones and over soft, sand-filled graves towards some bushes. He needed to reach the rear gate of the wat. There would be motos there. His foot snagged on a root causing a knee to buckle, and when his shoulder hit the ground hard his run was over. The roots of a banyan were draped around him. He pulled himself up with one hand. He stood side-on against the tree, one hand clutching a branch for balance. He could sense the footfalls of the monk approaching. In an instant he was beside him. Carey swung around and struck the monk with the heavy, handle end of his cane, striking his arm. The knife flew into concealing bush. Now in a practiced move Carey reversed his cane and rammed the monk's stomach. He doubled over and collapsed with a moan. Carey was not going to hang around. He hobbled quickly towards the safety of the wat roadway and that other sanctuary, Stonewall, with its infra-red surveillance cameras. He still had his keys.

IV

It was Carey's last day in Siem Reap, and he checked his flight time for the following morning. Drake had gone to work. Seyha had taken his grandson to the International School on her Honda Dream scooter, a parent-teacher day before exams. His right shoulder was sore from the night before, though ibuprofen pills had lessened the pain. He had said nothing to Drake about what he had seen and experienced. He had been the trespasser, after all. His only loss was the amulet necklace, which must have come off in the fall. He could always email his son later about the incident.

Bring up Buddhist corpse meditation, and the animist black art of making of Nam Man Prai, human oil for ritual use. Anyway, this was Cambodia, a freak show of culture writ large, Southeast Asia's historical sideshow of death, skulls, ghosts and slavery. Nothing would change that, not even the Wi-Fi-seeking hipster nomads besieging Siem Reap or the busloads of zero-dollar East Asian temple visitors. The best thing he could do today was get away from Stonewall and the goddam view of the mad monk's cell…go to the Water Festival in town and baptise himself with Khmer revellers, disappear among the riverside peasants, forget the horror. Yes, he thought, end this trip on an up note.

Sarouen's ride along the narrow river road was death-defying as he confronted oncoming buses, trucks, vans, cars, other tuk-tuks, motorcycles, bicycles and hundreds of pedestrians. The whistles of traffic police sorted out any standoffs, though the mood was festive, if frenzied. Sarouen never lost his cool. They stopped amid the multitude arriving at the Royal Gardens, across from the majestic Raffles Grand Hotel d'Angkor. Carey dismounted the rickety carriage, his left foot finding the step plate, his cane the ground while Saroeun supported an arm. He told him not to wait around like he normally did, he wanted the freedom to go walkabout and there was no way they could rendezvous later as the crowd was growing. Saroeun understood, and he had to move on anyway in the crawl of traffic. Carey would grab another tuk-tuk in town. Sarouen nodded with gratification and concern, pocketing a full day's fare in dollars and riel.

Carey decided to head straight for the riverbank to watch the bridge-to- bridge dragon boat races. He had never been in such a crowd, but his claustrophobia was offset by his intent of going with the flow of Khmer families, the safe anonymity that made him forget about dark matters. A tsunami of people moved like flotsam along an unseen concourse between stalls. Smoke filtered through carrying the enticing smells of grilled pork sausage, stuffed frogs, cob corn, river crabs and roti pancakes. It was sweltering so Carey bought an iced can of Angkor Beer, and pushed his way to the riverbank, the only barang. A color-coded flotilla of boat teams paraded up to the starting bridge to set up for their one on one elimination races to the downriver bridge, where King Norodom's entourage sat in their private stand. Carey was bedazzled by a kaleidoscope of moving colour, the mud-green river and brightly painted dragon boats, their crews in red, yellow, orange, green, blue and white T-shirts. A starter gun went off and the spectators lining both sides of the river screamed with pleasure. Southeast Asia was never boring…frustrating or shocking, yes.

He decided to plow on in the floodtide of Khmers drifting downriver, through the gauntlet of stalls, come what may…hopefully some breathing space. Maybe catch an Aspara Dance on the soundstage. He was jostled and bumped from behind now and then, pickpockets possibly, so he swivelled around at times to watch his own back. Then, on one such turn, he saw a face he recognized a distance behind him. *Jet-black eyes…Jesus Christ, the mad monk was following him. Canvas-colored baseball cap.* Carey quickened his pace, dividing the oncoming with his cane. He could see the dense human traffic thin out ahead behind the King's stand, where the esplanade turned sharply right. He was desperate to reach the more open Royal grounds, and not be stabbed here in the back, unnoticed.

Carey kept turning his head around. Nothing. He reached a grassy area where delighted families were sitting on blankets, eating fried funnel cake, watching musicians and dancers on the soundstage. Then Carey saw the monk again standing beside a lotus pond and stone Khmer lion, staring at him. *No robe, civvies, black top, blue jeans, gaunt, wiry.* There was nothing he could do, he thought, but mingle with the distracted audience, though few were standing and those that were, like him, stood out. His arthritic knees would render him useless on the ground. There seemed to be no uniforms around. *Fuck this.* Carey held both ends of his cane up above his head for the monk to see his defiance. But the monk had vanished. Best to remain sitting on a garden wall until dusk, he realised…then blend in with the families heading home early.

Carey made for town, at first following departing Khmers along a grand tree-lined concourse, then he cut across parkland and headed for busy Pokambor Avenue. He could easily spot anyone coming after him here. Fireworks whistled and exploded over the river…flashes of phosphorous light…nobody around him. All the shops along the avenue were closed, and most taxis were jammed up near the river…the few that passed him had passengers. Then a diagonal lane appeared to his right, and he knew from his rides this was a shortcut to the central market, two blocks long and dark but with welcoming streetlight glowing at its far end. Carey doubted the killer monk, on foot, could have circled ahead of him. He took one last panoramic look behind him, then took off, striding apace in sync with his heartbeats.

Carey was almost half way along the lane when a figure, a black cut-out of the monk edged with faint light, blocked the distant exit. Carey edged quickly into a passageway with a recessed gate between two buildings, a dead end, but so narrow that it would give him an advantage with his cane unless, of course, the monk had a gun. Carey twisted the rubber ferrule off the tip his cane, which he pocketed. He had filed and honed the end of his cane pipe into a round razor. He would have to go for the face, the head or neck. One chance. He angled his back against a wall and held his cane like a horizontal ram, left hand gripping the pipe a few inches from the T-shaped Derby handle, which was wrapped tightly in a golf-like grip by the fingers of his other hand. He was in position to swing it upwards. He could strike first if the monk came along close to the entrance. Silence, except for the growing purr of a four-stroke engine. He waited ... had the monk used a motorcycle to cut him off?

The monk appeared in the middle of the lane and just stood there, taunting Carey with stillness, ready to pounce like a black tiger. In one continuous move he drew his Naga knife from his belt, held it up high, and leapt forwards. Carey swung his ram up under the monk's chin before he could come down on him. The monk stumbled backwards and fell across the lane. He was wounded but not enough to stop him from getting up, still holding his knife. Carey dare not leave the passageway. The monk raised his arm again and gurgled -- "Eeee ..." -- as he charged towards Carey. Before Carey could swing his cane again, before the monk reached the passage entrance, a tuk-tuk passed between them at full throttle. A front corner of its carriage caught the monk, collected his spidery form and sent him flopping in a death-roll along the lane.

What the hell? Carey left the passageway and walked several metres to where the tuk-tuk with its lights off had stopped just beyond the monk's still form. Moonlit dust settled on him. Sarouen was sitting on his motorcycle, and motioned for Carey to get into the carriage. The monk was on his side, possibly dead, but Carey passed him without any intention of getting too close. He tapped his phone flashlight. This revealed a sculpted snake grinning with fang-like teeth, the handle of the monk's Naga knife, lodged in his side. He must have fallen on his own knife. Blood dribbled from his broken jaw and seeped into the dirt road. The bleeding slowed.

They took off without conversation. Sarouen flicked on his headlight when he turned onto busy Pokambor. The tuk-tuk zig-zagged along potholed backroads west of the river, almost bucked Carey out once or twice, then with relief they drove over the last bridge to Wat Leur. There was no light in the monk's cell window.

V

It was a blinding, windy morning, dimmed with pale limelight and fine dust, and inhuman heat rising already off Highway 6. Carey was on his way to the airport with Saroeun. He had left a note and gifts at Stonewall, anxious to get out of town without family formalities or having to explain events. That, and the fact he had overstayed his visa by a day, only added to his jitters after his fitful, almost sleepless night. He could see himself drowning in alcohol later, sated with Penang-style curry, during his five-hour stopover in the AirAsia lounge at Kuala Lumpur.

They parked alongside the end of the airport building away from the main entrance. Inside there would be some police. Sarouen stuck out his hand and said, "passport, ticket." He disappeared into the busy departure hall. Carey did not know Saroeun had made arrangements, set things up with immigration and customs …there would be no overstay fine and no line-up required. Sarouen returned after a few minutes with his stamped passport and boarding pass, then pulled the carry-on out of the carriage and set it down. Carey leaned his cane against the bag and took a deep breath of relief. He knew whose side he was on. Carey handed Sarouen a fifty-dollar banknote. Sarouen's round face offered a subdued smile. They just stood there eye to eye for a while, incapable of words, aliens from different planets at a waystation.

Sarouen reached into his pocket and held up something in his fist. Carey put his hand out. Saroeun dropped an unchained amulet onto Carey's upturned palm. The sculpted figure of the solitary forest magician, Pra Upukut, framed in a grotto of silver, stared up at him. Carey choked up and tried to stop his eyes from welling up with unbidden tears, to no avail. Sarouen stepped forward and held Carey in a strong embrace. Carey hugged Sarouen.

Carey watched Sarouen mount his bike, rev up his Dailem four-stroke, and wheel around out of the parking area. The Tuk-Tukker of Doom disappeared with dead set intent down Highway 6, into a mirage of Cambodian existence. Carey went through the glass doors into another, global dimension.

Chad A. Evans is a Canadian writer whose first book was the award-winning 1983 monograph Frontier Theatre, a comprehensive history of 19th century entertainment in British Columbia and Alaska. His drama, A Woman For Hanging, won the Australian Bicentennial Playwriting Competition in 1988, and was staged in Sydney. In Australia, where he resides, he is the author of several heritage planning documents and engineering patents. In 2015 Heaven Lake Press in Bangkok published 'Vincent Calvino's World', his noir interpretation of modern Southeast Asian culture drawn from a close reading of the works of Christopher G. Moore.

The Hill of Poisonous Trees

Matt Carrell

Phnom Penh, Cambodia – 1979

May 23, 1979. Ten years since Vannak Sang became a teacher of Mathematics at Phnom Penh's Chao Ponhea Yat High School. The same desk, the same chair, the same classroom as on his first day, but four years had passed since he'd taken chalk to the grubby blackboard that still hung on the wall behind him. Now it is covered with photographs of the hundreds who'd sat or knelt before him since that last class. Basic trigonometry if his memory served him right.

Vannak's shock on hearing of his new role was momentary. The only constant in his life had been change. The Cambodia into which he was born was a French colony, the early days of independence were chaotic and, shortly after his tenth birthday, neighbouring Vietnam was plunged into a brutal war that would last nearly two decades. Cambodia was nominally neutral but when the USA, the Soviet Union, and China are pulling the strings, *realpolitik* demands that you pick a side. Prince Sihanouk chose China, and in 1970 was deposed by American-backed General Lon Nol. Vannak never had to choose. Scoliosis, or curvature of the spine, made him ineligible for military service and the target of every school bully. Even teacher status had not protected him from the pointing fingers, callous whispers, and the barely concealed laughter of the more fortunate. Few of his colleagues took much interest in the political preferences of the misshapen maths teacher, so when the communist Khmer Rouge closed in on the city, nobody knew which side Vannak was rooting for.

Pol Pot's Khmer Rouge seized power in 1975 and four days into the new regime Vannak was offered his new role. Chao Ponhea Yat High School was renamed Security Prison 21 or Tuol Sleng, the Hill of Poisonous Trees. The second floor classroom, last used for a basic trigonometry class became a processing centre for those suspected of being a threat to the new order… the *Anka*. Intellectuals - soft hands and spectacles were enough to get one so classified - were high on the list. Almost all the teachers had been photographed, interrogated and transported within a week.

In the months leading up to the latest lethal spasm in Cambodia's history, Vannak had confided in only one person, Thom. He'd talked of the terrible poverty that was the fate of most of his countrymen, of the privileged lives of the city elite, of the hope that the advancing communists might bring change. As the Khmer Rouge took power, Thom revealed himself as an agent of the new regime and Vannak was spared. His past as a teacher of mathematics was glossed over, he was taught to use a camera and told to record the daily arrivals at Security Prison 21. Initially the cruelty of his new colleagues was anathema to Vannak, but as the days passed he'd recognised more of Tuol Sleng's arrivals. The baker who'd mocked his inability to reach a high shelf, neighbours who'd taunted him as he shuffled painfully down the street and the doctor who'd advised his mother to put Vannak in a sack and toss him in the Mekong River. It was Vannak who removed the doctor's glasses, broke his nose with a metal club and wrote the fateful words on his registration document. 'To Choeung Ek.'

Prior to the arrival of Pol Pot, Choeung Ek was a tranquil orchard about ten miles south of Phnom Penh. It is now the site of a Buddhist stupa that houses the remains of many of the nine thousand bodies discovered when the Khmer Rouge was finally defeated. Of all of Cambodia's "Killing Fields" it is the most infamous. Tuol Sleng was not a place of execution, it was where suspects were interrogated. There were only two outcomes for those brought to the prison. They could admit their guilt, possibly implicating others before being transported to Choeung Ek for execution. The alternative was to deny any wrongdoing, the interrogation would be longer, the torture crueler but the final destination the same. Choeung Ek.

Vannak was watching from the window when she arrived. Sita Khay looked bewildered as she was dragged from the truck. There was no fear, just the inability to comprehend how her life had been thrown into chaos in a few short days. Vannak's heart lurched. They'd been neighbours, he'd been smitten but she'd barely even noticed he existed. Maybe that was even worse than the taunts, the laughter. She turned and threw her arms round a tall, handsome man who'd almost fallen from the truck. Narith was carrying two babies, neither more than six months old. Twins. Vannak watched as the soldiers herded the new arrivals into a holding cell on the ground floor. At the entrance was a female guard with the insignia of a sergeant in the Khmer Rouge and a deep red scar on her cheek, a vivid souvenir of the battle for Phnom Penh. Her face softened as the traumatised parents shuffled past, each now holding a crying child. Vannak called his deputy, there were important instructions to be issued.

***

"Name?"

Vannak barked the question as the shutter clicked on his camera.

"Sita Khay."

"Oh of course, you're married now, I remember when…" Vannak paused, awash with a tide of memories.

"You remember wha…"

"Do you remember me?" His voice was urgent, harsh, angry.

Bewilderment had been etched on Sita's face since the second she entered the prison. The question only exacerbated her confusion.

"Where...? I don't know. I just…" Sita glanced helplessly at Narith as though he might offer some inspiration. There was only the look of a man who knew all hope had gone.

"You've never seen me before?" Vannak slammed his fist onto the desk.

Sita shook her head slowly. Vannak turned to his desk and looked at the two documents in front of him. On each he wrote the words, 'To Choeung Ek.' Then to the guard,

"They have two children. Take them all."

The truck in which Sita and Narith arrived was also their transport to Choeung Ek. They knew their fate but it hardly mattered, they were already dead inside. It was Sita that noticed the way the sergeant's face had softened as she'd carried baby Samang into the holding cell no more than an hour before. A tiny shred of humanity in a place that otherwise held only terror. The woman had a deep scar on her face, she'd seen battle but still could still show compassion. Or so Sita had thought. The same guard was on duty after their brief audience with Vannak, as they'd come to rejoin the twins for their final journey. She'd laughed in their faces.

"The twins. They're dead. Must have suffocated I suppose. It's what happens when you leave your kids in the company of strangers."

Narith tried to brush past the guard into the cell and took a rifle butt to the gut for his trouble. Sita collapsed to her knees and wept.

They arrived at Choeung Ek barely an hour later and joined a line of forty others marching silently to their death. To the right was a deep trench fifty yards from a small picturesque lake. As each prisoner reached the front of the line they were shot with a single bullet and dropped into their pre-prepared grave. To the left were the children, some little older than Sita's own boys. The Khmer Rouge saw no need to waste precious ordnance. Their executioner lifted them by the feet and dashed their brains out against a tree. The larger the child the more blows were required to finish the job. Suffocation was, in hindsight an easier way to leave this world.

Sita turned as she got to the front of the line, she reached out and felt the faintest of contact with Narith's hand before the trigger was pulled. She'd only be separated from her husband for the time it took their killer to reload.

Tuol Sleng sits at a busy crossroads in the heart of Phnom Penh, but the arrival of the Khmer Rouge kept civilians off the streets, particularly at night. The only people who could go about their business without challenge were the conquerors, and rank mattered. The old woman with the bicycle might have attracted attention, but she was talking to a sergeant in the Khmer Rouge, a battle hardened veteran, the deep scar on her cheek was testament to that. The insignia was enough to deter anyone who might have asked what was in the two small bundles she placed in the pannier on the back on the old woman's bike. Anyone seeing the exchange might have been suspicious had they seen the sergeant kiss her finger twice, each time touching her fingertip to the heart of one of the bundles. They might also have been confused by the message she conveyed to the old woman.

"The family name was Khay. Their names are Pich and Samang. Take care of them."

***

Matt Carrell spent over twenty-five years in the investment industry. In that time, he travelled extensively in south-east Asia. His first book was inspired by the story of a young woman trying to put her life back on track after a brush with Thailand's illegal lottery. The Hill of Poisonous Trees is the back story of the two young Cambodian men accused of the murder of a tourist in his novel, 'Blood Brothers… Thai Style'. He is the author of five novels and numerous short stories, one of which, Crazy Medicine, has just been turned into a film directed by award winning Richie Moore. Bitten by the movie bug, Matt is working on another short story adaptation and a potential TV series based on his novel, A Matter of Life and Death.

Snow

John Daysh

There is a Chinese guy tied up in my bathtub and I'm not really sure what I should do now. I will probably kill him but I can't decide how. I'm sitting here on my sofa hoping he'll just miraculously disappear but it is not going to happen because I'm the only one who knows he is here. I could drop him over the balcony. A fall of sixteen floors would do the trick, but I'd then be one of about twenty-five suspects, one on top of another in my apartment building – unless I could swing him out to the side so it looked like he came from the neighbouring stack of balconies. But for my shoulder I could do it.

He is small; just under five feet tall. I know this because my bathtub is five feet long and he is lying down dead flat. I put a pillow under his head and there was room for it to ride up the back of the tub. He isn't heavy either. Lighter than Sophia probably, and I manage to fling her about okay. Even now I can't bring myself to regret meeting her. She is going to turn me into a killer and I still want her. I will have to kill her Cambodian boyfriend as well, so killing his pint-sized thug will be no more than acclimatising to a state of mind I haven't been in since the time when I took pleasure in burning ants with a magnifying glass. So what started as a warning shot across my bow is going to end very badly, one way or another. He should not have sent one of his lackeys to intimidate me. If I let this one go he'll be back with a greater show of force than his three previous attempts to hurt me.

He has lost dignity, lost face and the only way back for him is to kill me. I see it in his eyes as I hose his excrement down the plug hole and leave him shivering in the cold bathroom, watching snowflakes drift past the window. I turn up the heat in the lounge and prepare a thick rail of coke and tighten the roll of a crisp one hundred yuan note. I leave it on the lid of my laptop while I find the Cartoon Network on the television. I love the cartoons and it is a killer line. I take half up each nostril and my front teeth are numb in seconds. This is the good stuff. I turn on some disco music, mute the television, and I laugh as Jerry whacks Tom over the head with an oversized frying pan.

It is only a woman who can transform me, an otherwise calm, rational and peace-loving man, into a state of bitter jealously and revenge. Sophia has turned me into a killer. But I think she deserves no less. When she squats naked on my chest, lights a thin menthol cigarette, and starts singing sweetly in Khmer, as I lie beneath her in post-coital bliss, I look into her eyes with a dopey grin and complete adoration. Her flawless doll-like face, perfect teeth, and deep brown eyes transfix me. She flutters her long fake eyelashes at me, flicks her dyed blonde hair, and I feel a hollowness in my chest as my breath catches. I am well and truly fucked and I know it and I think she feels it too. When she finishes her cigarette I know what she will do next. She will shuffle further forward and intoxicate me with her musky scent. She will lower herself, I will oblige and we'll be off again. Cigarette break in half an hour.

I change to a Chinese news station and watch coverage of the massive snowstorm wreaking havoc across the country stranding literally tens of millions of people trying to travel home for Chinese New Year. This could play into my hands. I chop another line on my laptop, nail it, and head out onto my balcony to catch snowflakes on my tongue. I wish that Sophia was here now. We would turn it into a game and we would giggle like children and then I'd grab her and pull her into me while she pretended to struggle before meekly surrendering to my warmth. I'd slip my freezing hands up her back and she'd squeal and thump me on the chest and then try to tickle me with her cold fingers. Then I'd take her inside and make love to her on the sofa and lose myself just like I did the first time.

Two days after moving into a new apartment after leaving my wife I was out on the lash with my best friend here. It was the eve of my birthday. I already knew my birthday was going to begin with a bang. It was just a matter of which beautiful young lady was going to provide it. Midnight arrived and my buddy and I toasted and gulped back another shot of tequila. The bar was tired and mostly occupied by fat middle-aged Germans and run-down Chinese women in their thirties and forties hoping to score some German sausage and a roof over their heads for as long as they put out. And then in walked Sophia. All heads turned. I met her eye and smiled and she sat at the bar stool at the window, her back to the door that she'd come through. She looked different to the thousands and thousands of Chinese girls I'd seen in Shanghai. The bland looking girl already trying to get my attention noticed and tried to put herself in the line of sight between me and the beautiful girl. I stretched up and leaned out over the bar looking around her, my Achilles taut, maintaining my smile as Sophia took control of my eyes. I felt a hand clamp onto my thigh, a last ditch effort to draw me back. I brushed it aside and seemed to move through her as I was drawn in by eyes that were autumn pools, shimmering above a cloudy depth. I drifted over, feet not touching the floor and sat next to her, our eyes running into each other's, smiles of realization sparking a flaring recognition. Her hand went straight to my chest flattening out below my throat as those deep waters searched me. I shrugged the bland girl's hand off my shoulder and leaned in, enhancing the pressure on my chest. She clawed her hand, squeezed and giggled like a schoolgirl. I leaned back a little and went slowly in again, eyes still entranced. She giggled again, blushed and dropped her eyes to her hands which she folded neatly in her lap. I backed away to take her in. She peered coyly out at me from behind her curtained hair which had drifted forward in protection. She giggled again, a high-pitched delight that widened my smile and changed my life.

I am fixating on my problem. My mind is racing. I can't sit still. I start pacing around the lounge. I am not feeling distraught or panicked though. I am at peace with what I must do, whatever it is. I feel a sense of power and I am invincible. I will have my Sophia back and she will be mine alone. I walk down the hall, through my bedroom and into the en suite. The little guy has shit himself again. Dirty fucker. I turn on the extractor fan and turn on the tap, swinging the handle around to hot. I check the nylon rope that is tied to the tap suspending his bound feet a few inches above the floor of the bath. He is going nowhere. I test the water with my fingers until it is warm and depress the mechanism that switches the water flow from the tap to the showerhead. I take the showerhead from its mounting and spray. He is naked from the waist down. I had to take off his pants the first time he soiled himself. His dick is tiny. I smirk. This is one of the reasons such men can be pitied. Without his money, Sophia's boyfriend would be lucky to get laid at all. The little man sneers at me through his gag so I slap his forehead and turn the water to cold.

After my birthday, I was hooked on Sophia and I think she was hooked on me. But I am not a rich man and my wife and I promised we wouldn't hurt each other by getting involved with anyone else so soon after our split. I kept her at arm's length, only inviting her to my apartment a few nights a week and refusing to be seen in public with her, apart from Chinese nightclubs where no foreigners go. She told me she understood. I didn't know what she was doing on other nights but it didn't bother me too much. I knew that I was her number one. She told me that if I would let her move in with me she would commit. In hindsight I should have said yes. But I couldn't leap into another commitment although I later realized that I subconsciously had. Then she disappeared. Went dark. When I called her I got a message in Chinese and English that the number was out of service. I tried every day for a month or so and then gave up. She'd gone.

The snow has just hit Shanghai today but is forecast to intensify over the next few days. It has started to settle on the ground. The roads will be chaotic. There is no infrastructure to deal with weather like this. It will not be cleared by machinery but with thousands and thousands of shivering men and women and their shovels. It will take days to clear once it has stopped. I dump another pile of my own white powder on my laptop, chop, snort, and then change the channel to Nickelodeon. I really get SpongeBob SquarePants. He knows his shit. I feel no hunger at all but think that the little guy must. I have not fed him in the forty-eight hours or so that he has been captive in the tub but he has managed to crap three times and piss as much. He must be hungry though and I don't think he'll have the time to process let alone excrete whatever I give him. He doesn't need it either. It's a kindness. That is all. I will make him some noodles and feed them to him as I point out the injuries he inflicted on me, which we both know are superficial in relation to his original intent. Fuck him. I should pity him but it is cold. Fucking cold. And the cold and the snow are not good for me.

A few months later I was having a pint with that same mate of mine and having not really given Sophia much thought of late. A sexy girl flashed me a smile and it got me started reminiscing about the good times we had shared. My friend knew how much I had liked her and he met her when we ventured out to various obscure Chinese nightclubs. My phone started vibrating and I checked the display. It was Sophia. I showed my mate and we shook our heads in amazement. I answered and she told me that she missed me. I asked her where she had been and she said she had been traveling. She said she was in Phnom Penh but would be back in Shanghai soon and she promised to call. Within a few minutes I just had to hear her voice but her number was out of service. I called several times every day for the next week. Nothing. It was like falling off the wagon.

SpongeBob solves his problem and I still can't figure out how to solve mine so I dip my beak in the charlie again trying to reclaim my analytical edge. I catch more snowflakes on my tongue on the balcony but my damaged shoulder starts to ache and the purple bruise just above my knee stings in the cold. I go back inside and pace around again trying to figure out a way to get Sophia's boyfriend over to my apartment so I can kill him. He is supposed to be coming back from Phnom Penh this afternoon. He is fucking Sophia and he thrice sent his man to hurt me. The third time the little man was stupid enough to come to my home. Now things have gone far enough that I have to be decisive in order to end this. He is fucking Sophia and claims her as his number one now so I have no qualms. I know it is only money. Sophia told me that he has a wife and a child but I can't worry about that. I'm sure they will be better off without him.

She turned up unannounced at my door late one night a week later looking amazing. Her striking but garish blonde hair had been softened to a sensual mousy brown, she had less make-up on than usual and wore a figure-hugging floral dress with an expensive leather overcoat. Exuding class. My Khmer Girl was back and I felt so happy. I didn't ask any questions; I just held her tight and then picked her up and carried her to my bedroom. We made love like starved animals and only when we lay side by side gazing at each other did she begin to tell me where she had been and why she had come back to me. He was rich, a business man with Chinese connections, and as soon as he saw her in a Phnom Penh nightclub he insisted on taking possession. He had a wife and a child and Sophia knew he had another mistress besides her. His Chinese business connections meant that he regularly visited China, especially Shanghai, so to keep Sophia away from the prying eyes and ears that permeated every aspect of life in Cambodia, he set Sophia up in a nice apartment in Shanghai, provided her with a healthy allowance and got her a nine-to-five job with a real estate agency to keep her busy. When he travelled to Shanghai, she would be there for him and when he travelled to Beijing or Nanjing or Hong Kong or Guangzhou on business he sometimes took her with him. He bought her a new phone and insisted she remain monogamous. She loved the money, the travel, the expensive hotels and dinners but hated him. "He has wife and children," she said, "and very small," she said as she grasped my penis, smiling mischievously. But he had money. More money than I could dream of making. I told her I wanted to kill him and she didn't believe me. I said it seriously but I was gently licking her nipple at the time.

The snow is no more than a light flurry now but on the balcony I can only see white below. Pudong Airport is still open but flights are being delayed. The flight from Phnom Penh should make it in okay. I surf through all of the channels and cannot settle on anything. My buzz is mostly gone so I smoke some weed and drift towards the other end of the awareness spectrum. I am tired and I am bored. I want to lie on the couch and close my eyes and fantasise about Sophia and I together and I want to open my eyes and have it as an instant reality. I cannot do anything before it starts to get dark. I lie down on the couch and close my eyes. I take long, deep, deliberate breaths that banish my buzz entirely as my mind sinks into the paralysis that weed provides. The snow is my blessing and my curse. I just hope that the airport does not close. I want to call Sophia but I am numb and I don't want to move and it is too early. I drift.

I had no control over when and for how long I saw Sophia. We snuck around like a couple having an affair which I suppose we were, or at least she was, but it never felt like that to me. Over the next few months she stayed with me whenever he was away. One time she was with me for two weeks and I was in heaven. I hated it when she turned up late at night because I knew he had been fucking her. I could smell his cigarette smoke in her hair. She was always damned horny on these nights because he couldn't come close to satisfying her and she hated him and loved me. It was Saturday morning when she got the message from him. We had been out late in a club, dancing all night, doing lines in the bathroom and drinking copious quantities of Johnnie Black and green tea. We fucked and then crashed and then fucked again in the morning. I was in the shower giving my nethers a good wash and I looked through the glass at Sophia. She was squatting naked on the bathroom floor, trembling with her head down, hair covering her face. She kept staring at her phone. I got out of the shower and started towelling off. I asked her what was wrong and she said he knows about you and me. She shook her head in confusion and said that it was impossible because he'd been in Bangkok and was going to Phnom Penh for a few days before he came to Shanghai. How could he know? I told her that he must have someone watching her. Her trembling turned to shaking and I dropped my towel and held her close. I was happy that he knew but I was scared too. I knew how wealthy he was.

I am awake again and the darkness is encroaching. The snow is still light but it hasn't stopped all afternoon and there is good inch on the balcony railing. My shoulder aches and I want my Sophia here. I will need her help to do what needs to be done. I don't want to pop my shoulder again. I call Sophia because she will be finishing work about now and she says she will come straight here because of the snow. She is worried about being followed but she doesn't know that he is tied up in my bath with probably less than a few hours to live. She knows about my shoulder and she knows about my leg, but she doesn't know that he came here two days ago. I told her I had gone to Suzhou to hide out for a few days and I would be back today. I rack up some more lines but decide to wait for Sophia to arrive. It is better to do it together. I turn on the television and watch a violent Japanese cartoon and I like the way it looks so easy.

A few days after Sophia's message I had my first run in with the little man. I was cycling to work in the bike lane, swerving around slower cyclists and being overtaken by bigger faster electric bikes. I had earplugs in listening to music, minding my own business when an electric bike pulled up beside me and kept pace. This isn't an unusual occurrence. The Chinese are generally happy and curious and often those who are fresh from the country haven't see a white guy wearing shorts that expose hairy legs, riding a mountain bike and wearing a helmet. They'll ride alongside me pointing and smiling and shouting "Ni Hao" at me. I'm used to it. But this guy was not pointing, laughing or shouting. He was sneering at me so I sneered back. Then he pulled in closer, hemming me in to the gutter and shoved a length of bamboo through the spokes of my front tire. I flew ass over tit and landed headfirst but with my head tucked to the side so that I landed on my shoulder, dislocating it. He sped off and I was left nursing a few minor cuts, grazes, and bruises but with my left arm hanging about six inches lower than it should. No one stopped to help, only to stand and look at me sitting on my ass, cradling my arm and wincing in pain. I knew no one was going to call an ambulance because then they would be liable for the bill. It took a few minutes but I managed to get up off the ground and retrieve my phone from my bike panniers. I called Sophia and she arrived in a taxi and took me to hospital. While I was being treated she got a message from her boyfriend asking if I was okay and hoping that I was not.

Sophia arrives and she wants to make love right away. Her boyfriend has cleared customs and is on his way into the city from Pudong Airport. He wants to meet her at her apartment. She has to go soon. I say no to sex and she is confused. I tell her we need to talk. We sit on the sofa and she sees the lines I have prepared. She thinks I want the charlie before we fuck. She hoovers her lines and I hoover mine. I don't know how to start so I take her by the hand and lead her to the bathtub. She recognizes the little man and shudders in revulsion. I tell her that this time he came to kill me and show her the knife he had. I take her hand and we go back to the sofa and sit in silence. She is manic in her channel surfing and she won't sit still. I tap my front teeth, which feel like two planks of wood. I tell her that her boyfriend isn't going to stop until I am out of the way. She doesn't say anything. I tell her that it is going to be either him or me and she shuffles around in silence, rhythmically pressing the up channel button on the remote. I know she is thinking about his money and her lifestyle and I know she is thinking about how much she loves me and the remote is taking a pounding. I tell her what I want to do and she stops and looks at me. I chop two fat lines for us. Outside the snow is coming down thick and fast.

They popped my shoulder back in, gave me some painkillers and sent me on my way. When we got home Sophia lovingly disinfected and covered the little cuts and grazes and rubbed tiger balm gently into my bruises. She called in sick and lay on my bed with me all day. She barely said a word. On that day I loved her beyond words. I could feel her pain and knew it was for me. We made love that night with her on top being as gentle as she could and when we finished she got straight off, went foetal with her back to me and started crying. I tried to console her but my heart wasn't in it. I felt pleased that she was feeling bad. The next day she went to work but I was too sore so I decided to take a gentle walk down the road to sit in a teahouse and read a book for the day. I hadn't gone far when the little fucker jumped out of the bushes and swung a tire iron at my knee. The bastard knew he had to aim a little higher to get me good because he was so short but he swung too high and caught me on the thigh. It hurt like hell but it didn't hit bone and I didn't go down. I lunged at him but he skipped out of the way and ran to his electric bike. I tried to follow but the pain hit and he was gone. I limped back home and seethed with anger. Sophia called ten minutes later, crying. She asked me if I was okay and I said I was. I was short with her because I liked that she felt bad. It made me feel loved and I knew it was driving her away from him and closer to me. I told her she had better stay away for a few days because it wasn't safe for her or me. If the little guy saw her coming here he would come at me again.

I tell her that I want her to call her boyfriend and get him to come to my apartment straight from the airport. I am worried that he will know that it is my place but Sophia says that he is always telling her that he is too important to deal with minor details. She will tell him that she is at her friend's apartment because of the snow. She wants to know what I am going to do but I tell her I don't know and that she should just trust me. She gets off the phone and says that he is coming in a taxi and should be here within half an hour. I fall upon her and fuck her well in case it is the last time. I don't care if the little guy hears us. He doesn't have long, the bastard. Then I dare her to stand naked on the balcony in the snow for ten seconds. She does it and I lock the sliding door and she squeals and jumps up and down pounding on the glass. I count to ten slowly and let her in. We are laughing and laughing as I embrace her and rub her freezing skin to warm her up. I bite her breast and she squeals again and punches me in the chest. We get dressed and have a few more lines while we wait for her boyfriend to arrive.

The little guy was hiding in the stairwell waiting for my door to unlock and for me to emerge. I had my back to him putting my key in the lock when he came at me from behind. If he had done it in silence he would have had me, but he sounded a battle cry and I instinctively spun around and saw the flash of steel and shuffled sideways. His knife just missed and stuck in the door. I head-butted him and he went down like a sack of shit, his nose a mess. I kicked him in the head to make sure he stayed unconscious and dragged him into the apartment down the hall, through the bedroom and into the en suite. I dumped him in the tub and bound his hands and feet. As best I could I put him in the recovery position and hoped like hell I hadn't killed him. I stood over him for a few minutes before I doused him with cold water and he started to wake up so I flipped him on his back and tied his feet to the tap. He gradually gained consciousness and when he saw me he lunged at me. His dilemma became apparent to him and he started shouting his head off. I didn't want to gag him because of his broken nose but I had no choice. I made sure he could still breathe gave him a pillow and decided not to go to work.

When the knock on the door comes I am surprised and realise that I am not quite ready. I expected to buzz him in from downstairs but he must have come in with a resident. Sophia looks panicked and I tell her to relax and just go and open the door, bring him into the lounge and I will take care of the rest. She goes to the door and I run to the kitchen and rummage around in the cupboard under the sink. I rush back to the lounge and flatten myself against the wall beside the door. He starts shouting and I hear him slap her and I hear her cry out in pain. I tighten my grip and wait. She comes into the lounge backwards, arms up, defending herself as he keeps swinging with an open hand. He goes past me without noticing and I step up behind him and hit him on the back of the head with a frying pan. He goes down and is out like a light. I look at the frying pan in my hand and am surprised that there was no loud clang, only a deep thud. Cast iron. It makes sense. Sophia looks at me and she has a red mark on the side of her face. She doesn't move. She is frozen. She looks down at him and I can see the anger start to bubble inside her. She quickly thaws and swings her leg and kicks him square in the nuts. She does it again and again and starts crying and I have to pull her away and hold her close. She trembles and sobs. I tie his hands and feet in case he wakes. Then I take a deep breath and pick up the frying pan. I walk to the bathtub and without pause swing at his head and this time enjoy the thud and how it jars my hand. He is out cold. He will never awake again and I feel a little bad about laughing at his tiny dick. Not his fault.

Sophia has calmed down and she asks me what we are going to do. I take her to the bathroom and I untie the little guy. She helps me sling him over my good shoulder and I walk out to the lounge and get Sophia to open the balcony door. I step out in to the cold and unload him so he is sitting onto the balcony railing and leaning forward against me, limp as his dick. Then I shove him as hard as I can and I lose sight of him as he falls with the snow. I turn and Sophia is staring at me with her hands covering her mouth, eyes wide. I say to her that he is next and nod at her boyfriend on the floor. Her eyes widen further and then a grin slowly spreads on her face and she starts jumping up and down clapping her hands, squealing with delight. We have trouble carrying him but we get him onto the railing in the same position but over to the left a little because I want them to land side by side. Sophia asks me if she can push and I smile and nod.

We put on gloves and scarves and jackets and go down in the elevator and outside. He must have landed on his feet because his legs are like concertinas and we can pretty much keep him upright with his legs folded beneath him rather than out front or back of his body. I find a long piece of bamboo used to help support a tree in its infancy and shove it down the back of his shirt and into the ground to hold him upright. Then we just pack the bastard with snow. He has the perfect physique, crumpled legs notwithstanding, and we build a beautifully rounded snowman in no time at all. I wonder where I am going to find a carrot when I realized that there was no way in hell that a Chinese/Khmer snowman is going to have a big nose…or round eyes for that matter. I use his own scarf, which I think is a nice touch. The little guy is spread-eagled on his back and Sophia throws herself on the ground laughing and makes a snow-angel beside him. We start covering him with snow and turn him into a snow angel too. Sophia takes great care in sculpting his wings while I construct a large erect penis for him. Then we have a snow fight and roll around together in the snow. We are wet and cold and we are happy and we are having fun. We have a competition throwing snowballs at the snowman from increasing distances and she wins because I have to throw with my left arm. The snow keeps on coming down and we are tired and out of breath from laughing so hard.

We go upstairs, finish the cocaine and take cash and cards out of his briefcase and go through his luggage and take his watches. She asks me where we will go and I tell her that we will go to Bangkok because it is the place where everyone goes to escape. As the taxi crawls through the snow on the way to the airport she asks me to give her a Chinese name. She was always My Sophia or My Khmer Girl. I have already thought about it and I tell her that her Chinese name is Xiou Hu. She asks me what it means and I tell her 'Small Lake' because her eyes are like autumn pools of water shimmering above a cloudy depth. She smiles the sweetest smile. I look into her eyes and I kiss her hard and I love her so much. Enough to kill for her.

***

John Daysh is the co-founder of Spanking Pulp Press, editor of James Newman's Joe Dylan series and author of the novels Cut Out The Middleman and Like a Moth to a Flame. He has worked as a freelance writer and journalist in South East Asia, and a teacher in Oman, London and China. He currently teaches film and literature in New Zealand, and lives with his imaginary pet giraffe, George, and his stable of well-trained gerbils who tolerate his sneezing fits.

Excerpt from The Cambodian Book of the Dead

Tom Vater

Cambodia 2001 - a country re-emerges from a half century of war, genocide, famine and cultural collapse.
German Detective Maier travels to Phnom Penh, the Asian kingdom's ramshackle capital to find the heir to a Hamburg coffee empire.
As soon as the private eye and former war reporter arrives in Cambodia, his search for the young coffee magnate leads into the darkest corners of the country's history and back in time, through the communist revolution to the White Spider, a Nazi war criminal who hides amongst the detritus of another nation's collapse and reigns over an ancient Khmer temple deep in the jungles of Cambodia.
Maier, captured and imprisoned, is forced into the worst job of his life – he is to write the biography of the White Spider, a tale of mass murder that reaches from the Cambodian Killing Fields back to Europe's concentration camps – or die.

IN THE SHADOW OF ENLIGHTENMENT

Battambang, 1997

In retrospect, Maier could see that the catastrophe in Cambodia had been the turning point. But in retrospect, everything always looked different.

War was never simple. As soon as the first shot was fired, carefully made plans changed beyond recognition. As soon as the first shot was fired, everything was unpredictable, and no one got away scot-free.

Most men were simply blown away by the wilful mayhem, like dry leaves in a fast wind.

Others found themselves in the horror of the moment and got stuck there, making the world die, over and over. A few went by another route, on and on, into themselves, until they experienced a kind of epiphany, a moment of arrival.

War correspondent Maier was about to arrive.

Maier and Hort sat on a crumbling wall near what was left of the railway station in Battambang, or what was left of this once-picturesque and industrious town in north-western Cambodia. Perhaps a school had stood here forty years earlier. A few metres of tired red brick work was all that was had survived the recent vagaries of history. At midday, the wall offered no shade. It was just a structure to sit next to. Better than being exposed, in a world of dust, misery and possible aggravation. A group of men sat next to the two journalists on low stools. They drank rice wine as if their lives depended on it. Perhaps it did.

Garbage and dust-devils blew across the shabby, run-down space between the wall and the railway tracks – scraps of paper, plastic bags, and diapers. Who had money for diapers around here? Where could you even buy nappies in Cambodia?

A young woman with a pinched face served the rancid drink from an old oil canister. There was only one glass, which went around in a circle. People in Cambodia drank quietly and with great concentration. Everyone was waiting. The railway station was a good place to wait. The trains were less reliable than the next glass, as the Khmer Rouge, Pol Pot's feared communist army, frequently mined the tracks between the capital Phnom Penh and

Battambang. The Khmer Rouge was the main reason why people were waiting. Despite UN sponsored elections, boycotted by the communists, the war just would not die. Most Cambodians wanted peace, and peace meant waiting.

Hort passed Maier a joint. "The war will be over in a few weeks, Maier. 1997 is our year. At least that what they say in Phnom Penh. Around here, people not so sure."

Hort laughed, as the Khmer sometimes do when they don't feel like laughing.

Maier wiped the sweat from his eyes, rearranged his matted beard and shrugged his shoulders. "Your country is sick of war, Hort. And you are getting married next week, when we are through and you have earned yourself a sack full of money."

The young Khmer was working as Maier's fixer and had been accompanying him for the past four years, every time the German journalist had been on assignment in Cambodia. Four years and six visits to this cursed country. And yet Maier had fallen into uneasy love with this sunny and wicked paradise.

Hort had saved his life on at least two occasions. In a few days, Maier would be the best man at his young friend's wedding, hopefully without making a drunken pass at Hort's attractive sister.

What would Carissa, beautiful and twisted Carissa, say if she found him in the sack with a young Khmer woman? What would be left, when the war really ended, when the international media left this tired land to its own devices? Maier had come with the war. Would he not also disappear with the war? Move on to the next war? Lack of choice wasn't the issue. War was always in vogue.
Hort interrupted him in his thoughts.

"As long as Pol Pot is alive, we not find peace. Why don't UN arrest and kill him?" Hort answered the question himself, "My people no longer have expectation that anyone come and help."
An old woman, her lined forehead almost hidden beneath a faded krama, the traditional chequered scarf many Khmer wore, her eyes black and numb like the tropical small hours, passed the two men slowly and silently spat on the hot dusty ground in front of Maier.
Hort's contorted stare followed her.
"I think I could do with a glass of rice wine myself."

Maier and his fixer were waiting for an officer serving with a regiment of government troops. Their contact was involved in peace negotiations with the last remnants of the Khmer Rouge fighters. The civil conflict, which had prevented recovery since the demise of the communists' agrarian utopia in 1979, some eighteen years before, was drawing to a close. The government in

Phnom Penh had some control over most of the country, or at least over what was left of Cambodia after a half century of catastrophic politics, war and genocide. Every time he made eye contact with a Khmer, Maier could see that that wasn't much.
The Khmer Rouge had retreated to the west, to the provinces bordering Thailand. Several conflagrations had taken place in Battambang in recent weeks. Nasty, dark stuff.

Maier knew there wasn't much time left. One of the great nightmares of the twentieth century was drawing to a close and Cambodia was moving towards an uncertain but less violent future. He'd come back to find out what that future might look like from the country's last battlefield. Finding out anything in Cambodia usually involved waiting. Maier had been waiting for three days. Today, Hort had assured him, the interview would materialise. Hort had been equally optimistic the previous day and the day before that.
A group of young men in torn work clothes, their dusty, hard feet in plastic flip-flops, walked past the wall, smoking cigarettes and talking quietly amongst themselves. Maier had picked up enough Khmer to understand that the conversation revolved around him. Was the tall foreigner a soldier? Was he looking for a girl? One look from Hort made them shut up.

"What gift do you give my future wife on her wedding day, Maier?"

The young Khmer could hardly wait to return to Phnom Penh. Two extended families were waiting on the groom and his tall, white employer – his protector. They had already put up the marquee.

"If you keep bugging me, Hort, I will buy her a sack of cold, fried frogs." Maier grinned at the young man – for his friend's assurance – as the Khmer did not always understand his sarcasm. How many miles had he already travelled with Hort, how many cruelties had he documented, while his fixer had stood next to him, his face expressionless? How many drunk and trigger-happy soldiers had they passed together at road blocks? Perhaps he really was the young Khmer's lucky charm.

Maier got distracted by a young woman in a bright purple sarong. He noticed the boy as well, but you noticed so many things. You had to choose, and Maier chose the woman. Hort, too, held his breath for a second. The woman passed the wall without looking at the men and crossed the railway tracks. Maier could not see her face, but he was sure that she was beautiful. He followed the languid sway of her hips and let his thoughts meander. The war was practically finished and he felt happier than he had in a long time. His plan to stop working in the war news business had become more appealing in recent months, but since his return to Cambodia, he had enjoyed his work, and after all, a plan was only a plan.

Later, as he sat on the back of a pick-up slowly rumbling towards Phnom Penh, he would suddenly recall the most important moment: the short cropped hair and the fixed stare, the dusty brown baseball cap, which the boy had pulled deep into his face and which had not suited the young Red Khmer at all. But you saw people with fixed stares everywhere, especially in this mad and lost part of the world.

The boy had just appeared on the potholed road. He wore a ripped T-shirt and black trousers and he was barefoot. Why had Maier not looked at him more closely?

The youth dropped his bag next to the woman who was serving the rice wine. She had her back turned to Maier and he barely noticed the brief exchange between the two. It looked like an everyday conversation. It was an everyday conversation. A few seconds later, the boy was on his way and Maier had forgotten him. He stared across the tracks, but the girl in the bright sarong had also dropped out of sight. Maier briefly turned towards the woman serving the moonshine. She had started a heated argument with her customers. He didn't understand a word the woman said. She had a strong accent, and whatever she was saying, quickly fell victim to the mean, silent aggression of the day. He didn't care. The smell of the tropics, saturated with reincarnation and ruin, this hypnotising combination of extremes, of promise and danger, of temptation and failure, had convinced him once more that he'd chosen the best job in the world. In a few hours, when the interview would finally be in the can, he would drink with Hort. He still had a small bottle of vodka in his bag, and they were bound to be able to organise a few oranges in Battambang. No rice wine for Maier. And in a few days, after the wedding, he'd be flying back to Hamburg. That was the plan.

"I'm really looking forward to your wedding, Hort. It will be a special day for me as well."
"The day you ask for my sister's hand?"
The years with Maier had changed the Khmer as well. Occasionally he tried his luck with irony and sarcasm, in a gentle Cambodian way.

Maier replied drily, "Carissa will cut my balls off. Or I'll have to flee and will never be able to return to Cambodia."
"That a shame, Maier. Maybe it better you keep your hands off my sister and follow your western lifestyle."

Suddenly, the three drinkers next to Maier wrested the sack off the wine-seller and jumped up. Hort jerked to his feet and gave Maier a hard push. The explosion killed his friend's warning. The bomb blew most of the wall straight past Maier. The woman who'd been selling the wine was torn to pieces. Screams and smoke. Maier lay flat on the ground for a few long seconds, not daring to move. Even the sky was on fire. Turning his head, he could see twisted bodies through the clouds of black fumes, shapes covered in blood and dust, frozen in black burns. A few small lean-tos that had been built against the wall were ablaze. Maier shook his legs and arms, everything was still there. One of the young men who'd been sitting behind him was alive. Caked in blood, he cried softly, as he tried to pull a friend from under the rubble. It was too late. A wooden beam had completely severed his companion's legs from his torso.

Hort had disappeared. Perhaps he had fallen before the explosion had gone off. But Maier knew that his friend had been sitting between himself and the woman selling the wine and had jumped up to warn him. The sudden realisation that his friend and fixer was dead came as a physical blow, as if some unchallengeable force had risen at speed from the earth below him and was suddenly ripping the skin off his back, racing up his neck as binary code made of needles and knives, and on, into his head where everything contracted in panicked spasms. He sat in debris for a moment, trying to breathe, waiting for something to come back, for time to go on. In the silence following the attack, a couple of dogs barked in the distance and the whine of a motorbike grew louder. Women cried, somewhere to his right. Otherwise, all he could hear was a high-pitched ringing tone in his ears. Maier forced himself up and climbed through the smoke across the strewn-around brickwork. He had to be sure.

The bomb had taken Hort straight through a big hole in the wall of a building that had been destroyed decades ago. A quick look was enough. Hort was dead.

Without a doubt, the bomb had been meant for Maier. The Khmer Rouge hated westerners, especially journalists. And the Cambodian army had known that Maier would be waiting by the station. Virtually anyone with a modicum of energy could get hold of explosives in this country.

Maier moved away from the carnage and disappeared as best as he could into the crowd that was beginning to gather by the railway tracks. He had to get away before the police and the military showed. He ran to one of the nearest shacks, dived into a small shop, pulled his cell phone from his pocket and called Carissa. Then he tied a krama around his head and jumped a passing pick-up truck bound for the capital.

He'd call his editor once he'd returned to Hamburg and hand in his notice. Maier was no longer a war correspondent.

INTO THE HEART OF DARKNESS

Phnom Penh, 2001

By 9 o'clock, the city burnt out. For a few short hours the daily struggle for survival of almost all the city's inhabitants ground to a halt. As soon the sun disappeared into the Tonlé Sap River, the shops closed and the pedestrians got off the river promenade.

The opposite side of the slow-moving water had already fallen into silent, mosquito-sodden darkness. Perhaps the river was not to be trusted: after all it changed direction twice a year. Yes, Cambodia was a special place.

Even the one-legged entrepreneurs slowly faded from the sidewalks and soon only hardened motodops, pushing ketamine, brown sugar, and girls, all at the same time if desired, cruised up and down Sisowath Quay. Homeless families, perhaps just in from the countryside looking for jobs in the construction industry, were camped in front of closing restaurants. These people had to share the concrete floor with cockroaches and rats, for as long as it took to find employment and a roof over their heads.

Maier sat on the back of Carissa's 250cc Yamaha dirt bike. The Kiwi journalist drove like the devil down Street 154 and didn't hesitate to take a cop's right of way on Norodom Boulevard.

"If you drive too slowly at night, you still get harassed by kids with guns."

Phnom Penh remained a wonderful, frightening backwater. If the Cambodian capital had been safer, investors would have built a sea of chrome-and-glass monstrosities. But there were enough buildings from the French colonial days and the optimistic post-independence era of the Fifties left standing to get a feeling for the city's history, even at sixty miles an hour.

The Khmer Rouge had laid siege to and finally taken Phnom Penh in April 1975. In the following weeks, the victorious revolutionaries emptied the city of its people. The entire population was driven into the countryside onto collectives to work as rice farmers. The stone-age communists were trying to stop US imperialism in particular and the entire capitalist system in general in its tracks. Overnight, schools, post offices, banks and telephone exchanges were made obsolete. Money no longer existed. The Pearl of Asia became a ghost town. For three years and eight months, the city stood empty. Only S21, a school turned prison camp, showed any sign of activity. Here, more than seventeen thousand people were interrogated and tortured, before being taken to the Choeung Ek, farmland fifteen kilometres outside the city, where they were beaten to death with sticks and thrown into shallow graves. The Khmer Rouge kept just a few government ministries open and a handful of friendly countries including China, Cuba and Yugoslavia continued to maintain embassies. Apart from a handful flights to Beijing every week, Cambodia was virtually cut off from the rest of the world. As a nation amongst nations, it ceased to exist.

The forced exodus of the Seventies and the lack of investment in subsequent decades saved the city's character from demolition. As neighbouring Bangkok grew into a Bladerunner-like cityscape, Phnom Penh remained provincial, because much of Cambodia's urban population had been butchered in the Killing Fields and many of the capital's current inhabitants were really landless farmers who'd drifted into town since the end of the war in search of work.

The side streets were deserted. After dark, dogs, cats and rats, all about the same size, ruled the garbage dumps, which spread across almost every street corner. Here and there, fairy lights glimmered in the darkness, beacons of hope and all its opposites to guide the night people towards countless massage brothels which could be found in the small alleys off the main strips. The red light was Phnom Penh's only vital sign at night. The best party going was at the Heart, as the motodops called the city's most popular bar without a great deal of affection.

"How d'you want me to introduce you to Pete?"
"As your victim. And as a potential business victim. You can tell him that I am on the way to Kep and that I am planning to invest there."

On Rue Pasteur, close to the nightclub, a small traffic jam clogged the road. Rich kids, the sons of the families who plundered the country, were trying to park their king-sized SUVs with horns blaring, while mouthing off to their compatriots. It appeared to be

a fairly well-established and reasonably safe ritual – the children of the privileged were all surrounded by their personal teams of bodyguards. The street was in a permanent state of détente, yet just a few small steps short of apocalypse. With these people around, there would be occasional fuck-ups.
A food stall was mobbed by prostitutes – taxi girls. The young Khmer seemed to eat all day long – perhaps a reaction to periodic famines, which had many villages in its grip, even today. Ever since the Khmer Rouge had taken over the government and had begun to beat all educated Cambodians to death, there'd not been enough food to go around. Some Khmer had not had enough to eat for twenty-five years.

The music in the Heart of Darkness was loud. The bar was packed three deep. A small laser, the first in Phnom Penh, swished like a searchlight across the crowded dance floor to the sounds of Kylie Minogue's "Can't get you out of my head" – the vaguely futuristic dazzle caused a slight culture shock. The Heart was a different world. Backpackers, worn out, sleazy ex-pats – leftovers from the UNTAC years – and young, rich local thugs gyrated in front of the massive bass bins. Everyone danced in his or her own personal hedonistic movie. Taxi girls threw Ya-ba pills, cheap methamphetamines from Thailand, into each other's' mouths. Bowls of marijuana graced the long bar. The smoke of a hundred joints hung above the cashiers like a storm cloud.

The Heart was a Cambodian institution, a collection point for all those who couldn't sleep at night and had money to burn.

Carissa made her way towards the bar. Maier followed her through the dense throng, her white head guiding him like a torch. The pool table was run by shredders, young and beautiful taxi girls who played the tourists for their wallets. On the wall above the table, a faded photograph of Tony Poe, a CIA operative who'd made his name collecting the heads and ears of his communist enemies during the Secret War in Laos in the Sixties, faced onto the dance floor. Maier had heard the stories from UN soldiers. Poe had been so awful, he'd eventually become the template for Marlon Brando's Colonel Kurtz in Apocalypse Now. Maier smiled to himself. That was how small and post-modern the world had become. The Heart of Darkness was probably the best-known watering hole in Southeast Asia.

But you had to take care in here. The squat Khmer bouncer who was in charge of bets at the pool table was not the only man who carried his gun more or less openly in his belt. Maier was keen to avoid trouble. After all, he'd only landed a few hours ago.

"Shit, it is loud in here."

"You're getting old," Carissa laughed over her shoulder and passed him an ice cold can of Angkor Beer.

Maier didn't like beer. Nor did he like Ya-ba and disco music. Ya-ba meant mad medicine. Just the right kind of drug for Phnom Penh.

"Holidays in Cambodia" by the Dead Kennedys blasted from the speakers. Maier could at least remember this one. Good sounds to kick back to and watch the dance on the volcano. And what a dance it was. Jello Biafra screamed "Pol Pot, Pol Pot, Pol Pot," and the girls, who'd probably never heard of the man who'd killed their mothers and fathers, uncles and aunts, gobbled more pills as the sweat of three hundred drunks dripped from the ceiling onto the dance floor.

By the pool table, a life-size sandstone bust of Jayavarman VII, the greatest of the ancient Angkor kings, stood, softly lit, in an alcove. The thousand-year-old god-king sucked up the chaotic scene in the room with empty eyes. Maier sympathised. In the Heart, he felt as old as a Khmer god-king. An even older French man, his shirt open to his belt buckle, had climbed the bar with two girls and waved at the crowd, a bottle of red wine spilling from his right hand. The hair on his head and chest stood in all directions and he looked like an electrified dancing bear. Perhaps he'd once been a butcher or owned a tanning studio in the banlieue. And one day that had suddenly felt like no longer enough.

Maier understood the man, though he had no desire to swap places. In the clouds of marijuana smoke behind the pool table, one of the young shredders began to open the trouser belt of a helpless, drunken and equally young tourist. Maier had just read in the Phnom Penh Post that the staff of the US Embassy was banned – by the US government – from entering the Heart. He had to laugh. Had this decision been made for security reasons or out of prudish concern for America's brightest?

"The English guy is already here, at a table behind the bar. And he's with bad company."

"With some of these nouveau riche thugs?"

Carissa leaned heavily into Maier and tried to make herself understood above the din of the music. "No, with real gangsters. People who don't belong in here."

Maier shrugged and pulled a face. "So what are we waiting for? Introduce me."

"Hey Pete."

"Wow, Carissa, babe, you look stunning, as always. May I introduce to you, gentlemen, Phnom Penh's classiest import from New Zealand."

Maier immediately saw that all the chairs were occupied by problems. The skinny Brit with the bright red hair and the sunken cheeks, a tough little pirate, had jumped up and embraced Carissa. Maier guessed him to be in his mid-thirties. Perhaps he was from Essex or some shitty London suburb, where he had probably burnt all his bridges. The silver chain around his wrist was heavy enough to sink a water buffalo. He wore a Manchester United shirt, with the collar up, and moved in a cloud of cheapish deodorant. He counteracted this with a strong-smelling Ara, the cigarette of choice for taxi girls and motodops, stuck in his nicotine-stained fingers. Two full packs and three mobile phones lay on the table in front of him. So this was the business partner of Rolf Müller-Overbeck: the wide-boy from the mean streets of Britain. Not completely unlikeable, but definitely not trustworthy.

The other two men at the table, both Khmer, were of a different ilk – one was young, the other old, though they came from the same dark place. They were smoking Marlboros and looked at Carissa as if she were a piece of meat. These days, Maier did not encounter men like these very often. There weren't that many. Both of them had been defined and moulded by war. They were men who killed and thought nothing of it.

Maier noticed that his presence had been registered. He could almost physically feel being observed and judged. Was he a potential danger or an opportunity to further their interests? What was the English guy doing with guys like this in a cosmopolitan filling station on a Saturday night?

The older man was in his mid-sixties. He had glued his short hair to his square, box-shaped head with gel. His neck was non-existent. He wore a black polo shirt and looked too casual in a

grey pair of polyester slacks. Like a toad on a golf course. This man had worn a uniform for most of his life.
The youngster next to him was his son, mid-twenties, wide hip-hop jeans, a Scorpions T-shirt, and a baseball cap, worn back to front on his equally square head, his thick, hairless arms defaced by backstreet tattoos. The boy had been born and had grown up during the civil war, a stark but no less assuring contrast to his formerly revolutionary father.
Luckily, all the chairs were taken. It was better to stand, around people like this.
Carissa exchanged kisses with Pete. "My old friend Maier is on the way to Kep, guys. He wants to poke around down there, see if there's anything worth investing in."

Pete's handshake was hard and dry. His dark eyes sparkled frivolously in his sunken face, which seemed deathly pale, despite a deep suntan. Pete looked like a guy who had nothing to lose and loved playing for huge stakes. Maier thought him largely pain-free.

"Maier, mate. Come and visit. An old friend of Carissa's is always welcome. And my partner is a Kraut too, just like you. At least you look like a Kraut."
Pete winked at him as if they were secret co-conspirators and whispered in a hoarse tone, "Kep was made for people like us. Nice beach town, built by the French, who are long gone, thank fuck. It's a bit shambolic down there, but things are getting better.

Haven't you heard? Cambodia's booming. Now's a great time to get your investments in, mate."

The old man had got up. Pete threw him a few clunky chunks of Khmer. The son had also stood up, showing off the pistol in the belt of his low-slung ghetto pants. The older man bowed slightly.

"My name is Tep. I am number one in Kep. My friends call me Tep."

Maier couldn't imagine that this man had friends. The handshake was soft and moist, like creeping death. Did number one expect a round of laughs? Maier extrapolated a little – the man had Khmer Rouge and genocide written all over his face. The old comrades from the politburo, those who had survived the vagaries of history, had become investors. The price of peace.

The younger man with the gun did not introduce himself, but that was OK.

For a long moment, Tep smiled silently at Maier. The sonic sins of a Britney Spears song hung suspended between the two men, creating a strange, trivial backdrop to the encounter. What was a man like that doing in a place like this? Tep should have died in the jungle a long time ago.

"I run a few businesses in Kep. I can help you if you need anything in Kep. Come to visit on my island. And bring your girlfriend."

The old man's English was simple and barely understandable. Carissa pulled at Maier's sleeve, as the detective tried to look as uninformed as possible.

"Beer?"
Pete had already ordered five cans of Angkor Beer and banged them on the table. Tep sat back down, a shadow of irritation shooting across his face, and turned to Carissa. The antipodean journalist was waiting for him.

"Aren't you a former Khmer Rouge general? And aren't you the guy who blew up the Hotel International in Sihanoukville? Perhaps you remember, a tourist from New Zealand died in that attack, General Tep?"

For a split second, the old man's eyes burst into flames. Pete laughed nervously, "Wow, Carissa, babe, Carissa, we aren't here to reheat old rumours, are we? It's great to see you, babe."
Pete, Maier decided, was capable of balancing a tray full of landmines, which was just as well in this place, at this moment.

A young Khmer with a skinhead, dressed in an immaculate white silk suit, dead drunk and sporting a slight similarity to the bust of the god-king, had pulled his gun at the next table. A flat-footed tourist had just stepped on his brand-new, imported Nikes. Enraged the young Khmer had spilt his beer onto a row of green pills he'd lined up on the table in front of him, which he now tried to rescue from the ash-sodden slop directly into his mouth. The hapless tourist had already disappeared into the throng.

There'll be trouble in a minute, was the only thing that came to Maier's mind.

The bald playboy swallowed his last pills and got up to scan the crowd for a likely scapegoat who was going to pay, one way or another, for someone else's clumsiness. Someone would have to pay. With a theatrical gesture he whipped his gun from his belt and waved it around the room.

Sometimes things happened quickly. The skinhead climbed onto his chair and began to scream hysterically. Tep nodded to his son and turned to Maier, "Don't make any problems in Kep. Investors are welcome, snoops and stupid people are not. You see."

The first shot, the one to drive up the courage, went straight into the ceiling. The Heart stopped in its tracks. The DJ cut the music. The house-lights flashed on, illuminating a few hundred twisted, strung-out faces in mid-flight. Carissa grabbed for Maier's shoulder and pulled him to the sticky ground. Pete had already

vanished. Punters rushed for the exit. The old general made no effort to move. His son had got up and walked a few feet away from the table, behind the fashionable rebel who stood on his chair, turning round and around, levelling his gun more and more towards the surrounding tables. From the floor, Maier had a perfect view of the young man's next moves.
Pop, pop, pop

The tourists screamed in panic. The playboy skinhead was dead by the time he hit the table in front of Maier, which collapsed in a hail of bottles, cans and cigarette butts.
Tep's son had shot him in the back.
Blood, beer, pills, and broken glass spread across the tiled floor. The dark red was striking on the immaculate white silk. That's how easy it was to die in Cambodia.
The boy helped his father get up and made a path for the old man to get behind the bar.
"Follow them." Maier grabbed Carissa. "There must be another exit."

The muggy night air felt good after the two beers he shouldn't have drunk and a murder he hadn't wanted to witness. But outside there was only Cambodia. Shots rang down the street. Car windows were smashed. A small gang of motodops raced down Rue Pasteur, into the darkness. Girls screamed. Saturday night in Phnom Penh.

"So this is the most popular nightclub in the country," he said, more to himself than anyone around him.
The windows of the police station that stood, hidden behind a high wall, directly opposite the Heart, remained dark, despite the gunfire. No policeman who earned twenty dollars a month would get involved in this weekend orgy of adolescent violence unless there was money to be made. The situation would eventually bleed itself to death.

The general pulled his polo shirt straight and stared down the road, an expression of faint amusement on his flat features. The old man did not seem overly concerned about his son's state of mind, after the youngster had just killed a man in cold blood in front of several hundred witnesses.
"Thanks, Mr Tep, your son saved our lives."
The general looked at Maier for a moment, his eyes fixed and devoid of message.
"Kep is a quiet town. You can relax. Come and visit on my island. Ask local fishermen how to get to my villa on Koh Tonsay. Germans always welcome. And forget what happen here tonight."
His car pulled up.
Carissa had freed her 250 from the chaos of parked bikes in front of the Heart and Maier lost no time jumping on the back. A few seconds later, they crossed Norodom Boulevard.

"Fucking hell, Maier, as soon as you turn up, the bullets start flying. The article I'm going to write about this tomorrow will be sensational. Son of former KR general shoots son of oil executive in Cambodia's most cosmo nightclub. That'll make waves. You'll have to drink beer without me tomorrow."

"I don't like beer."

Tom Vater is a best-selling writer working predominantly in Asia. He is the co-owner of Crime Wave Press, a Hong Kong based crime fiction imprint. Tom has written for The Wall Street Journal, The Times, The Guardian, The Nikkei Asian Review, Marie Claire, Geographical, Penthouse and many other publications.

He is The Daily Telegraph's Bangkok destination expert and the Thailand correspondent for Reise Know How, Germany's largest independent travel publisher. He has authored and co-authored a dozen or so non-fiction books, including the highly acclaimed Sacred Skin –Thailand's Spirit Tattoos.

He is the co-author of three documentary screenplays including the highly praised The Most Secret Place On Earth, a feature on the CIA's secret war in Laos.

Tom has published three crime novels, including The Cambodian Book of the Dead and The Man with the Golden Mind, featuring former war correspondent turned PI Maier. A third Maier novel, The Monsoon Ghost Image, will be published in 2017.

www.tomvater.com *www.crimewavepress.com*

The Dark Son

Phillip Coggan

Glossary:

Koan kroach: a human foetus, preserved by smoking, worn in a bag around the neck of its "father" as a talisman. It must be taken from the womb with the mother's permission – she must say explicitly that she agrees to give up her unborn child. Her death is not an essential part of the making of a koan kroach, but it is almost an inevitable by-product. The "father" (possibly its true biological father, as men who desire a koan kroach sometimes marry gullible girls) is its only family, and it is totally loyal to him. Its function is purely protective – the koan kroach cannot be forced or tricked into doing harm. By night it comes to its father in dreams to warn him of the plots of his enemies, and by day it jumps in its bag if danger is near.

Kru, kru boramey: a *kru* is a shaman, and the *boramey* is the spirit which possesses her or him. When the kru is in a state of possession her words are those of the boramey. All kru are "white" and use their powers for good. Me Sar, whose home is Ba Phnom, a mountain in Prey Veng province in southeast Cambodia, is one of the best-known and most powerful of boramey.

***

Khla turned up after the Khmer Rouge left. Nobody knew for sure where he came from, though some people said he used to be Khmer Rouge himself. Well, nobody would worry too much about that, but the rumours said he'd been a KR spy. The spies, they had power. At night they used to lurk under windows and listen for anyone who talked in a way the KR didn't like, like saying there wasn't any food to eat, or complaining about the husbands and wives KR had chosen for them. If a spy wanted to kill someone, he did. Some people said that Khla had once eaten the liver of a man. I don't know if that was true, but Khla was like that.

At the beginning his name wasn't Khla, he started calling himself that later. It means Tiger. He started off as a village policeman, and he was savage like a tiger. An animal. The district chief noticed him and promoted him. When I say the district chief noticed him, I mean he noticed that Khla was afraid of nobody and nothing. He was a man who dared. This district chief, he had some enemies, and he wanted Khla to take care of them. And he did.

We have a saying in Cambodia, "act as if your heart is not cut off." Our monks and elders teach us not to let anger rule us. That's why we smile all the time. If a man harms me, I smile. I smile because my heart is cut off. If I dare to have my revenge on that man, I have to do it when my heart is not cut off. I smile and then perhaps I drink and one day perhaps my heart is not cut off. This Khla, his heart was not cut off.

The governor of Kampong Cham province heard about Khla and made him one of his bodyguards. Everyone in Kampong Cham was afraid of the governor's bodyguards, and of all the bodyguards they were most afraid of Khla. One night Khla was in a beer garden. There was a new beer-girl that night, very pretty. She was serving at another table, but Khla saw her and liked her. He decided he wanted her. He called out, "Pretty bird, come fly to my nest." That was the kind of coarse man he was.

There were three men at the other table, Royal Gendarmerie. The gendarmes aren't afraid of anyone, just like Khla. "Hey, dog-face," they said, "go find your own girl." They were arrogant, because they were gendarmes and there were three of them. Khla grabbed the girl's hand and pulled her and she tripped and fell into his lap, and one gendarme jumped up and went to pull out a gun. Khla was faster. He shot that gendarme dead. That was the sort of man he was.

But the gendarmes were too powerful even for Khla. The governor couldn't protect him and he had to run away. Nobody knows where he went, but he was away for two years. People said he went to Ba Phnom and studied magic with a sorcerer. Maybe that's true, because when he came back he had tattoos all over his shoulders and back and chest and amulets around his waist and his neck. Some of these tattoos and amulets were to make him strong and to make him brave and some were so bullets couldn't harm him and land mines wouldn't blow up if he stepped on them. So Khla would lead his men against the enemy through the rubber plantation with the landmines, and one man would be blown up on this side and another man on that side, but never Khla. He was more powerful than ever, and more arrogant.

Khla had been poor before he ran away, but when he came back from Ba Phnom he was rich. Nobody knew where the money came from, but it was a sign that he was a powerful man. The governor made him the head of his personal security unit. Contemptible Khla was now Colonel Khla.

The gendarme he'd killed had a brother who was also a gendarme. This man believed he could defeat Khla's power. He made a plan. He went to a kru and got a powerful amulet and then to the temple to have it blessed. You see, that man had gotten power from the kru to bring success in everything he did and he'd had it blessed by the monks to bring good luck, and that was how he was going to overcome Khla's power. That night he fired a rocket at Khla's house. But Khla's power was greater. The rocket swerved aside and hit the house next door. A little boy living in the house was killed, but Khla wasn't touched.

That man failed because Khla had a koan kroach on a string round his neck. There's nothing more powerful than a koan kroach. Khla wore it always, and in the daytime it would warn him of danger by jumping up and down, and at night it would speak to him. It warned him about what his enemy was planning, and it told him he didn't have to worry, his protection was too strong. So that evening Khla invited all his friends around to play cards and drink whisky and see his luck and his power. He told them what was going to happen. They were all sitting round playing cards when the house next door blew up and Khla laughed so much he had to lie down on the floor and kick his heels, and his enemy ran away to Siem Reap. Khla hunted him down and killed him.

The governor got into the rubber business with some local big men. When I say the rubber business, I mean he was smuggling rubber illegally to Vietnam. The trucks would go in convoys with a truckload of Khla's men to guard against bandits and to make sure the police didn't stop them. That was Khla's job now.
Anyway, this time I'm telling you about, there were three trucks of rubber plus Khla and his men in a fourth truck. They got to the Mekong at Neak Loeung about mid-afternoon in the rainy season and the ferry brought them to the landing on the far side, the Prey Veng side, and it was raining, just a drizzle. The three rubber trucks came off first, going slow-slow up the bank to the police post at the top, and at the top a police lieutenant came out in the rain in a plastic and his officer's cap and rubber flip-flops. He had nothing on his feet but rubber flip-flops, you see, because in those days the police were poor. He didn't even have a gun in his hands. Behind him came two little policemen in their plastics with their carbines cross-ways across their chests and the lieutenant held up his hand in front of Khla's three trucks.

The people who'd just got off the ferry and the vendors at the landing all stopped what they were doing. They got ready to run, but they wanted to see what would happen. They knew Khla, they knew he was a man who dared, because that was his power, the power to dare. They knew this policeman, too. His power was different. He was a serious man, a man who did right. That was this policeman's power.
The policeman went to the cabin of the lead truck. The rain wasn't very heavy but the driver had the window up and the rain was speckled on the window. He was smoking a cigarette. He didn't even lower his window for the policeman, because he was Khla's man. The policeman rapped his knuckles on the glass and made him wind it down.

"What's in the trucks?"
The driver took his time. He looked at the policeman and he looked all round. He was insolent, because he was Khla's man and Khla had power.
"Who's asking?"
"Show me your papers," said the policeman.
"Ask the boss." The driver pointed his thumb over his shoulder without looking. He didn't even take his cigarette out of his mouth. He blew some smoke in a circle and laughed to himself as the policeman walked away. He knew what would happen.

Khla's truck had stopped when the rubber trucks stopped. Khla couldn't believe his eyes, this little policeman without boots to his feet, stopping his trucks. Khla got down from the cabin of the truck and stood in the rain and shouted at his men to get down from the back. They crawled out from under the canvas. There were twelve of them, all in boots, and he lined them up in the rain and led them up to where the policeman was standing.

The policeman had ordered his two men to search the back of the truck, and they'd just untied the canvas when they saw Khla's soldiers. The soldiers pointed their carbines at the two policemen. When the policemen saw that they dropped the canvas. They wanted to run away but they couldn't because Khla's men were surrounding them, so they just stood there with their butts shaking.
The lieutenant wasn't afraid. He stood there in his rubber flip-flops in the mud and waited as Khla stamped up to him. Khla stood so close his breath was in the policeman's nose.

"You dog, what do you think you're doing?" His speech was coarse, because he was an arrogant man.
The policeman said, "All trucks that cross on the ferry at Neak Loeung must be inspected."
"Not my trucks!"
"I have my duty," said the policeman.

"Not my trucks," Khla said again, and before the policeman could say anything Khla hit him on the side of the head with his open hand. He was so fast, nobody saw it coming. The policeman staggered and Khla hit him again and again, one-two, and the policeman fell down in the mud on his back. He started to get up, but the mud slipped on the knees of his uniform, and Khla kicked him and he fell on his face. He started to get up again and Khla kicked him in the face. After that he stopped trying to get up, he just lay there in the mud on his belly with blood coming out his mouth and his nose.

Khla said: "What makes you think you can stop my trucks?"

The policeman said, "I." He didn't say any more, because Khla kicked him in his private place and the policeman curled up in a ball with his hands between his legs and groaned with his face screwed up.
Khla said: "Now you need to learn your lesson."
Khla had his gun in a holster on his belt. He took the gun out and he pointed it between the policeman's eyes. He said: "Don't stop my trucks." Then he fired.

He didn't shoot the policeman. The bullet went into the mud right next to the policeman's eye. That was the moment the policeman lost his mind. He squealed and kicked like a dog that's been hit by a truck, and started to shake all over.
Khla fired bullets into the mud all around that policeman, and when he'd shot all around the policeman he put his pistol back in the holster and stood there with his legs apart and said, "Am I a good teacher?"
The policeman didn't say anything, he was shivering and his pants were brown at the butt and he made a bad smell.
Khla kicked him in the ribs. "I said, am I a good teacher?"
The policeman made a sound, but not like a word, but Khla pretended he'd heard him say yes. He grinned. "Ok, seeing I'm a good teacher, get up on your knees and thank me."

The policeman just lay there shaking. Khla nodded at his men and two of them lifted the policeman to his knees. The policeman knelt in front of Khla between the two soldiers and he was

shivering and crying, there were tears running down his cheeks with clean tracks in the mud.
Khla bent down and grabbed a handful of the policeman's hair and lifted his head. "Thank me," said Khla. "Thank your teacher for teaching you a good lesson."

The policeman's lips started moving and he put his hands together palm to palm and thanked Khla. He didn't say anything, he was crying in the rain, and he thanked Khla.
Khla's men dragged the policeman to the side of the road and threw him in the ditch and the convoy drove off to Vietnam. Then the people who'd been watching went back to their lives and the ferry crossing started up again, but very quiet.

There'd been someone else watching. That policeman, he had a son, just twelve years old. He'd always been a strange kid, that one. Never smiled, never played games. Never spoke unless spoken to, but when he said something, people listened. When he was a baby he had that way of looking at you that babies have. Other children lose that look as they grow older, but this boy never quite did.
The boy was a novice in the monastery, and he learned the chants so fast the chief monk said he must have been a monk before. He was there at the ferry crossing because his father wanted to teach him that it's possible to be a policeman and still follow religion. People say the police are corrupt, and so they are, but this one wasn't. That policeman had been through the Pol Pot time and he believed that if Cambodia was to become a great country we needed religion. That was why he had his son there with him, to teach him that a man could serve his country as a policeman and still follow the Five Precepts. That little kid saw all that Khla had done.

The two policemen took the lieutenant back to Prey Veng town, along with the kid, and all the way the kid's father didn't say a word, he just sat straight and stared at nothing. They took him to his house and helped his wife take him inside, and then they went off to report to their chief, although nothing would happen, because of Khla's power. On the way they dropped the kid off at the monastery.

Next morning he'd vanished. Left his robes folded on his bed and vanished. For two weeks, three weeks, people looked for him, but after a while they stopped looking. No, his father didn't look for the kid. He lay in his bed and stared at the ceiling and never spoke a word and his wife fed him soup with a spoon. He stayed that way till he died.

Months later, so early in the morning the sun was still rising, a kid walked up to the barracks in Kampong Cham and asked to see Khla. The kid was filthy, like he'd been sleeping in ditches, and dressed in a pair of shorts as filthy as his skin. The sentry thought he was just a beggar-boy, maybe mad, because he didn't seem quite normal, something strange about him. The sentry asked the kid why he wanted to see Khla and the kid said it was because he had a message. The sentry asked what the message was but the kid said he couldn't tell him; it was only for Khla. The sentry told him to go away, and the kid sat down on his butt outside the gate.

All morning the soldiers and the trucks went in and out and the kid sat there watching with his butt on his heels, but he never moved from the gate. At midday the soldiers brought him some food because they felt sorry for the crazy beggar-boy. That evening when the sun was setting they told him again to go away, but he shook his head and said he had to see Khla. It got dark and he was still there so the sentries let him come in the gate-house, and that was where he spent the night.

Next morning, he told them again that he had a special message for Khla.

I guess he scared them a bit. They took him to Khla's bungalow and told him to wait at the foot of the steps while someone told Khla how this mad beggar-boy had arrived the previous day and how he'd hung around all day because he said he had a special message. Khla told them to bring the kid in.

They brought the kid in and he stood in front of Khla's face. Khla had forgotten the little monk at the ferry, probably he'd never even noticed him. He didn't recognise the boy now, because of the rags and the dirt, and because the kid's hair had grown back. He didn't look like a novice monk any more.

Khla asked the kid what he wanted. The kid answered respectfully to Khla like he had with the soldiers. He said again that he had a message, and that Khla should send the men out of the room because it was for Khla only. Usually Khla wouldn't let some stranger alone in a room with him, but this was only a kid so Khla sent the soldiers out.

When the kid and Khla were alone in the room Khla said, "What is this message?"

"Sir," the kid said, "your life is in great danger."

Khla's eyes opened wide. It sounded as if the kid was threatening him, but how could a little kid threaten powerful Khla? He guessed someone must be behind this, some secret enemy. He grabbed the kid by the shoulders and shook him so his teeth rattled. "Who told you to say this to me?"

When Khla was angry a man's butt would start to shake, but not this kid. He wasn't frightened and his butt didn't shake.

"Sir, the message is not from a man."

"A woman?" Khla was puzzled. No woman would dare to threaten him.

"Sir, not a woman." The kid was polite, his voice was clear and firm. "It was a boy, sir, a boy like me."

"A boy? What boy?"

"Sir, I can't say. He came while I was sleeping."

"He woke you up?" Khla still didn't understand. He still thought the kid was talking about somebody human.

"Sir, he did not wake me up. He came while I was sleeping under the Buddha tree in the monastery and said I was to come to you and give you his message."

Khla drew his breath in when he heard the kid say this. The Buddha tree is a place where spirits gather, especially at night. Nobody who wasn't crazy would sleep there.

"A spirit?"
The kid nodded. "He called me by my name and said I was to hurry and tell you that in two days your enemy will close the trap."
Khla's blood ran cold. Many times the koan kroach had come to him when he was asleep and said to him, "Father, your enemy is making plans against you." Now here was this boy who knew more than Khla, because his koan kroach had not told him anything.
Then he remembered that the soldiers had told him the boy had been waiting outside all day yesterday. When did the two days start? He grabbed the kid by the shoulders again, but this time he was gentle. "When did the spirit come to you?"
"Sir, the spirit came to me early yesterday morning, just before the sun rose. I came to tell you at once, but your men wouldn't let me in."
Khla was dumbstruck. "Who is this spirit?" he asked.
He was sure the spirit was his koan kroach, but why had his koan kroach gone to this kid, instead of to him?
The kid said: "Sir, the spirit is my brother."

Khla assumed the kid meant that he was the koan kroach's brother. He didn't stop to think. If he had, he would have remembered that a koan kroach has no brother or sister or mother, no family except its father. But he didn't think. That was Khla's weakness, you see, he didn't think. He yelled for the sentry at his door. The sentry thought Khla was being attacked and came running. Khla pointed to the kid. "Give him some breakfast. Give him everything he wants. He's my son. Do as he says as if he were myself."

Khla turned the base into an anthill. He doubled the sentries at the gate, everybody had to be armed and ready for combat, all men outside had to be found and brought back. He marched up and down ordering and supervising, and all the time he couldn't understand, because now when he needed help and guidance from his koan kroach, it was silent. He could feel it in the bag where it hung round his neck next to his skin, but it didn't jump like it did when there was danger about. He couldn't understand what this meant.

When everything was ready and the sentries were at the gate with machine-guns pointed out at the road and he was ready for every enemy, he thought: "Who is my enemy?" He took the koan kroach in his hand and prayed: "My son, help your father, tell me who is my enemy."

The koan kroach was silent. Of course, the koan kroach didn't speak in the daytime, only at night. Khla tried to think for himself who his enemy might be. He had many enemies, but not many who would dare to attack him. He thought of two names. The chief of the Royal Gendarmerie hated him because of what had happened all those years ago, and also because of the arrogant way Khla and his men treated the gendarmes. The chief of the gendarmes was his enemy and he had men and weapons, but Khla had the governor's protection and was safe even from the gendarmes. But the governor had thrown a party last month and his enemy had been seated closer to the governor than he had himself. Yes, when he thought of this, he started to be sure that the governor and the Gendarmerie commander were conspiring against him.

The second name was a kru called Yeay Sar. It wasn't clear to him why Yeay Sar hated him but he knew she did, because he'd gone to consult her last year about some land and she'd told him to go ahead and buy it, and after he'd paid the money a minister's brother had produced a title deed and taken it off him. Yeay Sar had no men or guns, but she was powerful, powerful enough to prevent his koan kroach from warning him of the plans of his enemies.

But which was it?
Perhaps both together!
He had to strike first!

Walking up and down he thought of a plan. He would take Yeay Sar and bring her to his headquarters and force her to release his koan kroach from whatever spell she had put on him, and then his son could protect him against the governor and the Gendarmerie. Yes, this was what he should do.

Now that he had a plan he immediately started giving orders. He ordered six men into a truck, ready to go to Yeay Sar's village. Then he thought: what if my second enemy attacks while I'm away? He ordered another six to take a second truck and go at once to a café where he knew the eldest son of the Gendarmerie commander would be taking his breakfast; they would capture his enemy's son and bring him back to the base to be held as a hostage. You think this was a stupid idea? It was, but the kid's words had unbalanced Khla's mind.

The koan kroach still didn't give any warning signs. It had never failed to warn him of danger before. He was sure this was Yeay Sar's doing. Yes, he saw it now, the Gendarmerie commander had paid Yeay Sar to put a spell on the governor to turn against him, and another spell on his koan kroach to stop it warning him, but his koan kroach was warning him through the kid instead. But he could outwit his enemies. He would force Yeay Sar to lift her spells. And he would take the kid with him, so his koan kroach could warn him through the kid.

A sergeant ran off to fetch the kid, but came back alone. He saluted. "Sir, the boy's gone."

Khla's butt clenched. "What do you mean, gone? I told you to watch him!"

Then he realised that he hadn't ordered anyone to watch the kid, just to give him whatever he wanted. The kid was just a beggar-boy and crazy, he'd probably wandered off as soon as his belly was full. He cursed himself, because he knew now he should have been more careful. But he had no time to look for the kid, he couldn't give his enemies time to mobilise.

Yeay Sar lived in a village outside Kampong Cham town, not far in kilometres but the roads made it more than an hour's drive. The ruts and potholes started even before they'd left Kampong Cham, and got worse the further they travelled. The truck dipped and swayed and Khla, sitting in the cabin next to the driver, had time to think. He told himself he was rattled. Be calm, he told himself out loud. Think. The strange kid arriving out of nowhere, the silence of his koan kroach, yes, of course he was rattled. He needed to keep a clear head. What if the spirit that came to the kid was not his koan kroach? What if the spirits themselves were misleading him? But the warning sounded genuine, just the sort of thing his koan kroach had been telling him for years, just what he'd expect from his enemy the Gendarmerie commander. Yes, he decided, he was right, he had to attack his enemies before they destroyed him.

Yeay Sar's house was built of timber and raised up on stilts, with a yard of packed earth and a large tevoda-shrine in the corner next to the gate. It was a little better than the other houses in the village, but not by much. Yeay Sar respected the gods and followed the Buddha, and although she had many followers and received lots of donations she kept nothing for her own use. Everything she got she passed on to the village monastery for merit. Her house was in fact directly opposite the monastery gate, and Khla could see the new shrine hall with its new roof and a new house for the abbot and a teaching hall with walls covered in paintings of the Buddha's life, all built with donations received through Yeay Sar.

When Khla burst in on Yeay Sar she was not Yeay Sar the kru but Me Sar the boramey. Humans are only human, we live this little while and then we die and after some little while we are reborn, but the boramey are spirits. From their compassion they come to help us, and because they have no human bodies they chose special humans to be their vehicle. That's what it means to be a kru boramey. Yeay Sar was an old granny with white hair who spoke softly to everyone, but when the boramey inhabited her body the granny was not present.

Khla took six men and stormed up the steps to Yeay Sar's house. He found Me Sar in Yeay Sar's body with her hands in her lap, giving advice to a man and his wife about their baby who was not thriving. The man and his wife were afraid, but Me Sar wasn't afraid. Me Sar has lived tens of thousands of years already. She has power. Her eyes glared at Khla, and then at Khla's six men, and then at their boots. Khla's men became ashamed that they hadn't taken their boots off to enter the shrine room. They shuffled and tried to edge away from their leader and would have liked to become invisible.

Khla wasn't afraid. He pointed his finger at Me Sar like the insolent man he was and said, "Why are you my enemy?"
Me Sar didn't answer a word. She closed her eyes and began swaying gently backwards and forwards, and her lips began to move and her fingers began forming signs in her lap.
"Stop that!" yelled Khla. He was afraid she was putting a spell on him. He opened his holster and took out his pistol. "Stop at once or I'll shoot you right now!"
Me Sar continued to sway, her old woman's eyes invisible behind the lids, and her lips and fingers moved faster and faster.
Khla shot her in the head.

The sound of the shot in that small room was like a tree-trunk snapping. For a moment everyone was stunned, and then the woman began wiping herself and screaming and wouldn't stop, because she was covered in blood, and her husband stared at the pieces of Yeay Sar on the altar and leant over and was sick on the floor. The soldiers went very white. They'd seen plenty of killing in front of their eyes, but this was different. They knew you can't kill a boramey.

Khla stood there, the gun in his hand, staring at what he'd done. He knew it too. He'd crossed a line. Yes, perhaps this was the moment when he knew that his daring had carried him too far.

On the way back to Kampong Cham Khla said to the driver: "I had to do it, she was putting a curse on me, didn't you see?"
The driver nodded. He was careful to let nothing show in his voice or on his face. He kept his eyes straight ahead.

Ba Phnom was where Khla had found his own master, the sorcerer. Khla's master had warned him, the power of strength should work with the power of religion, not against it, even for black purposes. Ba Phnom is the home of Me Sar, and the sorcerer had warned Khla to respect Me Sar. Had Me Sar come from Ba Phnom to punish him?

Khla said: "If she'd just come with us she'd be sitting in this truck right now. Don't you see?"
The driver nodded. He kept his eyes on the road and his hands on the wheel.
Khla took the koan kroach from round his neck and held it in both hands and closed his eyes. "My son, please speak. I have no one but you, I am in my hour of greatest need, won't you speak to your father?"
The koan kroach was silent. Khla closed his eyes more tightly and prayed harder. "Why are you silent, my son? I've been a loving father to you, I've cared for you and raised you up since the moment I took you from your mother's belly. Tell me what food you want and I'll find it for you. Tell me what toy you want and I'll get it. Only speak to me. Let me hear your happy laughter and the sound of your pretty voice. Let me know you're here."
But his koan kroach was silent.

A thought came to him and he went cold all over. A koan kroach has to stay with its father. His koan kroach could never leave him and go to the kid. The kid's message could not be from his son. The message was from his enemy.
Then he thought: This kid was not innocent. He was involved in this plan. He is my enemy. But who is this kid?
The dipping and rolling of the truck made it difficult to think, but he thought hard about who the kid could be. He began to remember. The kid was about twelve years old. It was twelve years ago that an enemy had tried to kill him with a rocket grenade. His koan kroach had warned him then and turned the grenade aside. He'd been unharmed, as his koan kroach had told him he would be.
But his enemy, the one who had tried to kill him that night, had had his own charm, and that charm had been that someone would die that night. And someone had died. A boy from the house next door had died. Khla had paid compensation to the boy's parents, even though he hadn't caused the boy's death. The parents had

been happy to accept his money, or if they weren't happy they were too scared of his power to do anything. But what about the boy who died?
And so Khla came to know that the kid's message was nothing to do with his son, his koan kroach. His koan kroach had been silent because there was no message. It was the kid who was his enemy.

As Khla was thinking these thoughts a call came over the radio. Kampong Cham was calling to tell him that the base was surrounded by the gendarmes. The gendarmes were demanding that they release the Gendarmerie commander's son. The situation was tense. Khla's men were at their posts and ready to open fire as soon as he gave the order.
Khla asked, "Is the kid there?"
"Sir, we have their boss's son under guard in our mess hall."
"Not him, the other one. The one who brought the message."
"No sir, negative."
"Stand down," said Khla.
"Sir?" The operator was puzzled. "Please repeat, I do not understand."
In the distance Khla could see a crossroads and a line of men. They wore the battle dress of the Royal Gendarmerie, and although the distance was still too great to make out details he could see a truck behind them, and mounted on top of the truck was a heavy machine gun. The gendarmes were fanning out into the rice fields, and he knew that they would not try to take him alive.
"I said stand down. Lay down your weapons. Release the prisoner. No fighting. That is all."
He hung the mike on the hook and ordered the driver to stop the truck.

Khla stood his men in a row under the sky. Birds cried out from the trees, rice fields and clumps of sugar-palm spread to the horizon, and a little herd-boy stared at them from on top of a water buffalo in a pond. It was a world Khla didn't belong to any more, if he ever had.

Khla made a short speech. This was not a fight they could win, he told his men. Guns could do nothing now. Let each one look to his own salvation. Then he got into the cabin behind the wheel and we watched him drive off alone towards his enemy. Say what you like about Contemptible Khla, he was not afraid.

Philip Coggan first visited Cambodia in 2002. In 2015 he published "Spirit Worlds: Cambodia, the Buddha and the Naga", a non-fiction guide to Cambodian religion, with John Beaufoy Press. The story in this collection is a spin-out from that book and will be included in a collection to be published in 2018. He divides his time between Cambodia and Australia.

Raindrops

Voleak Phan

(Editor's note: This was our first-place prize-winner in the joint competition between Saraswati Publishing and Asia LIFE magazine.)

**The flower jompa that is mentioned in the story has a very pleasant smell.*

Kac Keeng Kong Kert! Kac Keeng Kong Kert![i]

Veasna woke up to the sound of roosters crowing, signalling the morning of another new day. Supposedly, it would be a promising day for a twelve-year-old like him, what with school to go to, friends to play with, and food to eat. But Veasna was not normal and hoping was most pertinent in his case.

He got up groggily to light a lamp in the semi-darkness of early morning. He rolled the carpet he had been sleeping in and laid his folded blanket on top of his pillow. With one hand holding the dimly lit lamp, he tiptoed towards the dishes nearby and washed them. Then he climbed down the stairs and grabbed a broomstick to sweep the ground. All the while, his mother was preparing his sister for school. She beckoned her daughter to climb on the motorbike and did not even glance at Veasna. Jompa turned back to wave at him.

Later that day.

"This is *kor…khor...ko*[ii]," said Jompa with her fingers pointing at the letters on the page. Veasna shook his head in confusion as he tried to copy the letters. They were sitting on a bed underneath the mango tree outside of the house.

"*AH*[1] SNA! You stole my money, did you? Where is it? Give it back?" snarled his angry mother as she grabbed him by his shirt and searched his body. With quivering lips, Veasna shook his head vigorously in denial.

"You won't tell me huh? You won't tell…"

1. *Kac Keeng Kong Kert - It's what Cambodians refer to as the sound of roosters crowing. It's equivalent to Cock-a-doodle-doo in English.*
2. *kor…khor...ko - They are three consonants from the Khmer alphabet, out of 33.*

3. AH - *It's a derogatory prefix to call a male. Usually, only the elders can call children using that when it is most insulting. But close friends also use it to call each other, playfully, especially if they are of the same age.*

Her voice trailed off as her gaze fell upon a bamboo stick nearby. She seized the stick and started to whip her son.

"You liar! You have become a thief, huh? I work so hard to raise this family, and this is how you pay me? Let me teach you, pathetic child!"

"Errr…mmmmmm…" cried Veasna, who pressed two palms together in a praying manner, begging for mercy.

"Mother, please don't hurt brother. He was with me the whole time; he couldn't possibly steal your money. You might have misplaced it somewhere," said Jompa.

"Shut up Jompa! I am sure he stole it. Let me teach him how to ~~tell the truth." Veasna was crying~~ hard and his eyes pleaded with his mom, who only looked at him menacingly; there was no mercy in those demon-possessed eyes.

Blood started to ooze from his wounds. His mother was getting exhausted as her whipping lessened its harshness. Just as she was about to whip him using the last of her strength, Jompa seized her brother's hand and blocked him from the terrible blow of the whip. She screamed as she had never before in her life as pain ripped through her body.

"Stop it. Please, stop it," Jompa cried, hugging her brother. Seething with anger, her mother threw whatever she could grab and cursed. The neighbours heard the commotion; some peered out of their houses to look, but none of them dared to intervene. They either didn't care or were afraid to interfere with another family's business.

Sobbing so hard, Jompa asked, "Why? Why are you so cruel to my brother? He's your son, too!"

"WHY? Because he is a mute. He is so stupid and slow like a cow. A disgrace! A distasteful disgrace! I should have killed you at birth." All the while mother pointed her finger at him as if accusing him of some crime he didn't commit.

"He didn't choose to be born this way. My…my teacher told us not to judge people…"

"I don't care what your teacher said!" her mother yelled. She stormed to the kitchen and came back with a bundle of clothes, which she threw at Veasna.

"Get out of my house. I am so sick and tired of raising you. You're useless to me, as if I am not poor enough! I don't want to deal with you anymore. GET OUT!"

"Mom, no! Don't do it!" begged Jompa. Veasna crawled to her and bent his head to her feet with his hands raised to his forehead. Fury and disgust engulfed the woman's soul so much so that she acknowledged him with a kick to his stomach and walked away.

Veasna could only watch with teary eyes. Then, he turned and checked on his sister's wound.

"I'm fine," reassured Jompa. She used her shirt to wipe the blood from his arms. "What are we going to do? She means what she says…you'll have to…you'll have to…" She broke down into an uncontrollable sobbing. Veasna hugged his sister, and they clung to each other for comfort.

After a while, Jompa said, "I will go with you." Veasna shook his head.

"You can't stop me. I have made up my mind." Seeing the adamant look in her eyes, he yielded. She went to grab her belongings, and together hand in hand, they walked out.

Suddenly, Jompa was tugged away from Veasna.

"Where do you think you are going?" said her mother.

"He has no one; I need to be with him," argued Jompa.

Seizing her by the arms, she dragged Jompa away, who screamed and kicked at her mother. Veasna rushed to free his sister, but his mother pushed him aside. He fell and banged his head against the pillar. Dazed, he struggled to get up as his sister was pulled further away from him. He hurried to her one more time, and their hands found each other. Jompa clasped her brother's hand tightly one final time as her mother yanked her from him and pushed her inside the house.

Veasna fell down on his knees and cried. He looked inside his hand and found a necklace there. On the necklace was a rusty *jompa.* He clutched it tight to his heart as he took tentative steps away from home, from his sweet little sister, whom he would never see again. His hunched silhouette walked off into the distance as the sun cast its final light and plunged the earth into a veil of darkness.

As for Jompa, she didn't know what to do besides sobbing over the loss of a brother very dear to her.

"Oh cruel world! A heart holds love, yet the heart of the woman I call mother is anything but kind." She paused. Her gaze was so distant. "*Veasna*…what will yours be like?"

Veasna

It was a small village, but seemed so vast. He felt his way through the dark interior of the night, oblivious to the pain his wound caused him, not knowing where to go.

Suddenly, he was surrounded by a gang of boys. They called him names and taunted him, but he only walked away, terrified of them and everything around him. But they didn't let him go as one of them saw the necklace. He didn't know what happened as a feeling of numbness possessed him when his head hit the ground. Their feet were on his hand, forcing it to open, only to no avail. He only knew he needed to keep it safe; it was his *jompa.*

(4) - It refers to one's destiny. It's also a common name in Cambodia, thus, it's the namesake of the protagonist.

But then, another group of boys appeared from the corner of the road and chased Veasna's tormentors away.

They inspected the inert Veasna.

"Just leave him here. I don't want to get in trouble," said one of the boys.

The tallest boy who was the leader pondered the suggestion. "No, we should help him. He can be useful to our business."

For days, Veasna stayed in a ramshackle house, where he was taken care of by the boys. To him, they were his saviours; he had food and a place to sleep. When he had recovered, they brought a school uniform to him.

"Put that on, *Ah* Heng," said the leader. They called him by that name, hoping that he was the luck-bringer. The leader took Veasna by both shoulders and looked intently into his eyes.

"Listen to me, boy. Your job is to go to the back of the school we will bring you and deliver this package to the students you meet there. Then, you come out as quickly as you can with the money they give you and make sure you don't stop to let anyone else talk to you. Do this right and you'll get more food and some sweets tonight."

Veasna nodded and smiled at the leader.

"Good. Now go."

Veasna carried out his mission cautiously. When he handed the package to the boys at the school, they grabbed it hungrily and took the pills. After that, they looked blissful and gave him money.

He didn't know what the pills were for, but they definitely made you feel better. More than once, he had missions like that. When he failed to deliver the packages, they didn't let him eat. Sometimes, the leader beat him up. In pain, he would take the necklace out from its hiding place and clung to his jompa.

It was another raindrop on the same old wound.

Voleak Phan is 18 years old and from a village just outside of Siem Reap town. She has studied on a full scholarship for 9 years at Jay Pritzker Academy. Since she was young, reading has been her favourite past time. She loves fantasies and adventurous stories. Her favourite novel is The Kite Runner by Khaled Hosseini because it is a piece of work that is emotional but also compels you to think a lot about life, love, and friendship. Recently, she wrote a short story in Khmer for the Let's Read competition, and her story was selected to be published as an e-book for children in Cambodia. After high school, she wants to study at a university in the United States, majoring in Sociology. She also hopes to be a successful author in the future.

Shifting Fortunes

Joel Quenby

I. The Producer

"AAAAAY!" screamed the stringy *'moto'* driver as Jack Lilywhite slipped out of the elevator.

He'd been in Phnom Penh months yet still found this alarming alert-cum-sales pitch as unsettling as ever. He grimaced, squinting into the starkly sunlit foyer for his usual driver.

It paid to retain a familiar face in this city.

Mercifully, Mr Piseth was waiting quietly as ever amid the gaggle offering his default-setting: patience offset by a timid smile. Jack caught his eye and nodded.

The overenthusiastic chorus – which had swollen into gibbering, Tourette-like barks of *"tuk-tuk!"* – faded to a mutter. Eyes returned to the elevator door as the pair exited the building into the blazing morning.

Ambling towards Mr Piseth's rust-crusted motorbike – seemingly comprised of mix 'n' match components – Jack passed the Khmer a plastic-coated business card.

The squat, middle-aged man halted to scrutinise it at close range, tilting the card toward his nose, carefully reading the address aloud, twice. He slowly passed it back to the malnourished though younger, taller western man, still reciting it under his breath.

Jack had been on the receiving end of this routine numerous times.

"You *know*?" he intoned gravely, eyebrows aloft.

"Yes…I know…*this one*?"

Jack's heart sunk.

"OK, no problem. We go. *You tell me.* OK?"

Resigned, Jack mounted the geriatric steed behind Mr Piseth, who passed him a flimsy blue plastic helmet, sporting, for his peace of mind, a crack running virtually the full length of one side.

He recalled the time they'd zipped past a helmetless Caucasian – arms splayed in crucifix repose, flat on his back, an unhealthy distance from his motorbike, which lay on its side, wheels spinning. A horseshoe ring of onlookers scrutinised him like a venue of vultures.

"Why aren't they helping him?" Jack had yelled into Mr Piseth's ear.

"They are waiting…" the driver bellowed back.

"Then – if he not moving – they check his clothing," he added, yanking on his pocket to illustrate.

"American!" exclaimed Mr Piseth, sounding strangely pleased.

"*How* do you know that? You know him?"

The Khmer garbled something but whatever it was got lost amid the engine buzz and wind rushing in Jack's ears.

Jack squeezed Mr Piseth's shoulder in solidarity with the driver's struggle starting the engine. Once rattling, they traversed the sprawling carpark, weaving between other moto-traffic congesting the complex's gates – then out onto the broad, Gallic expanse of Norodom Boulevard.

The route passed grimy slums punctuated by glittering, tourist-brochure temples, their spires insistently poking the sky. They arrived at their destination – six kilometres away – a full twenty-five minutes later. Although his intentions could never be faulted, Mr Piseth was a hesitant navigator even in his sharpest moments, which this decisively wasn't.

The sun beat slick lines of sweat sticking Jack's dark fringe to his forehead and the back of his button-up shirt to his spine. He brought the trip to a close in the traditional manner:

"Okay! Okay! *Okay!* Here! *Here!* Okay! Stop! Stop! Here! ... *Okay*!"

Patience had never been the journalist's strong suit – or even present much in his deck. And what little he possessed steadily melted during the two needless loops of the *cul de sac* that was the flag-lined embassy row – adjacent to where the mighty Mekong River swirled ceaselessly in its mysterious convergence with the Tonle Sap.

The inimitable riverine phenomena literally passed Jack by. He was contemplating throwing himself off the bike so he could walk the remainder of the way. He settled for ignoring Mr Piseth's 'pity-me-with-a-special-tip' face; instead paying the regular seven-thousand riels. Mr Piseth's standard disappointed façade was betrayed by the hungry gleam in his eye as he swiftly pocketed the greying, powdery bills.

"Maybe 30 minutes, okay?"

Relief swept over the man's face; he nodded keenly and gestured towards a junction where a bunch of other drivers awaited custom beneath the shade of a frangipani tree.

As a tourist-luring focus of urban regeneration, the central riverside district was one of the first earmarked for gentrification, once the influx of foreign investment had created the means in the post-war years.

It was once the preserve of traditional wooden houses on stilts and the (still-ubiquitous) two-up two-middle two-down Southeast Asian shop-houses. Nowadays the area was up and coming; trendy bistros and subtly lit cafes jostled for prime position alongside sparkling white spas, patronised ostentatiously by *nouveau riche* socialites in chauffeur-driven imported marques.

Jack had precious little regard for these modern additions at the best of times. His attention was focused on his forthcoming interview – with a fellow English expatriate – while concurrently scanning the faded lane signs; a growing sense of unease forming a knot in his gut as the seconds ticked into minutes.

He eventually found the right building tucked fifty metres down an incongruous lane. Jack was unsurprised to arrive at a converted, three-storey shop-house. It was shuttered so he had to call Matthew Hastings on his mobile; the sexagenarian Brit brusquely ushering him – "Yes, yes, *come on in*".

'He's annoyed I'm late,' he realised with a glance at his watch as he ascended the rickety, bare-wooden staircase.

He'd have to strain to pull his subject round; better emphasise the body language mirroring during the opening questions. It'd help if he could raise a smile, too, but, having clocked the furrows of Hastings' frown, Jack wasn't holding his breath.

The first two floors were unoccupied save for a few chairs, the odd table and sheets of dusty cobwebs.

The third-floor office comprised some weathered work-stations loosely arranged open plan-style in what would have originally been the master bedroom. Two local ladies were present: the middle-aged one typing intently; the younger woman gathering a tea set.

Hastings made a beeline for the little ante-room off to one side that served as his office.

Shafts of sunlight glinted through the shutter slats drawn over the street-facing window. Jack could see particles of dust floating and bobbing in the moodily lit room; he romantically envisaged a tense negotiation with a fedora-donning 'Deep Throat' character in some hard-boiled detective thriller.

Wiry of frame and boasting a full head of neatly trimmed, not entirely grey hair, Hastings possessed a darting quality to his movements that suggested a similarly nimble mind. His close-set eyes might've been described as rodent-like by someone unkind; though he certainly looked sprightlier than his 64 years; and gave the impression of not suffering fools – especially journo-fools – gladly.

The Cambridge-educated television producer was known back in Britain, primarily for revamping one of its best-loved soap operas and reinstalling it atop the ratings tree. (Like millions, Jack had watched the soap; it was almost *de rigueur* on campus.)

"So I first came to Cambodia six years ago on a contract from the BBC World Service Trust to make a drama focused on promoting health," he was already saying as he rounded his battered teak desk.

Jack fumbled for his Dictaphone among the rumpled receipts, disparate currencies, hollowed-out cigarette shells, and abundant fluff jostling in his ragged shoulder bag. The younger Khmer woman seemed to float into the room, placing the tea tray delicately on the desk.

"Sooasday…Orkhun tran [Hello, thank you very much]" murmured Jack.

She responded with an ethereal smile that normally would've made his day. Jack had an expressive face (overly so, he opined; he *never* won at poker) that normally would've betrayed this, but now his jaw was set with the seriousness of work. He sipped the gently steaming concoction from a little, handle-less ceramic cup; it was some kind of lukewarm herbal *chai*.

"A hundred episodes; that's *finished*," said Hastings, briskly.

Jack riffled through his notebook, dropping his pen. Stooping to retrieve it only achieved kicking it further away, into a whirring spin, like some wayward spinning top. Hastings ignored it.

"I decided to stay on here, so I founded my production company, Mekong Khmer Films – and have been running it ever since."

Jack was finally composed.

"How did your company become involved with the *landmark* Khmer Rouge tribunals?"

"Well, we initially won a bid to produce some pre-trial short films, bankrolled by the British government.

"It was part of their funding for developing countries. We came up with a semi-dramatised treatment to explain what is essentially a complex, convoluted trial system – *I mean, it's had international legal experts scratching their heads* – in simple terms to ordinary, uneducated Cambodians."

The resulting series was entitled, appropriately enough, '*Time For Justice*'. Ever efficient, Hastings had couriered all six films plus various supplementary research materials, unprompted, over to *The Phnom Penh Post's* newsroom to help Jack prepare for their interview.

Among the bumf was an illuminating VCD (a Southeast Asian home video format not produced in the west). It contained videos of screenings of '*Time For Justice*' held in various rural villages as part of a nationwide, NGO-funded educational outreach programme.

Here was priceless, fascinating three-dimensional feedback. Screenings were usually projected at night (drive-in movie-style – without the cars, Jack noted) on whatever outdoors common ground served as that village's focal point.

"No gain in keeping, no loss in weeding out."

That had been the *leitmotif* motto of Pol Pot, the rubber plantation worker turned prime minister, who was, by many accounts, charming, generous, loving – *almost grandfatherly* – even as he administered one of the most heinous genocides in human history.

Two million dead. One in every four Cambodians. The Marxist formerly known as Saloth Sar headed the Communist Party of Kampuchea – the infamous Khmer Rouge Maoists – that wiped out most middle-aged Cambodians. The ravaged society left behind was characterised, scarred, by a striking age disparity overwhelmingly weighted towards younger generations.

Jack could clearly see this imbalance reflected in the audiences: *Where were all the grandparents?*

There were, of course, some; in fact, they stood out. Hastings' emotive narratives evidently jolted horrific memories in the few elder viewers, all too evident in the post-screening debates. One leathery, bespectacled old man stood out for Jack…

The village is gathered as if it were a school assembly. The wispy, weather-beaten old man sits cross-legged in the front row. When he first opens his mouth to speak, betel juice trickles out through cracked lips, like the first trickle of lava from a long-dormant volcano. His voice eventually emerges as a hoarse whisper; forming words seems an agony, each syllable accompanied by the widening of his eyes, as if greeting every tortured sound like a just-rediscovered friend.

"This film reminded me of what Pol Pot did," he exclaims.

"It was the same as in the story. My brothers and sisters all died."

He begins to cry. Scrapes his spectacles off his face, his body juddering with long-supressed emotion.

"I cannot speak because I am overcome," he eventually sobs.

A jeans-clad teenage girl subsequently says: "Now I believe this regime really did exist. It's shocking to hear older people talk about what happened to their families.

"When I was first told that so many people were killed, I didn't believe it."

Such footage exposed the painful generation gap between the survivors and their children and grandchildren, who were often in the dark about their grandparents' ordeals.

And the perpetrators – Pol Pot's child soldiers? By 1997, the year before the loveable tyrant died, numbers of remaining Khmer Rouge stragglers had dwindled to 3,000. They now ran restaurants; drove moto taxis; lived supposedly productive lives. (Jack couldn't help wondering what Mr Piseth had been doing at that time…)

Despite education campaigns such as Hastings', a pre-tribunal nationwide survey found eighty-five per cent of respondents 'had little or no knowledge' of the forthcoming trials. (Court officials disputed its findings – but Jack, ever the reluctant cynic, could well believe the idea of collective unconsciousness; tragic, considering the atrocities that had gone thus far unpunished).

He glanced down at his notes.

"The Human Rights Centre at the University of California calculated that as much as *seventy percent* of Cambodia's population is aged under thirty – and most of this generation has virtually no knowledge of the Khmer Rouge years."

"It is a problem," replied Hastings.

"That's why we commissioned an initial focus group to assess the level of knowledge and understanding of younger generations. A significant section of respondents believed the genocide was *totally made up*, though I don't think the intelligent younger folk think it's fictional.

When the British Embassy in Phnom Penh secured additional government funding to produce a television programme covering the long-overdue hearings, Hasting's production company was invited to advise.

"I suggested a summary of the weekly highlights presented in bite-sized chunks – again aiming at rural Cambodians."

Hastings tone, and his general demeanour, had softened perceptibly as the conversation progressed.

"This really is new territory for Khmer broadcasting," he mused.

"The presenters of our show – Neth Pheaktra, who also works at the *Post*, as you know; and Ung Chan Sophea, who's a reporter for the French newspaper *Cambodge Soir Hebdo* – say Cambodians aren't used to *'serious'* television presenters.

"Pheaktra told me: *'Lots of TV presenters talk a lot, and they're always joking – but they never actually say anything,'* which was interesting.

"He sometimes gets recognised on the street, you know. And people ask him why he never smiles on TV.

"And Sophea told me that some of her friends had been completely cynical about the show's prospects – you know: *'It's useless trying to do a trial programme'*, which was dispiriting – but they changed their tunes after they'd watched it.

"They now think it's a worthwhile, interesting endeavour. So there's a minor victory for us."

Jack thought these court cases represented pivotal bookmarks in modern Cambodian history; bittersweet notes of progress in a nation still reeling and struggling to rehabilitate its crippled economic and human resources.

Jack had watched episodes covering the trial of 66-year-old Kaing Guek Eav, better known as 'Duch' – widely feared as Pol Pot's notorious former chief torturer.

He'd ruled *Tuol Sleng* – the former school codenamed in stark, communist notation as S21, where up to twenty thousand Cambodians were tagged, snapped and tortured in under four years – with a sadistic ferocity. This made him a bonafide member of genocidal royalty; the highest priest of pain.

Jack had tuned in while the unassuming-looking, frail geezer – with a long but not haggardly visage and silvery crop – was shown a series of photographs in the dock. Apparently they depicted babies being smashed against trees. Mercifully, the camera angle prevented viewers from sharing the horrific spectacle.

'He's enjoying this,' Jack had sneered. *'He's reliving it.'*

"I didn't recognise that *at first*," Duch had responded, haltingly.

The camera cut to a shot of the dual row of Cambodian and foreign judges. Some frowned; others remained impassive.

The footage then flipped back to the accused, capturing his oily, reptilian pride as he continued, in a measured tone.

"It was done by *my subordinates.*

"I do not blame them because this was *under my responsibility.*"

When the programme cut back to a well-lit TV studio, the slick, business-like Pheaktra and Sophea proceeded to quiz a Cambodian legal expert on the case. Their guest didn't particularly inspire confidence, rather resembling a clichéd mad professor with flyaway, frizzy hair and crumpled, ill-fitting attire. Jack expected him to whip out a Groucho Marx nose at any moment or perhaps squirt the co-presenters with water from a novelty bow tie.

"Some of Duch's evidence seems carefully calculated rather than spontaneous. Is that a fair statement?"

"The way he answers each question *cautiously* may make the judges and observers sceptical about what he says..." started the expert.

"His name's Sok Sam Oeun – the show's resident legal commentator," Hastings was saying.

"You know, he told me: *'If we don't have this programme, some victims won't ever know the outcome of the trials.'* Which seems just *crazy* when you think about it.

"It just so happens that television is the best medium for getting this vitally important message out. Outreach people have previously done sterling work in spreading the word – but one showing on CTN (Cambodian Television Network) gets up to a million viewers…"

Jack had drifted off momentarily; worrying about his girlfriend, Tong, back in the northeast Thai city of Udon Thani. It happened at regular intervals every day.

They'd been together six years; she'd initially accompanied him to Cambodia upon his accepting the job. They'd lived together at his ramshackle, somewhat eerie, second-floor apartment. While Jack was out at work, Tong helped out at the local Thai restaurant which, as luck had it, happened to be on their street.

Her impromptu employment had come as a massive relief to him; he'd fretted about how Tong, who'd never been abroad, would adapt. There was also a history of political enmity between the neighbouring countries; reinforced upon their arrival at the airport.

Shuffling along the immigration queue, the Cambodian visa official on duty had tossed the already nervous Tong's passport at her with utter disdain.

(They'd had a bumpy flight in – and the poor girl had been in tears, so terrified she refused to look out of the window as they flew over green, the shades of green of the irrigated patchwork rice paddies forming the outskirts of Phnom Penh, further in over the capital's slums, colonial suburbs and golden-spired temples bisected by the snaking, glinting Mekong…)

Then this nationalistic bullshit. *Welcome to Cambodia.* Jack had silently seethed.

Khmer political culture is steeped in resentment. A national inferiority complex pervaded; a deep feeling of being *culturally lesser* – fuelling a seething nationalism. Under Pol Pot this manifested as a psychotic, primordial racial hatred of the Vietnamese. He'd truly believed co-existence was impossible; Cambodia would disappear off the map unless the aggressors were slaughtered.

There had to be an Armageddon. Every Cambodian must kill thirty Vietnamese.

The simmering rivalry extended to Thailand, expressed most prominently via an oft-rancorous territorial dispute over the world heritage-listed 11th-century *Preah Vihear* temple on the border between the two nations. Soldiers from both countries patrolled its ancient perimeters; a situation that occasionally tipped over into fatal violence.

Cambodia had even defined the standoff *'an imminent state of war'*.

Upon alighting the arrivals hall, they'd commandeered a rattle-and-hum *tuk-tuk,* its dash overflowing with regionally familiar Buddhist trinkets. *"Phut sawasdee Kampuchea [Say hello to Cambodia],"* he'd prompted, gently – and she'd repeated it softly and so fearfully he'd melted.

He'd worried about leaving her alone all day in their dank apartment, which she'd surely think was haunted … then she'd scored the unexpected job, a blessed relief –and everything had been going better than expected.

Then she was diagnosed with terminal ovarian cancer. That was four months ago now. Jack's world caved in.

Things had obviously been *not right* for a while. She'd ignored the growing bulge in her abdomen. Then there were repeated return-flights to Thailand for hospital appointments – their Cambodian counterparts just weren't up to scratch yet, incoming expats were routinely informed.

The Thai doctors had dropped the bomb after several consultations. Then it had taken Tong time to disclose her mortal diagnosis to Jack (over the infuriatingly impersonal medium of Skype, although the pixelated video feed had still captured the new light of fear and desperation shining in her eyes).

The *knowledge* nagged the back of his skull; knowingness occasionally drifted out of focus, almost tantalisingly out of reach … Then the realisation thudded resoundingly back into prime position: front and centre of his consciousness.

It caused an involuntary heave of grief swelling from his guts and congesting in his throat. A spontaneous gulp rocked him. He hoped Matthew hadn't noticed.

"I spent some time in Israel," gulped Jack *apropos* of nothing.

"There's a tangible sense that the young generation is inheriting some kind of genetic post-traumatic stress syndrome… in Israel, it breeds an aggressive, confrontational culture.

"I see something similar happening here – but in Cambodia I notice fear rather than aggression. *Do you see it in their eyes?*

"There's a nervous deference you don't encounter in Thailand. You can almost hear Cambodians' nerves jangling."

Hastings fixed Jack with a queer expression.

"Yes, I *think* I know what you mean," he replied, slowly.

"I think it's highly likely a form of mass hysteria has evolved and become imprinted in the collective national DNA …something *so monumentally destructive* is bound to produce a knock-on psychological effect.

"In fact, an academic told me Cambodia won't recover for *at least* a century.

"But let's not forget that where fear flourishes, violence is often not far away.

Violence begets violence – and, sadly, it is the primary characteristic – you could say the defining principle – of modern Cambodian society."

Jack brooded. There was reportedly an overabundance of guns in the capital. A local legend had it that a former Khmer Rouge guerrilla was dozing against a bar after a few too many when he was rudely awoken by a cat yowling on the doorstep. He simply spun round in his barstool, whipped out his revolver and shot the cat dead then returned to his golden slumbers.

So the story went.

Little wonder this place was referred to as the *'Wild West of the East'*.

Even celebrations reflected, and often ended in, death.

Far too many people were killed, farcically, by falling bullets – a corollary of the all-too-popular habit of young men drunkenly firing their pistols in the air emerging from bars after a session.

It, all of it, created the uneasy but certain impression that life was cheap here.

Hastings' eyes gleamed earnestly.

"It's certainly a fearful legacy."

II. The Astrologist

Jack emerged from Matthew Hastings' shop-house into the glare – and was immediately set upon by a phalanx of beggars, bookselling street urchins, impoverished women clutching babies bundled in rags, and one-legged landmine victims.

A passing motorbike screeched to a halt at sight of the melee; the driver unceremoniously tipped forward an oversized woven wicker hamper.

When the Vietnam War spilled into Cambodia in 1970, Richard Nixon unleashed merry hell on the country in his pursuit of fleeing North Vietnamese Communist rebels.

A poor soul – *a literal basket case* – being ferried from one port of begging call to the next, rolled forth. The unfortunate blob had a mound-like head, misaligned eyes, a loopy, demented grin with lolling, canine-like tongue flopping from a corner of his twisted mouth.

It – he – propelled himself along the cracked pavement with a flick of his whirling flipper-claws. He came to a juddering halt inches from Jack's feet and extended a flipper, eyes bulging at right-angles.

The reporter couldn't help but flinch. Was this the result of Agent Orange? Anything to make it vanish – which was basically the service being offered here. And it was a pretty watertight formula – as evidenced by Jack's reaction, which mirrored most: scrambling for his wallet for a fistful of small denominations to call the doomed mutant off.

Jack glanced up and mercifully caught Mr Piseth's silhouette beneath the sun; the driver raised his hand before turning over the throttle and heading over. Judging by his grin, Mr Piseth found something pretty amusing. Jack just wanted out of there.

There wasn't time to check in at the office; it was on to the next appointment. The newspaper had arranged a reading with a local soothsayer, who'd been garnering attention as a television spiritualist. Jack took his cracked helmet and seat behind Mr Piseth; the pair pulled onto the riverside road, climbing gears.

Jack was an atheist led in his thinking by rigorous, torch-bearing Darwinian evolutionists like Richard Dawkins and professional sceptics like James Randi.

The closest he'd ever felt to anything approaching *'spiritual'* had typically occurred during moments when he was dwarfed by the majesty of nature. In ski-lifts strung between the Rocky Mountains; traversing vertiginous vistas on the Annapurna trekking circuit in Nepal; or simply staring up at the stars accelerating away from him at light-speed in galactic exodus on clear summer's nights.

Transcendence was generally unforthcoming in sacred environments. Sure, sites of worship often produced daunting, admirable architecture; wandering between the ancient Khmer temples in Siem Reap inspired a similar kind of mystical wonder as the huge, intricately filigreed Egyptian mosques he'd visited.

Jack had marvelled that it was devout faith that had produced such cultural masterpieces.

His adventures in Southeast Asia had presented him with new, diverse models of religious devotion. Buddhism was woven into the fabric of everyday life at all levels – invading, informing, fuelling public and private spheres as well as politics. Separation of church and state evidently wasn't much on the agenda.

Southeast Asian Buddhist faith was fluid and adaptive; able to pick, choose and absorb elements of other creeds – bits of ancient animism; tropes from Hinduism – as it saw fit.

The local culture was shot through with diverse, cod-spiritual influences. From miraculous animals to mystical pendants via lucky numbers, magical totems and voodoo tattoos, most Cambodians are fanatically superstitious. The culture is riddled with folk illogic.

In Phnom Penh, tellers set up booths – decorated with cabalistic diagrams of palms, astronomical wheels and zodiac symbols – in public squares, markets or malls. Others stalk the riverside or temple grounds with folding tables or groundsheets, ready to pounce and unpack incense, candles and cards from a briefcase.

Jack thought he was onto a winner with 'Grandfather Floating Stone', mystic correspondent for '*The Moon Magazine*' and Apsara TV's '*Serey Sour Sdey Pordermean (Happiness News)*' – until the show had been dropped due to lack of sponsorship.

Jack wondered if he'd seen that one coming, as they pulled up at the artist formerly known as Long Bora's residence: another standard shop-house halfway down a nondescript terraced lane of identical, mostly heavily shuttered, shop-houses.

Home security was evidently a civic issue. Jack recalled how the heavyweight locks had stood out when he'd first arrived from Thailand. They set him on edge.

This place was open, though seemingly unoccupied. Jack dismounted the bike and, after making the requisite arrangement to meet Mr Piseth in an hour, slowly entered between the open French sliding doors.

The off-white plaster was fading and cracked in the corners. A transistor radio blared crackly Khmer rock in the empty ground-floor room. A bamboo mat lay unfurled in the near corner upon which lay a pile of padded triangular cushions and a low wooden table.

In the opposite corner a sprawling, heaped-up, multi-faith shrine composed of Buddhist, Brahman, Hindi and other less recognisable *'exotic'* religious icons – Jack knew the multi-armed, elephantine *Ganesh,* of course – lay loosely collected, strung with brightly coloured jasmine garlands. Incense sticks protruded from opportunistic cavities in the *omni-god* assemblage.

Overhanging from facing walls, lest anyone forget his spell in the limelight, Grandpa Floating Stone displayed his media credentials in jagged Khmer script on a tacky, fluorescent yellow banner. It dangled over a soft-focus self-portrait, in which he bore medals and an expression of deadly earnestness.

Trading on his famous pseudonym – coined after a rock he claimed to have found bobbing buoyantly on Oudong Mountain – had been good for business. Long Bora claimed to be getting twenty to thirty clients a day. Perhaps he conducted readings remotely, Jack mused.

His mind flipped back to the unconscious foreigner sprawled on the road.

"They are waiting to see if he moves…"

Presently the growing growl of an approaching motorbike sounded. The engine cut out; there was a light padding of footsteps.

A handsome, tawny Khmer with fulsome hair and a wispy moustache and goatee in his mid-twenties, sporting a pair of box-fresh white Adidas (immediately marking him out as at least middle-class to Jack), strode confidently in, eyeing Jack. He offered his hand. Jack noticed a tribal tattoo dotting the underside on his forearm.

I'm Phap Sina. I'm here to translate for you."

"Ah, Sina. Nice to meet you. How are you today?"

"I'm fine, thanks. So…where is the fortune teller?"

"Good question. Maybe he couldn't guess we were coming."

If Sina got the joke he didn't appreciate it; he whipped out a bright red Nokia mobile phone from his jeans pocket and tapped away at the keypad. Presently he was engaged in conversation. (Jack was reminded how little of the Khmer language he'd picked up compared to Thai, which seemed accessible by comparison.)

"He says he's coming. Maybe 15 minutes. He was visiting his mother-in-law."

Jack rolled his eyes. Sina motioned towards a couple of foldable plastic picnic chairs set against the wall.

"So is translating your main job?"

"No, I'm a project assistant for NGO Active Help Cambodia. I just do this if I have some free time."

"Ah, okay. So do you visit fortune tellers yourself?"

Sina nodded.

"Most people believe in it – even if they don't actually use it."

"People go for advice on many things. It could be business or building a new house. Sometimes it's about investments or about marrying the right person. Gamblers ask for the winning lottery numbers."

Sina reached into his denim shirt and pulled out a gold pendant on a silver chain engraved with anachronistic, swirling script.

"This protects me against evil spells. My witch can make people hate or love each other – *or even kill*."

Jack grimaced. He was starting to feel suspiciously hot under the collar.

"Never ask three Cambodian people to stand together for a photograph."

"Oh, really – why?"

"Cambodians believe the person in the centre is *cursed to die young*."

That brought ghastly literal meaning to the phrase, *'Cut out the middleman'*, thought Jack. Where was the dial for the fan in this room? It was sweltering; becoming unbearable.

In his research Jack had read of Meach Ponn, 75-year-old former professor at the National Buddhist Institute. He'd said fortune-tellers were plying their trade here more than two millennia ago.

"When the Buddha was born in 623BC, his parents invited eight Brahman fortune-tellers to predict his son's future," he'd told *'Asia Life'* magazine.

The CIA's online fact-file said 96.4 percent of Cambodia's population were self-professed Buddhists. With karma set to decide their fates, many of the devout regularly flocked to check their astral accounts, creating a cultural landscape ripe for all manner of fortune-tellers, soothsayers, witch doctors, astrologers, numerologists, mediums, mystics, clairvoyants, psychics and quacks.

Cambodia's futures market is a lucrative industry.

Jack recalled watching a documentary about Peter Sellers. Famed for almost preternaturally inhabiting his roles, the indulgent yet insecure actor was obsessed with astrology, clairvoyance, the occult, and all manner of obsessive-compulsive, superstitious mumbo jumbo.

The psychologist in the doc had interpreted Sellers' reliance on quasi-spiritualist phenomena in terms of insecurity:

'I think people who are deeply superstitious,' she had said, *'don't feel in control of themselves or anything else – therefore have to litter their lives with talismans in order to make themselves feel that, somehow, they're keeping the unsafe world at bay.'*

But that was a Westerner's interpretation of a Hollywood actor; how much it applied to everyday life in Southeast Asia was negligible.

Jack readily admitted to being cynical; he'd even studied 'cold reading' – a technique used by false prophets conflating sleight of hand, cheap wordplay, and basic intuition. He was, therefore, hardly the most receptive subject. He was, however, genuinely intrigued, so that would have to suffice.

"Er…do you normally pay your '*witch*'?"

"There's no fixed price. The *donation* is up to you. It depends on how much you believe and how happy you are."

"So how much do you think would be a normal price?"

"Don't know this witch…Maybe three to five dollars."

That sounded reasonable, thought Jack… He'd been trying to ignore it – but by now it was undeniable: the sickness was on him. It had swollen from hot flush to fever in minutes. His head started pounding; his stomach knotting into sheet metal; his thighs began to ache. *Since when did thighs ever ache?*

His brow prickling, Jack shortened his breathe to a shallow pant in an effort to stave it off.

'Do you know where the bathroom is?" he yelped.

Sina frowned.

"First time here. Usually in a place like this…" he motioned towards a far corner opposite the shine.

Jack got up quickly, heaved and stopped dead in his tracks. He took a measured breath through his nostrils, his head swirling, then shuffled towards the door, chin to his chest. He pushed tentatively, trying to choke back the warning waters leaking from the walls of his mouth.

Mercifully, it was indeed a standard Asian squat job. Jack lunged inside and struggled with the flimsy plastic lock, which half dangled off its hinges. Beads of sweat were now breaking all over beneath his clothes. Suddenly a cold flush flooded over him; the sweat turned to ice and he started shivering.

He fished rapidly through his shoulder bag's detritus – *where was it?* – and, after what seemed like minutes but was probably seven seconds, pulled out a half-squashed 'hard pack' of Marlboro Lights.

He dipped in with trembling fingers and extracted a rolled up clear plastic baggie, followed by a fold of tar-stained, crumpled aluminium foil. He unwrapped it to reveal a tin-foil straw and another curled strip.

His sigh morphed into a dry heave then a warning mouthful of puke. *Better hurry.* Instinct took over; in auto-pilot mode he methodically essayed a well-practiced routine.

Snapping open the baggie, Jack squeezed out a small white rock and cracked a chip off with his fingernails then crumbled it onto the pleated foil. Flipped the foil tube into his mouth, gripping it with his lips. Out came the lighter, with the front metal guard stripped off to modify it for a lower-than-usual flame.

He flipped the wheel with his thumb, dipped his head to hover the foil straw over the foil, and raised the struggling flame.

The white granules crackled, bubbling into a burnished, bourbon-coloured oil. Jack tiled the foil; coils of vapour lifted from the gluey golden blob.

Jack inhaled, gulping at it.

Moments after the smoke hit, his stomach softened and loosened.

He took another couple of runs. His body returned to room temperature; the thud in the back of his head ceased; the aching thigh subsided. He sighed again, this time without the retching. He unbolted the bathroom door with a yank and wobbled back into the front room.

Having been summoned by telephone rather than telepathy, Long Bora was finally here.

He was in his early thirties, sporting an outgrown crop of black hair and, like Phap Sina, a thin moustache and goatee combo. He was decked out rather splendidly in a pristine white, starched cotton smock with a raised collar (reminiscent of Brian Epstein's iconic 'moptop'-era Beatles suits, Jack noted), military-style shoulder flaps and polished, gold-effect buttons.

He also had a lazy eye. It gave him an otherworldly air; surely a selling point in his line of work, mused Jack.

Long Bora beckoned him to the low table. The assorted deities loomed over the setup as if observing. Jack, mute, nerves jangling slightly, knelt.

He was asked to shuffle then split a deck of cards and pick a couple. Long Bora then asked for the Chinese zodiac sign of his birth year: the dragon. The Cambodian earnestly consulted some symbol-laden charts and began reciting his reading, adopting the dispassionate monotone used by Buddhist monks during worship – their ceremonial drone.

Phap Sina translated: "Previously, you were confused about *all the troubles and stress.* You've got *too much* to think about."

More shuffling and droning.

"You have been planning to ask me something, but you're not sure if you will yet."

True enough, Jack had come to probe the sage. But then, as a hesitant foreigner, doubt was probably pouring from his every pore. A strange pinging noise sounded. Long Bora yanked out a touchscreen phone.

"Your recent bad luck has *vanished.* You will be *thinking and planning* until the end of the year. Though you've accomplished some things, *real success* will come *early next year.*"

Jack thought that sounded like a stab at what someone his age, or any age, might want to hear.

The touchscreen re-emerged. Long Bora kindly kept his call short then resumed fishing for clues about Jack's career.

Did he ever consult overseas business partners?

"Well, maybe, sort of; I guess."

This fuelled the Big Reveal. Jack would have success in one of two fields: "NGO work or import, export."

He'd blown it, Jack thought triumphantly.

Long Bora eyed him wonkily then exchanged a rapid-fire Khmer babbly with Sina, who'd been fidgeting, increasingly bored. Jack assumed from the soothsayer's stiffening and grave expression that he'd checked the inaccuracy of his prediction.

"He says he made a mistake about the NGO work. He thought it was that at first – but now he says *your fate will mix with someone in the diplomatic field.*"

Clearly more nonsense – but the nape of Jack's neck prickled weirdly.

"You must be *extra careful* about this situation. He says it's quite serious.

"And is there anything else he can do for you?"

The opiated reporter knew there wasn't – and he'd heard just about enough by now. Bora was unfurling a cloth with an array of random trinkets on it – a greedy glint in the eye facing Jack.

He decided, against his better judgment, to ask for some nominal relationship advice.

For matters romantic, the esteemed fortune-teller turned to Chinese chiromancy – palmistry – to back up further platitudes.

"When it's good, it's *really good*, but it can suddenly turn *very bad*, often over something small that shouldn't cause a big problem, but *still does.*"

That, thought Jack, describes just about every relationship ever. A sneaky *'Barnum statement'* designed to sound specific – while actually applying to most people, most of the time.

Southeast Asian cultures traditionally frown on emotional disclosure – even within family units. One foreign writer had interpreted readings, such as this, as offering rare chances to reflect and confide. Tellers' warnings upheld the concept of karma and their upbeat advice often encouraged *calm, sociable* behaviour.

Long Bora had indeed recommended patience as a romantic virtue. Jack began to consider the value of emotional counselling in a nation reeling from civil genocide – with just 20 practising psychiatrists (according to the photocopied edition of *Lonely Planet* he'd bought from one of the marauding book-vending urchins).

Patience may well be a virtue but it had always been a failing of Jack's. He deemed it high time to go.

"Sorry, Sina – one last thing: Can you ask him for his best price on the handkerchief and belt"

Bora glanced at the sanctified keepsakes, mulling it over before stating his fee in grave tones.

Jack registered shock and embarrassment on Phap Sina's face.

"He says US$70 ... I did not expect anything like that much."

III. Bon Soir

Jack came to slumped forward on the blue, cracked faux leather couch in his apartment.

One hand still rested on the keyboard of his laptop. The movie's end credits were rolling. He stood up unsteadily, spun out, and almost folded over. He gradually tried to straighten himself – then vomited copiously.

The one thing he'd managed to eat today. What nutrients and vitamins he'd partially ingested from the *amok* fish curry and rice splattered over his dark hardwood floor.

His eyes watering, face pallid, Jack skidded in the puke *en route* to the kitchen to fetch the manky mop.

He stopped off in the bathroom, stood reluctantly before the mirror and raised his shirt. A pustulous boil glared back from his reflection. His ribcage jutted. He looked like a Prisoner of War freshly liberated from Auschwitz.

The mop stood by his little gas stove.

Tong, on her last morning in this apartment, had cooked him a fried breakfast – bacon, eggs, tomatoes, mushrooms, toast – before he went to work and she made for the airport…

Jack gulped, blinking – then sank to his knees, slumped against the door and allowed himself a momentary bawl.

Minutes – could've been ten or thirty – ticked sullenly by. Jack might've remained slumped there feeling pathetic forever but for the pinging sound of the incoming text message rousing him to movement.

'Heart of Darkness? 30 mins ;-)'

Nathan Green. The *Post's* perpetually out (to lunch, dinner, drinks, on the town, of his head) Kiwi reporter.

The idea of blowing this joint before it depressed him to a Plath-like resolution – using Tong's breakfast stove – was sufficient motivation for Jack to rise.

He did so, returning to the bathroom to splash water on his face and neck and wipe the crusted vomit from his lips. He sprayed aftershave all over and dabbed toothpaste on the boil. *For good luck.*

He groggily descended the steep, narrow staircase, exited the gate and went through the motions of securing the trio of locks – two Yale padlocks and a stiff sliding bolt.

The Heart of Darkness was aptly named – and fittingly located. The place felt like it was on the wrong side of the tracks – lurking halfway down an unlikely, dark alleyway-like lane that felt like a dead end after a wrong turn on the way to Hades.

Saying the place had edge was an understatement; it was rightfully notorious for its seedy air of menace.

Still, there weren't many late-night joints that weren't last-chance saloons or blatant brothels or the kind of haunts hideous western men who normally disliked children, except occasionally to fuck one, frequented. And the music the resident DJs played here was generally the best of the city's clubs.

As usual, a crew of mean-looking, long-haired young men waited by the entrance to frisk the queuing would-be clubbers. An inimitable dual-language display board set the house rules of the game going on inside; Khmer script above with the English translation below:

~ No Taking Gun
~ No Taking Explosive Weapon
~ No Taking Knives
~ No Hat While Dancing
~ No Putting on the Thong

Welcome to the Heart.

Jack duly received a rougher than usual (yet somehow still nonchalant) frisking from one of the thugs manning the door.

Inside, once their eyes had adjusted to the murk, the keen, bright-eyed clubber was presented with the kind of intriguing, labyrinthine split-level layout of shady nooks, sudden alleys and darkened corridors shared by most of the world's best dive-clubs.

The walls were splatted with fluorescent wall graffiti; people huddled in out-of-eyeshot crannies. There were separate dancefloors – pounding techno reverberated off the walls – and a strictly monitored, more competitively hustled than usual pool table interspersed with side booths, scattered seating areas and twisty, precipitous staircases.

It was the kind of place you could, perhaps should, get lost in. *Or be eaten alive by.*

Jack peered into the throng for Nathan. The place was heaving for a Thursday. A heady mix of expats, sexpats, backpackers and package tourists, bargirls, and local gangsters mingled like some writhing, pulsing, gigantic pupae. Steam ascended from the heaving mass of sweaty, pressed flesh.

He made a beeline for the nearest bar.

When he extended a hand to stake a claim at an almost-vacant spot at the bar, some baby-faced backpacker wearing a singlet and baggy 'ethnic' cotton fisherman's pants, clearly out of his mind, dancing on the bar like an inebriated gymnast juddering on a beam, trampled on it.

"Oi! Dickhead!"

Blissfully unaware, the bloke continued sashaying dangerously close to the ledge. Jack was tempted to yank him off by the ankle but refrained.

Minutes of vainly attempting to attract a bartender passed before Jack, almost triumphantly, received his G+T. He held the ice-clinking plastic cup against his forehead and set off for the nearest staircase.

This was already too much; he needed space.

He fought his way, nudging and elbowing, to the central spiral staircase looming over the ground-floor dance-floor, made his way up, and stopped for a breather (if you could call a cigarette, which almost induced another round of vomiting, that).

He made a desultory round of the mazy upstairs section, looking for a familiar face. At one point, leaning against the quieter upstairs bar beside some random stranger, he topped up the guy's glass of beer from the large bottle while its owner lit a cigarette. Having observed this small gesture of kindness from the corner of his eye, the man blanked Jack and turned his back on him.

This was doing him no good whatsoever, realised Jack. He may as well just go home. He'd make one final, probably futile circuit in search of Nathan then call it a night.

Descending the black wrought-iron spiral staircase, Jack thought he spotted Kerry Symondson, daughter of the British Ambassador, Sir Clive, who'd been stationed here for years.

He squinted at the woman in the bohemian paisley print dress and slicked-back, dark blonde locks.

Yep, it was her.

Jack had interviewed Sir Clive for a luxury lifestyle magazine cover profile – the kind of coffee-table glossy the hi-so set subscribed to in order to gloat over their own hallowed images in the *'Out & About'* events gallery section.

Clive Symondson, in contrast, had a wonderfully self-deprecating, humorous outlook on such fripperies. Jack had enjoyed their acerbic verbal jousting session – the old fellow with the naughty glint in his eye dropping outrageous but carefully worded hints during a prolonged cat-and-mouse battle of wits.

That interview – one in a monthly series of ambassadorial head-to-heads that Jack had filed for the vanity publication – had come as a refreshing reprieve from the staid, diplomatic politician's answers these occasions inevitably produced.

A couple of week later, in what would normally have been regarded as some kind of breach of protocol, the silver-haired charmer had invited Jack to an informal dinner at home.

There he'd met his daughter Kerry, a sparky 24-year-old aspiring filmmaker. They'd hit it off after dessert; bonding over an epic, to-and-fro game of tipsy chess that had stretched deep into the balmy evening. She was whip-smart, which Jack loved; even better, she was possessed of a filthy sense of humour – she'd won his heart in a beat when she cackled at one of his lame jokes.

He knew his secret crush was best left platonic. He didn't want to risk screwing up their friendship – plus she was out of his league anyway.

On his next birthday, giddy on Veuve Clicquot at the bar on the flat rooftop atop the legendary Foreign Correspondents Club, he'd bellowed in her ear that they were *clearly spiritual siblings* – a mantle she'd readily accepted, face ruddy from champers. From that point on, whenever they'd met it was them against the shitty, old, circle-faced world.

They'd celebrated their eternal pact by bellowing a rousing rendition of *'We Are Family'* over the balcony into the tropical night.

They'd been better times.

Kerry glanced up and spotted Jack descending the staircase, unsteadily, she noted. She wondered what ridiculousness he'd been up to this evening; it could be *literally anything*. She usually found his errant nature entertaining – when in the mood. He'd certainly been through the grinder lately, what with the terrible news about his poor girlfriend.

She wondered, all the same, if he was in a state conducive to productive conversation. Only one way to find out.

She raised her arm in a beckoning wave but he'd already seen her (Jack had, sadly, strained to neutralise his face before she'd looked up; when the expression he'd otherwise have worn would've beamed to her that he was more pleased to see her than anyone conceivable else). He was heading her way, weaving between the drunkards, dancers and dilettantes among puffs of dry ice.

"Hello stranger," she smiled.

"Alright, Kezza?"

"Not too bad, mate. Fancy seeing a nice boy like you in a place like this. You got a drink, yeah?"

Jack pursed his lips in mock consideration.

"Seem to…for the next two minutes, anyway."

"Well, I'll do the honours in a second; I need another '*biere*'. Any, er, news?"

"Not really."

"What about Tong?"

"Same. It's not going to change; just get worse. So no news is good news, I s'pose. *Doesn't feel like it though."*

"Oh, mate, *I'm so sorry*. If there's anything I can do – as always."

He squeezed her shoulder; Kerry pulled him in for a little, one-armed hug of reassurance. Though what she could reassure exactly, she wasn't sure.

Her brother was a trainee at medical school and, when prompted, he'd emailed her that ovarian cancer was virtually impossible to eradicate; under a microscope the malignant cells divided and spread at an alarming rate. She'd kept that to herself.

She knew, knowing Jack (and knowing he took thorough care over the accuracy of his reporting – if not himself), he would've looked into it anyway.

"They've already asked her how she wants to approach the treatment. Does she want chemotherapy or just to be *'made comfortable…'*

"*She's twenty-seven, man.* What the fuck's she supposed to say to a question like that?

"Jesus. So, ah… what *did* she say?"

A rogue tear ran down one of Jack's cheeks.

"She said she'd try it."

"Oh…*Come here*!"

She grabbed him, pulling him in once again – felt him trembling with supressed grief – and gave him a proper, tight squeeze. It was all she could do. *It wouldn't help, she knew, but what else was there.*

Changing the subject was probably called for at this point, she decided.

"You haven't got a joint have you?" she whispered in his ear over the squelching bassline of the drum 'n' bass cacophony. He often did.

"Erm…I think so. Lemme check."

Jack pulled away and searched his front shirt pocket for his dog-eared cigarette pack. He lifted the lid and peered in.

"Yep! Fancy it?"

"Let me get another couple of drinks in first then we'll go out, yeah? What you having? That a G and T?"

"Yeah, but think I'll move onto beer with you. I'll have a Tiger please."

"Done. Watch my bag. I'll be back in five."

"You'll be lucky. It's fuckin' heaving at the bar. Might be quicker to go upstairs."

"Alrighty then."

She handed him her shoulder tote. Jack hooked it over his shoulder and turned towards the DJ booth to discard his empty cup on the jutting front lip. As he turned, the bag swished into a dancing couple, knocking the drink out of the girl's hand.

Judging by the intoxicated leer on her face that was probably a good thing, Jack thought. Her indignant visage told him otherwise.

She was all dolled up; her dyed blonde-ginger locks done in waves that had probably taken hours, and she proudly donned a glamorous, sparkly-gold ball-gown – offset by a deepening scowl.

That peculiar feeling – *deja-vu?* – washed over him. He realised he recognised her. She worked at one of the morbid, depressing hostess bars where expats went to moan about local inefficiency on Street 104 – a riverside lane packed with bars and cheap hotels.

He'd bought her a drink sometime or other, and at the end of the evening had slipped her a small tip. He recalled distinctly how she'd jumped up from her lethargy, bolted for the door and returned three minutes later overburdened with transparent plastic bags of snacks: pork rind; noodle soup; segments of durian for dessert. *What was her name again?*

She was making a half-inebriated lunge at him – but halfway through recognition dawned. The anger visibly melted, leaving a far preferable beaming smile in its place.

"Joooohhhn! You remember me?"

Er, sure. Never forget!"

Jack placed Kerry's bag protectively between his feet and leant against the DJ booth. She was in his face now, still smiling.

"I not see you *long time*. Why you not come see *me*?"

"I'm sorry, I've been busy. Work, you know…"

"Never mind! Come! Dance!"

She grabbed him by the crook of one arm and attempted to drag him into the melee. Jack, who enjoyed cutting the occasional rug but was not currently in the throes of a boogying disposition, resisted.

"No – I'm not drunk like you! Maybe in five minutes…"

"Not five minute. *Now*!"

Jack rolled his eyes. It might be easier to throw a few token shapes until Kerry returned; then he could break away.

He reluctantly shuffled a couple of paces towards the throng, as fractal fluorescent red lasers flickered over like prison searchlights, and made some desultory physical acknowledgment – a gesture, at best – of the pumping, four-to-the-floor bassline.

Jack felt like a dad dancing after one too many at a wedding – an impression perverted somewhat when the young lady spun round and thrust her derriere into Jack's groin and started grinding.

Usually this was to be encouraged. Just not tonight.

Within seconds, a muscular, shaggy haired Khmer man in his mid-twenties had appeared next to them – and stood watching intently a metre away.

Jack, swaying as the girl – *Keo was her name* – tilted back into him, clocked the man in his peripheral vision and instantly froze.

The guy bore an expression of pure, intense hatred. He was wearing a white singlet – a 'wife-beater' thought Jack, dourly – and ripped jeans. Sweat beaded on his forehead. His bloodshot eyes were trained on Jack with an unblinking fire. His arms pinned to his sides; his hands clenched and unclenched repeatedly.

He was beyond wired. So overstimulated, he was literally frothing at the mouth; flecks of glowing white spittle pooled at each corner of his snarling oral cavity.

Jack had no idea who this man was. But violence emanated from his every pore. Keo was still dancing with her back to him, oblivious. Jack urgently squeezed her shoulder and she spun round to face him.

He leant into her ear.

"Is that your boyfriend?"

She glanced up, noticing the man – who was now gnashing his teeth in barely contained fury – for the first time.

"No, I don't have. I don't know him."

"What's his problem?"

"I don't kn-ow."

"Er…I think you should ask him."

She frowned slightly but turned towards the guy and spoke with him in their native tongue. Jack's heart sank further as he scrutinised the way the guy spat his words. She turned back towards him; he stooped in to listen.

"He says…*he wants to kill you.*"

Jack's innards froze.

"*Why? I don't know him.*"

"Don't know," Keo shrugged.

She hardly seemed concerned – but then she wasn't the one staring down the barrel of imminent attack.

Enough of this. One glimpse at the thug was more than enough to tell Jack he obviously meant business. He decided to leave immediately. Whatever was going on, this definitely wasn't worth the risk. *(Thanks, Nathan, for inviting him to this shit-fight; they'd be having words in the office – if he made it out of the joint in once piece…)*

"I better go home."

Jack didn't wait for a response from either of them. He whirled and departed, eyeing the guy warily in his peripheral. Mercifully, the would-be aggressor stayed rooted to the spot, still glaring daggers.

Jack hastily bumped, pushed and picked his way through the numerous oblivious people obstructing his route to the exit. This was a situation in which he could justify treading on a few toes. Which he did.

When he – *at last!* – reached the exit he felt *almost* secure enough to risk a wary glance over his shoulder. He did it anyway.

His mysterious newfound enemy was nowhere in sight.

Jack, almost gasping with relief, hurried out, breaking out into the open air as if a convict hurrying out of the prison gates upon release.

He glanced at his watch: 11.56 pm.

Mr Piseth was long gone; *hopefully supping some tasty morsel in the warm bosom of his family,* Jack thought enviously.

He squinted into the gloom. There wasn't a single *moto* – always the quickest, cheapest option – in sight. There were, however, a couple of dratted *tuk-tuks* vying for his attention, partially obscured by a bush.

The stragglers were beckoning Jack to their rusted chariots like dispirited rejects from a postponed Mexican wave.

(He usually relished spurning their efforts, which didn't discourage most drivers in the slightest. During tourist slumps the desperados would literally sprint at Jack, eyes bulging and flip-flops flapping, gesticulating wildly at their vehicles babbling "Tuk-tuk!" repeatedly like overexcited halfwits.

It made for an intensely unsettling start to the day; although occasionally he found one who actually knew the way. Too often they'd just say 'Yes!' to everything then set off in whatever direction they were facing – in the hope that you'd eventually direct them.)

Jack hopped into the first *tuk-tuk* he reached and carefully enunciated his address, resisting the urge to indicated his street number with his fingers.

The driver – wearing a baseball cap low over his eyes – nodded silently; the ignition rattled and churned into life.

The 'drive home after midnight' often fostered an existential experience. It was something about the peace created by silence of the darkened, usually bustling streets. They'd pass the vacated Victory Park bookmarked by the ominous shadows cast by the looming Vietnam-Cambodia Monument; the odd vagrant in tatters, quietly carrying their bundles to their shaded sleeping spot.

There was a stillness that settled the mind.

Jack had never been so glad to arrive back at his glum dump of a haunted apartment. They'd arrived without a hiccup let alone a wrong turn – and nary a hint of the all-too-common crawling at a snail's pace in hopes of a navigational hint.

The street was dark, deserted.

Jack pulled the usual dollar-fifty – the fifty composed of numerous crumpled and faded *riel* – from his wallet and passed it over the metal rail dividing the front seat from the rear as he absconded the auto rickshaw.

The driver quickly counted the bills, shuffling them rapidly.

"No! Two dollars!"

Oh, for chrissake.

"*You, no!* I know the price."

The driver leapt out of his seat, flinging the banknotes melodramatically onto the street. Jack turned away and started towards his gate, wishing there weren't three damn locks to negotiate.

The driver ran from behind and obstructed Jack while he fumbled for his keys. He then shoved him – and whipped out a lethal-looking homemade weapon. It looked like a prison shank from Hell. From what Jack could pick out among the gloom, there were both a glinting blade and a hypodermic needle lashed to a makeshift wooden handle.

Not this. Not now.

It could happen if you didn't agree a fare before setting off. Newbie expats were routinely warned about it.

Jack quickly pulled out another dollar from his pocket and tossed it towards the driver. The heavy-handed Khmer followed the arc of the bill with his eyes; he scooped it and the others up and skulked back to his steed, muttering dark curses.

Rattled, Jack pulled the bunch of keys clipped by a chain to his belt loop, with shaking hands, from his pocket.

Epilogue.

THE PHNOM PENH POST
Shooting Shutters Doors At City's 'Heart'
BY SAING SOENTHRITH AND COLIN MEYN | AUGUST 12, 2009

The 24-year-old British daughter of the British Ambassador to Cambodia, Kerry Symondson, was shot inside the popular Heart of Darkness nightclub in the early hours of Thursday morning. She was flown to Bangkok where she remains in critical condition.

The latest violent incident at one of Phnom Penh's most well-known nightspots has created headlines around the world.

Symondson, a filmmaking student at the Asia Euro Institute and daughter of His Excellency Sir Clive, who has been assigned to Phnom Penh since 2002, was shot in the head with a handgun at about midnight, Chea Rotha, deputy municipal police chief, said.

Police say they are looking for a suspect who had been seen at the club sporadically 'for a number of weeks' – often accompanied by the son of an unnamed high-ranking government official.

Chea Rotha said the shooting happened after Kerry's bag was snatched at the DJ booth. She argued, then got into a struggle with the thief. One of his friends retrieved a high-quality gun from his car, brought it back into the club and shot her.

Phnom Penh Police Commissioner Heng Pov said police were investigating but declined further comment.

Deputy National Police Commissioner Sok Phal said he had heard about the shooting but didn't have clear details, and referred further questions to Heng Pov.

As part of their investigation, police have closed the Heart of Darkness on Street 51, which achieved fame in the 1990s as a must-visit spot for foreign backpackers and has become popular with the children of high-ranking officials.

There have been a number of incidents involving weapons in recent years.

"The Heart of Darkness gave our police a headache many times," so it has been closed on the orders of Heng Pov, said Chea Rotha.

Post reporter Nathan Green, a New Zealand national, was coming out of the nightclub's bathroom at 12 am.

"I heard a shot, and saw people scream and flee the dancefloor, to reveal a body slumped on the ground. I ran over and as I got closer, saw it was Kerry, who I've socialised with previously. The bullet apparently scraped the side of her head – but there were gallons of blood."

Five minutes later, a black sports car screeched away from outside the club, knocking over several parked motorbikes, he said.

A few minutes later, what appeared to be the same car arrived near the club, and a man holding a two-way radio and dressed in khaki bodyguard uniform stepped out, which was when Green decided to leave.

The British Embassy declined to comment on behalf of Sir Clive, who is in Bangkok. Anthony Davies has temporarily assumed ambassadorial duties until further notice.

A man identifying himself as the manager of the establishment said he was uncertain how the shooting happened.

"We security check, but bad people are still sometimes able to conceal weapons at the bottom of their legs where security guards cannot find them", he said outside the premises on Thursday afternoon.

Brit Joel Quenby moved to Thailand in 2002 and spent a decade writing, editing, testing boundaries and patience while living way beyond his financial means. He's written travel guides; started a couple of successful magazines; and hacked out award-winning ad copy. The main achievement from his brief, catastrophic foray into Cambodia was creating 7Days weekend magazine while working as a section editor at The Phnom Penh Post.

Happy Ending

John Burdett

Once upon a time Jack Bell fell in love with a Khmer girl. His face glowed, his eyes shone, he became tolerant of his enemies and generous to his friends, who hardly recognized him.

The affair was not without complications, though. "I'll do anything you want except sex," she said. Not the kind of offer you hear much on lower Sukhumvit, and not one Jack had hoped for at that fateful moment. He had been on his young and carefree way to a massage parlour off Soi Cowboy, where he could be confident of a 'happy ending,' but lightning struck before he reached Asoke. You could hardly miss her: she stood on the sidewalk in the gold and purple silks of her Thai folk costume as a kind of mascot to lure Westerners into the very respectable nuat shop where she worked. Her jet-black hair formed a bun on top of her head held by a gold pin in the form of a bird's wing. She led him into the salon where the beds were ranked neat and tidy in full view of the street.

He was pretty much gaga by the time she had him in the white cotton pants and jacket. When he lay on the bed and one of his hands began a journey of reconnaissance, she held it tight for a moment and whispered those intriguing, maddening words: I'll do anything you want except sex. At first he supposed she meant not here in the shop and was ready to take her anywhere she liked for 'short time'. He would have forked out for the Mandarin Oriental just to impress her. By the end of the massage, however, something beyond common lust had taken hold of his mind. As he put it later to himself: "Instead of playing with my dick she went straight for the jugular."

Which was not quite fair: she told him her life story only because he asked, so desperate was he to prolong the moment. She was penniless from Battambang in Cambodia, but skilled with people and smart. A devout Buddhist in the Theravada tradition, she was working in the no-sex massage parlour to earn enough to pay her way to Sri Lanka, where they also followed the Theravada system, but where women were allowed to ordain as full Buddhist nuns.

That wasn't what clinched it for Jack, though, who didn't give a damn about Buddhism. It was the other stuff that pierced his heart: Jack's fault for asking so many questions - he couldn't help it, he was hypnotised. She replied without adjectives or emotion, a Buddhist girl answering painful questions honestly; she didn't seek sympathy. It would have been rude not to answer him. He was a customer after all.

This was before everyone owned a mobile phone. She slept on the second floor of the massage shop with the other girls - they used very thin roll-up mattresses and lay together side by side like sardines. She was not allowed to receive phone calls at the shop unless it was an emergency. More massages were Jack's only recourse. At the fifth session, when she was digging her elbows into his abdomen, he decided to risk everything and invite her to share his apartment until she was ready to leave for the convent in Sri Lanka. He did, as it happened, have a spare bedroom in the cheap suite where he was staying on Soi 6. You could have knocked him down with a feather when she answered with a simple 'yes,' and a smile, as if she had expected the offer.

That only added to Jack's anguish, of course. She was not a virgin - Jack knew that. He knew why she didn't do sex. After all she'd been through, what woman would want to have sex with a man ever again? So the rage of his lust transmuted into something of a quite different order. Despite himself he found his eyes following her everywhere in the tiny apartment like a dog. Because she was perfect. She was as compulsively tidy as any Thai girl and just as funny. No woman had ever cracked him up the way she did imitating a monkey trying to snatch a nut out of a trap.

He saw her naked only once; the scarring made him so angry he could have killed a thousand Khmer Rouge. He fantasized about mowing them down with a machine gun.

Three months was all she gave him. She even managed a sad face when they said goodbye at the airport, although he knew she was intoxicated by the promise of pure freedom that Buddhism bestows on its faithful. He kissed her on both cheeks and burst into tears. "It's not fair," he blubbered, "if you can't sleep with me that's one thing, but I can't even desire anyone else after you."

She kissed him once more on the cheek, said something in Khmer - or was it Pali? - that he didn't understand and was gone.

That all happened a very long time ago. Now, nearly forty years later, he is going to the airport to meet her again. Not the same airport, of course; in that length of time everything changes. Bangkok is hardly recognisable. He takes the Skytrain to Suvarnabhumi. She has promised him only a few hours in an airport lounge, it would not be proper for them to be seen to spend too much time alone together - considering.

He watches her walk through the gate, still light and young on her feet, but with the unmistakable ravages of age in her face. Instead of kissing they bow deeply to each other with palms pressed together in the Buddhist way. She is in the robes of an abbess of a Buddhist nunnery in Sri Lanka, which she has made famous for its rigour and enlightenment. Now she is going to oversee the construction of a Buddhist convent in her own country, Cambodia, where she has become a hero and a celebrity.

She isn't the only one in robes. After a shock to the heart such as Jack endured, a lesser man might have wasted himself on debauchery. She chose her victim shrewdly, though. After she compassionately destroyed him he rebuilt himself in her image and ordained. He has even risen to the position of Meditation Master in the Thai forest monastery where he lives. He is known for the rigour of his practice and the clever little meditation tricks she taught him. Not to mention the priceless insights into the dark side.

John Burdett practiced law for 14 years in London and Hong Kong until he was able to retire to write full time. He has lived in France, Spain, Hong Kong and the U.K. and now commutes between Bangkok and Southwest France. He is best known for his bestselling Sonchai Jitpleecheep series of books.

SARASWATI PUBLISHING

PHNOM PENH, CAMBODIA

Printed in Great Britain
by Amazon

62728529R00180